Fathers and Sons and Other Village Idiots

Underdogs and Angels in 1969 South Brooklyn

A Novel
by
Billy Warren

This is a work of fiction. All characters, places, and events are products of the author's imagination, or in the case of historical persons and events, used fictitiously.

Billy Warren Books
Copyright © 2024 Billy Warren
All rights reserved.
Do not reproduce in any fashion without the permission of the author.

Contact information at billywarren.com

ISBN: 979-8-9913561-0-7 (Hard Cover)
ISBN: 979-8-9913561-1-4 (Paperback)
ISBN: 979-8-9913561-2-1 (eBook)

DEDICATION

My mother, Natalie, and father, Charles,
were very dedicated to the raising
of my sister, Geri, and me.
My sons have been dedicated to being village idiots,
just like their dad.

Despite the fact I love them all very much,
my debut novel is not dedicated to any of them.

It is dedicated to my wife, Theresa,
who has enriched my life
beyond my wildest hopes.

Fathers and Sons
and
Other Village Idiots

Underdogs and Angels
in 1969 South Brooklyn

Billy Warren

Billy Warren

"Do you know what really makes man free?'

'What?'

*'Will, your own will,
and it gives power which is better than liberty.
Know how to want, and you'll be free,
and you'll be master too."*

**Ivan Turgenev,
First Love and Other Stories 1881**

Billy Warren

Prologue

In 1969, my grandfather wrote down some notes during the last year of his life. He must have had some sort of epiphany because he transformed from being a cautious man to one whose favorite mantra became

Life's too precious to be careful with.

Before reading the events in his notebook, I had remembered Grandfather's first funeral far more vividly than his second. We should all be so lucky to have divine intervention give us a second chance.

He, himself, doubted the existence of this heavenly intervention and if real, would have resented god's interference. Maintaining his free will was paramount. After reading it, I'm not sure what to believe happened.

It has been more than a half century since 1969. Last month, I found his journal in my mother's attic. The blood stains on its cover worried me.

Whose blood was it?

Billy Warren

The Journal of Baranski

New Year's Day, 1969

My name is Kazimierz Adama Baranski, and these will be my notes during the last months of my life. Don't ask me how I know. I know and don't like it. It might mean I'm going to hell.

For the last decade, I have done much in defiance of my god, yet on this first day of my last year, I am thinking about kissing his dupa. Outside on 23rd street, as New Year's Eve partiers start their year, I'm making a promise to my beloved wife. Writing it down somehow makes it seem more real.

My Beloved Marysia,

If there is no heaven, then it does not goddamn matter what I do down here.

But what if there is, and you are there watching and waiting for me? My love, I fear that my life is about to fail our family, myself, and you. I sit alone at your vanity with only our wedding picture and your hairbrush to quiet my distressed mind. The brush still clutches strands of your hair from nine years ago as your so-called treatments ravaged your body as much as your cancer.

Through our window, I see our neighbors stumbling back up their stoop stairs from the sidewalk. A few minutes ago, they were banging their pots together to celebrate the arrival of the new year. Much has changed since you were taken from me. There are many new strange faces who live here now. They don't look like us. I don't know most of them, and they don't know me. No one out there looks for me. They don't wave to a dying man sitting behind the window before them. Our sons,

Henry and Otto, probably sit on their barstools adopting their father's worst habits.

Sadly, our house, once so full of happy sounds, is in a winter of quiet despair. Our former daughter-in-law, Louise, lives in Staten Island with her mother, while Louise and Henry's only son, Duke, may not return home after graduation from university.

In springtime, I remember the happiness of hearing your voice calling to me from the kitchen. In summers, it was Louise singing in the apartment above, while on the stoop, Henry and Duke watched the perpetual stickball game of summer. Spring and summer were the happiest seasons of our lives. The ones that I will remember with the most sweetness. I never choose to think about autumn, the season when that SOB took you away.

It is a cold winter day once again, and I realize now that I am running out of time. It's the beginning of my fifth year, and the little prick told me that if I made it to the end of my fifth year, I am as healthy as any other old man. The fifth year, he also said, would be the most dangerous. Little Prick always wants to take away all my hope. My five-year follow-up is in June, if I can make it. It is getting hard to swallow once again. Little Prick didn't do a good job.

Do you wonder why I resist dying, when I could easily yield and be with you sooner? I know my reason. I fear dying before I am redeemable. I have not been to church since your funeral and may not be admitted to heaven.

If I want to be with you forever, is it possible to trick that SOB into believing I belong there too? God may be harder to fool than my bookie or Little Prick. In order to redeem my life, what must I do that I am freely willing to do? I refuse to be extorted by the Church to behave to their liking.

On this desperate night, I realize that I need help from someone. I don't like this feeling of dependency, but if I want to rest with you in peace forever, I need to do some good.

If you still believe all that crap that they taught us in Catechism classes, then please pray for me because I can no longer pray for myself. No angel, other than you, will listen to me.

This act of writing to you tonight has kindled an ember of hope in this season's freeze. To carry my quest forward, I shall try to write in this notepad as much as I am able. I love you, my darling. To demonstrate my resolve, here's a meager poem to get my final journey started.

final turn of wheel
desperate resolution
hope in winter chill

Your loving husband,
Kazimierz

Thursday, January 2nd

The *New York Daily News* is what I purchase every day from Frankie's newsstand on the corner. Even on Wednesdays, when the store is closed, Frankie leaves my paper in his house vestibule on 24th Street. Along with my paper are a few others. Each paper has a customer's name on it and is folded up and rubber banded. Sometimes inside the paper might be an envelope. The envelope might contain cash for payout on a bet, or more frequently, a note with a number. The amount the customer owed him. Frankie is the neighborhood bookie. His newsstand operation does little to hide his bookmaking. Payoffs to the local cops do more.

This morning, I got myself out of my warm bed and got my copy. My paper had an envelope inside with a note that had a very big number written on it. The number was bigger than last week.

I ripped up the note and set the newspaper on top of the kitchen table unopened. With the coffee pot percolating on the stove and babka warming in the oven, the stovetop timer finally rang. With my filled coffee cup, I sat down and unfolded the paper to its centerfold. Normally, I would read the paper from back to front to read the sport pages first, but this edition was special.

The centerfold didn't have what I sought, so I closed the paper then leafed page by page from front to back. When I reached the back page, I knew the paper had failed me.

If I could have screamed out, I would have cursed, but being a speechless fool, I could only look up in silence and watch the winter day blowing through my backyard. It's just maddening.

Normally, each New Year's Day dawn, the *Daily News* would send a reporter down to the beach to photograph the Coney Island polar bears plunge into the icy ocean. This event had been happening since before I arrived in the country in 1910. I blame myself. I should have gotten my lazy dupa down there to witness this annual plunge.

On many a new year's morning, I would sit on a splintered boardwalk bench to watch those wonderful idiots. I always wanted to take that dip with them and promised to take my sons in as well. I broke many promises to Henry and Otto. For a few years, they took their sons to watch. The dads made the same promise to them. Someday never came for any of us.

At first, we were all too young, then too responsible, and finally, in a flash, I became too old to take such a risk. One of my many regrets of being a poor father, unfulfilled promises. Maybe all fathers belong in hell.

I remember those wonderful idiots each New Year's Day dawn. The sand beat on my face as I sat was watched from my lonely bench. Nearer the surf, this pack of polar bears lit fires in trash cans, then waited for the summon from the alpha bear.

A conch shell would sound, and everyone began throwing off their clothes. Most wore bathing suites but not all. In recent years, the papers reported the police seemed to be caring more about that. Jesus Christ, it's only naked blue bodies. Nothing there to likely to impress or offend anyone. All screamed from the biting sting on their hides.

As they entered the cold waters, they shrieked even louder as if they were going to die. Their screams sounded so joyous to me. I envied them as they got knocked over by each other or a crashing wave. With near freezing waters dripping from their hair, they gasped and screeched as if they were newly christened babies.

The thing I remember most was their laughter. They were alive and happy. I wasn't. I was dead in spirit much before my time. My caution has become soul-killing. At 76, this icy plunge might kill me. I regret that I didn't follow the wisdom of my favorite drinking toast. "If you ever get to it, and don't do it, you may never get to it to do it again!" I had missed my chance to do it. A broken promise even to myself.

My dad broke a promise to Mom and me. He promised to love us, and he failed us. It really was no secret; I hate my father and hope that he is burning in hell.

All this reminds me of my greatest secret. One I never told, even to my Marysia. I've grown weary of hiding it. Writing it down might somehow help me. Maybe it won't. What would people think of me if they knew my secret? I need to take a bath and think about what good will it do for me to reveal it in my notebook.

Friday, January 3rd

M y hot bath last night reminded me of my first bath in America. That one probably wasn't all that warm, but it was much more satisfying.

As I say frequently to anyone who will listen, my father was an SOB, and all these years later, I still hate him for what he made Momma and me do. He tried to kill our souls, and perhaps we killed him instead. Nearly 60 years later, I still don't know.

In winter of 1910, the lands of Poland were controlled by other countries. We were living in a German-controlled village just outside of Poznań, where Father occasionally picked up work as a stone mason. When he couldn't find work, he'd go out and drink away what little money Momma or I had earned that day.

I was almost 16 years of age and dreamed of going to university someday. One day, I made the mistake of telling my father that I wanted to be a writer and go to Warsaw or Moscow to study the works of great writers like Ivan Turgenev.

"A Russian?" he snarled. He was already drunk that early evening, but even if he wasn't, he hadn't been a gentle person to me since I was a little boy. His first blow to my face knocked me off my feet.

His anger that day was especially bad. He picked me up and threw me across the room. This was where most beatings usually ended, but this time he followed after me to start striking me further with his huge fists and boots. Fortunately for me, Momma returned from her trip to the market.

She could not pull him back, so she grabbed a cast iron pan from the stove and hit him hard on the back of his head. He fell to one knee. As Momma pulled me away, slowly, he started to get back up. If he got up, I knew that he would beat her too, so I grabbed the pan from Momma's hand and hit him again as hard as I could. This blow to his temple put him face first down to the floor.

Blood poured from the side of his head, and he no longer moved. Momma and I looked at him and then at each other. Behind her tears, I only saw horrible fear. No one should feel such fear.

In the past, the neighbors learned to never come when they heard these fights, and this time was no different. After some minutes, he lay motionless, but he was still breathing through the blood coming out of his nose and mouth. We knew we needed to get out of there fast.

Momma told me to pack some clothing in whatever sack I could find and wear as much as possible. She took some food from the shelves, and all the money in her secret money box—he hadn't earned any of it. Within minutes, we were leaving. As I closed the door, I looked back and saw his body move.

Throughout the night, we walked toward Poznań, finally reaching it the next morning. We bought train tickets to take us north to the coast where Momma had a sister. We reached Ciocia's house safely and stayed with her a few weeks. During that time, Momma and I were able to secure some immigration documents to come to America. Apparently, she and Ciocia had been writing to each other, and they seemed to have this plan already worked out. From her various jobs, Ciocia had saved quite a bit. Momma not so much.

Fathers and Sons and Other Village Idiots

The plan had been for all three of us to go to America together, but Ciocia was not prepared for our early arrival and was having second thoughts. The problem was that Ciocia hadn't yet heard back from our sponsor already America. They were to supply an address that would get us past immigration in New York.

We stayed another few weeks in the north before it was decided that Momma and I needed to go without Ciocia. She gave us all the money she had saved, and we departed.

Our part of Poland was under German control, but with documents in hand, we easily moved eastward. The question was, would Father be trying to find us?

We ended up in the seaport of Hamburg, where we rented a room. We took turns going out of the room because one of us needed to stay with our belongings. Thieves seemed to be everywhere. Eventually we secured third class steerage tickets on the *Graf Waldersee*, a steamship bound for America the following month. For the next month, we both jumped whenever we heard a loud noise in the hallway. Each night, I fell asleep fearing that tomorrow Father would find us.

Unfortunately, when the departure day came in March, Momma had the beginnings of a bad cold. She was worried that the steamship agents would not allow her to board. If we were rejected for health reasons by the Americans, the steamship company would have to take us back. Somehow, we managed to get past those agents. Maybe it would have been better if we hadn't been allowed on board because Mamma would not survive the ocean crossing.

We sailed down the Elbe River. Our first stop was the next morning in a little town on the North Sea. The following day, we reached a town in northern France. As Mother's fever rose, the steamship headed east into the dark North Atlantic's wintery seas.

A Polish woman traveling alone noticed Momma's distress. She developed a bond with Momma and soon began caring for her. The three of us became so inseparable that others may have thought we were family.

Sadly, Momma didn't appear that she could fight her illness. Officials and the crew didn't notice that they had a very

7

sick person in steerage. We never asked for help until it was too late. Even when we finally did, not for my mom, but for someone else.

As we crossed the stormy ocean, Momma and this other woman became concerned that, at Ellis Island, we might get sent back to Europe. The two of them came up with a plan to exchange identities just in case that were to happen. By the time we finally sought medical help for Momma, she went to the infirmary using the other lady's papers. I didn't really expect her to die, so I went along with it. One of the last things she said to me was that I needed to trust this lady. Mamma said she must be an angel sent by God to help us. We were all together when Momma stopped breathing. I have never told anyone about all this, for fear I would be deported with this woman as well. For all I knew, I might be wanted for murder in Poznan.

During the remaining voyage, I found out more about my pretend mom. She had lived in Brooklyn before, but when her family decided to move further west, she decided that she needed to return to Poland to look for a sister she had left behind. She failed to find her and was returning to America to rejoin her husband and children, who had already relocated to Buffalo.

I had continued to go along with this exchange of identities because I knew I could never go back to Poland. If Father had survived, it would be more dangerous for me there. Because no one was sure what illness my mom died of, they buried her body at sea. There would be less questions that way. A few years before, our ship had a plague outbreak. The captain was taking no chances getting through New York Harbor's pre-landing health inspection. On March 31, 1910, the ship passed through preliminary inspection and was allowed to enter upper New York Bay. I had arrived in my new world.

Many of us from steerage pushed our way up onto the main deck to see our new land. While it just turned spring, it was cold and blustery on the deck. We steamed through the Narrows, the waterway between Staten Island and Brooklyn. I stood by the rail on the left side of the ship and looked forward. I saw the Statue of Liberty towering above the harbor. Being lit by a gray morning dawn, she appeared to be stepping forward from the mist to welcome me. As we sailed before her, a man nearby began to recite a poem. As he spoke, my new mother translated for me. It was a poem that I have since memorized.

Not like the brazen giant of Greek fame,
With conquering limbs astride from land to land;
Here at our sea-washed, sunset gates shall stand
A mighty woman with a torch, whose flame
Is the imprisoned lightning, and her name
Mother of Exiles. From her beacon-hand
Glows world-wide welcome; her mild eyes command
The air-bridged harbor that twin cities frame.
"Keep, ancient lands, your storied pomp!" cries she
With silent lips. "Give me your tired, your poor,
Your huddled masses yearning to breathe free,
The wretched refuse of your teeming shore.
Send these, the homeless, tempest-tost to me,
I lift my lamp beside the golden door!

Emma Lazarus was the poetess of this verse. Her words gave me such strength and hope back then. I wish they still could today, but after so many years, I have begun to question whether America has given up on her ideals and on me. Nevertheless, I do still love my Mother of Exiles and what she is meant to stand for. Maybe my quest should be to fight for her promise. I just don't know.

As we approached Liberty Island, my surrogate mom suddenly grabbed my arm and dragged me around the rear deck to the other side. I still remember the great sense of urgency in her grip. Once on the other side, she pointed to the shore and spoke.

"This is Brooklyn before us, and there are Catholic Poles living there." I only stared out.

"Today, we will part, and you will need to find those people by yourself.

"Do you see that church steeple right there? The big one with two smaller steeples on each side" She pointed back across the waters. There seemed to be church steeples everywhere in the land of Brooklyn. It took me a minute, but I finally picked out the one that she was pointing at. She continued to instruct me, and this is some of what she said.

"That is the Polish church, Our Lady of Czestochowa, the church of the Black Madonna. That is where you need to go. I don't know how, but that is where you need to go." She further explained that she needed to continue immediately by railroad to rejoin her family.

A few minutes later, she pointed up the river and said, "Look over there. You can cross on that bridge." She was pointing at the Brooklyn Bridge.

"I am your mother until we walk off the dock, but after that, you are on your own. I liked your mother, but this is all I can do for her son. My family may get a forwarded telegram from the steamship company notifying them that I am dead, so I must hurry west to arrive before it. You cannot come with me to my new life. You must create your own."

We landed at a Manhattan pier on the Hudson River. The first- and second-class passengers exited ahead of us and walked right off and into America. Because we traveled steerage class, authorities put us on a barge to Ellis Island. We were ragamuffins and apparently not to be trusted.

In the main immigration building, there was a steep flight of stairs leading to second floor examination rooms. Uniformed officials waited at the top of those stairs, watching the ragamuffins ascend. If you showed signs of breathing problems, an official would mark your clothing with a big P and sent in one direction. If your behavior was deemed as odd, they would mark your shoulder with an X. In seconds, you could be judged by a clerk on whether you might be sick or insane. These hasty decisions could change lives. Momma would never have passed this early stair test, but this lady and I, as mother and son, ascended without difficulty. I tried to look not crazy, but I was frantically worried that this country would not let me in. Fortunately, my pretend mother knew how to navigate through Ellis Island and gave the name and address of our supposed sponsor in Brooklyn. This satisfied the inspector. After hours of further interrogation and

Fathers and Sons and Other Village Idiots

examination, we were eventually ferried back to a pier in Manhattan. It was nearly dusk.

After passing through the pier's iron gates, we both stood firmly in America. My surrogate mother handed me all of our money and Momma's papers, we briefly hugged, and then we quickly parted. The harbor wind blew her up the street and out of my life forever. I hope she had a good life. I still think of her as an angel sent to me in my time of need.

I turned to see others from my steamship being greeted in their native languages. I realized, for the first time in my life, I was completely alone. No one in the world knew or cared where I was.

Within minutes, the larger crowd of steerage passengers disappeared. Soon, I had men walking up to me speaking very poor Polish. They kept offering me work and some of them tried to grab my arm and pull me into a wagon. I saw these same men speaking broken Italian and trying to grab at the young Italian boys too.

On more than one encounter, I needed to push back hard to get them to release me. One of them managed to grab Momma's clothing bag and ran off with it. I could not stop him. I thought I noticed a policeman walking a block away who took no interest in my struggles. He was there to protect citizens not ragamuffins. This was my welcome to America.

Maybe I had done some damage to my attackers, and they decided I probably was more trouble than I was worth. The assaults stopped. I gathered my bearings and found my bridge as it started to rain, which quickly turned to cold sleet. It took me over the East River into Brooklyn.

There, I walked along the waterfronts following the shoreline. I heard many strange languages on the docks. A few were some that I had heard Momma speak, but most were unknown to me. I felt like I was walking in circles and decided to walk up the slope to get a better view of where I was. I wish my surrogate mom had given me an address or street name, but she hadn't. I only had the church steeple to guide me.

I wandered onto 4th Avenue and looked down it. The buildings along this great avenue seem to go as far as I could

11

see to the south. I started to walk south into a chilling evening. My clothing was soaked through and through.

In the store windows were signs that I could not read so I never went into any. I was getting very hungry but too afraid to show my money or to sleep anywhere with fear of another attack. I continued to walk past a great many churches, and at each corner I looked down towards the harbor. Eventually, I started seeing the glowing torch of the Statue of Liberty, though I was not quite in front of her. I walked further, until Lady Liberty was directly down the street, but there was still no church, so I walked on. I passed the corner of 21st Street and 4th Avenue and saw a steeple a few avenues up the hill, but it was not the one I had seen from the boat. I feared I had somehow missed it. It was dark and getting very late. The streets were emptying.

I then reached the corner of 24th and 4th and looked down the street towards the harbor. There was a church on the left about halfway down. I left 4th Avenue to go look more closely. The highly ornamented walls were made of gray stone and brick like the Catholic churches in Poland. I looked down to read the sign near the door. It was written in Polish. *Matka Boska Częstochowska*, Our Lady of Czestochowa.

I looked up to the triple spires that rose towards heaven. This sight assured me that this was the church I had seen from the harbor. I had found my Black Madonna. I wept as I climbed up her stone steps and went from the cold rain into the warmth of the church's embrace.

Our Lady of Czestochowa does stand under the perpetual gaze of Lady Liberty. These two women had been my beacons to my new village.

I walked inside in a pretty sad physical state. I hadn't eaten or slept in over a day. I'm sure I stank from my ocean's voyage and my clothing was soaked though. I shivered from the cold, as well as a fear inside me. God may have protected me through my journey to this church, but what would happen next to me?

Standing in the vestibule, I looked down the main aisle to the altar. There was a painting behind the altar, and it drew me forward. It seemed impossible to me then, but the painting somehow looked familiar to me. While I walked forward, a nun of the Order of the Holy Family of Nazareth came up to me. I recognized her habit. This order was common in Poland.

The church fed me that night, got me a bath, and gave me dry clothing to wear. They setup a cot in a storage room for me. I told people that I was an orphan since my mother had died on the voyage across. No one questioned my story, and I never said much more about it. No one has ever known my full story. No one ever came to deport me.

With time, under the protective gazes of my two Ladies, I felt safe in my new village. A feeling that I only felt before as a young child before my father turned mean. I came with Momma to America to pursue freedom, and the Mother of Exiles was offering this to me. I also desired peace for my soul. Black Madonna offered that.

In Poland, I knew of this Black Madonna of Czestochowa because I had met her before. My name, Kazimierz, is forever joined to hers. I have been told that my name means *one who reveals or creates peace*. I have also heard it said that Kazimierz means *destroyer of peace*. My life has created both for me and others.

The story that my mother told me about my name was that the original Black Madonna painting in Poland was a sacred icon of the Catholic Church, and that it was painted by an apostle. Once my parents took me to see the original in Czestochowa. When I had walked into this Brooklyn church, there she was again. The connection between us was that centuries ago, King Kazimierz of Poland proclaimed the painting to be the Queen of Poland.

Today, Brooklynites call the Our Lady of Czestochowa parish OLC. The good people of the OLC saved my life that night. They found a job for me. Soon I was able to rent a room in a Polish men's boardinghouse on 4th Avenue. As I got older, the men from my boardinghouse fraternized with the Polish women from the women's boardinghouse. This is how I met my Marysia.

From the moment, I first heard her name, Marysia, I was enchanted. The rhythm of her name was so poetic to me. In

Polish folklore, her name portrays kindness and warmth and grace. When she spoke to me, I fell in love with her for eternity.

Marysia was from the Polish countryside and had just immigrated to my Brooklyn Polish village. After the "war to end all wars", Marysia and I were married in OLC by a newly ordained young Irish Priest, Father Edward McCormick, who was fluent in Polish. There was a shortage of Polish Catholic priests in the diocese, so this Irishman would need to suffice for us.

With the war over, Marysia and I went on to have a wonderful life together in our new village in South Brooklyn. Not a wealthy life but a very happy one in our community. All my life, I went to OLC as much as work would allow. I was grateful that we were safe. My sons were baptized and later married by Father Ed, who was once my best friend.

Marysia had her funeral mass in OLC. Father Ed presided over the ceremony. I have not been there since that day and wanted nothing to do with the SOB who took her from me. Decades after my two Ladies had saved me to find my Marysia, the love of my life, I face a dilemma. In order to be with my love, I need to negotiate with the one who took her away. I may still be doomed.

On my first night in America, I had a bath that quieted the shivering in my body. I have never forgotten the peace of that first night. I desire and pray that yesterday's hot bath can once again mend my soul. I need to find some path forward to a redemption of my life.

Marysia, I will not fail you this time.

Saturday, January 4th

This is my favorite quote.

If we wait for the moment when everything, absolutely everything is ready, we shall never begin.

Whether it was the events that happened back in Poland, or my lack of education or talent, I never became a writer.

Nevertheless, I read obsessively and over time, Ivan Turgenev became my muse. I own a few of his books, and the Park Slope library at 9th Street and 6th Avenue have many others. I think that it is time for me to revisit Ivan—just one more time.

Since I lost my speech some five years ago, I now carry a small notepad to communicate with others. It was Little Prick's incompetence that took my speech, but it has finally made me into the writer I always wanted to be.

Take for yourself what you can, and don't be ruled by others; to belong to oneself—the whole savor of life lies in that.

It's remarkable that Ivan Turgenev wrote those words over one hundred years ago and that I sit on another continent still pondering them.

Sunday, January 5th

My little Brooklyn village is nestled within the mountains of humanity called New York City. I bought this house on 23rd Street over four decades ago, so more than half my life has been under this roof.

In Poland, my village had many churches, even more taverns than churches, a social hall, shops, homes, and two stone gateways into it. But a village is much more than just structures—mine had priests and prostitutes, politicians and leaders, bartenders and drunks, gossips and recluses, and constables and shysters. My Brooklyn village has all the same from churches to taverns to priests to mobsters.

My village does not have an official name on any map, but ask anyone here where they live, and all would say "South Brooklyn," and they would all be wrong. It's far from the southern edge of the borough. The designation stemmed from colonial times when it was the southern portion of the original village of Brooklyn.

South Brooklyn originally contained the areas of Park Slope, Bay Ridge, Gowanus, and Red Hook. Despite being in the middle of them all, calling 23rd Street any of those names would be misleading. Park Slope and Bay Ridge have stately brownstone houses on tree-lined streets. Red Hook by the docks has warehouses and factories. Gowanus has its canal where criminals might dump a body or toss a gun that needs to disappear. Twenty-third street with its three-story asbestos shingled walk-ups, sits in a gap between them all.

In Poland, in order to trade with anyone passing through, Momma spoke many languages—Russian, Yiddish, and German to name just a few. I know that she'd have done well in this Brooklyn village because it is equally as diverse.

On the corner of 23rd Street and 5th Avenue is my son's tavern, *The Polish Eagle*. It also contains a social hall and funeral parlor. He bought the businesses after he returned from the war. Kitty-corner from it across 5th Avenue is Wilfredo's Hispanic market. Next to Wilfredo's is one of my most favorite places, *The Melting Pot* diner. It's run by a crazy Greek fellow named Georgios.

On Monday mornings, the Melting Pot becomes an intellectual oasis for a bunch of aging philosophers. While we drink our morning coffees and eat our pastries, we solve the world's problems. Surprisingly, the world has not come to seek our sage advice.

From front to back, on one side of the Melting Pot, seating extends backwards with a row of red cushioned, chrome-plated counter stools before a counter. On the other side, an equally long row of vinyl-covered booths line the wall. Maps and icons of many countries hang over the booths. These were token gifts from international travelers passing through the diner. When any stranger walks in, Georgios would immediately challenge them with a question.

"My fellow world citizen, where are you from?" This morning, a dark-skinned stranger only made a gesture of incomprehension. Georgios grabbed his arm and dragged him over to a big multi-colored globe near the cash register. He pointed to himself and tapped the stranger on his chest, then pointed to New York City on the globe. He then pointed only to himself and then pointed to Greece and traced the path of a ship between Greece and New York. With his hand folded before him, he looked at the globe and waited for the stranger to respond. The man looked at the globe, pointed to Egypt, then traced an arc to New York City. He must have flown.

Upon learning the country of origin, Georgie quickly ran to the back of the diner, all the while scanning the sidewall over the booths. In seconds, he found what he was looking for, an Egyptian currency bill tacked onto the wall. He shouted and waved for the man to come look. When the stranger saw the bill, he laughed with a nodding of his head. Georgie quickly shouted for all to hear his welcome in Greek, *Kalos Irathate*, which means *Welcome! I wish you great success of it!* As Georgie ran behind the counter to fetch his new guest a cup of coffee, he exclaimed in English, "It is well you came."

Georgie is a fervent evangelist of the Age of Aquarius—a time he claims when mankind would assume its destiny with revelations of truth and enlightenment.

With the day's entertainment over, the philosophers returned to their dissection of world events being presented in their morning papers. Outside the window, life continued undisturbed.

Thursday, January 9th

Winter can be a difficult time for me. Often, I don't go out for days or even weeks. Marysia knew all about my melancholies and would force me outside, even during stormy days. I needed to force myself out today. I felt her gently pushing me out into the cold.

When I reached the Melting Pot this morning, I was surprised to see the usual Monday morning boys on a Thursday. They were sitting around the window table reading their newspapers. As I received a cup of coffee from Georgios, he commented on the table's occupants.

"Look at them, Kaz, all with their noses inside their various propaganda sheets." He shouted over to them. "Somebody say something worthwhile." He was met with silent indifference, so he walked over with me and continued his rant.

"David with your elitist *New York Times*. Sal with your capitalist *Wall Street Journal*. And now here comes Kaz, with his working man's rag, the *New York Daily News*. What stories are in those pages today that were not in there yesterday? Is there new news, or just samo-samo about who should we be fearing and hating right now? It's just samo-samo.

"Well David, how does the war go today? Well let's check today's body count." With this, he grabbed David's paper and mimicked like he was reading it. "Oh yes, more are dead today and the Paris peace talks are stalled—we are losing the war." He then reached across the table to grab my paper. "But here it says we are killing more of them than they are killing of us, so this means we are winning the war. Rah for America. Let's hate those little yellow bastards.

"My fellow citizens, there is no enlightenment in these toilet paper sheets. Show me one new story in today's papers that was not just some variation of a story you read yesterday." With that, I grabbed back my paper and opened it to its centerfold. I pulled it apart on the table for all to see, then slammed my hand in the middle of it. Everyone looked to it, then slyly smiled and awaited a response from Georgie.

The centerfold photographs were of Apollo 9. Nine would be the preparatory flight for the moon landing scheduled for this summer. As the table began to stare up at Georgie, he knew a response from him was being expected. He didn't smile, but he also didn't frown. Instead, he squeezed around the chairs to where I sat. From behind my chair, he took the sides of my head with both his hands then bent over and kissed it on my bald spot.

"You, world citizen, get a free piece of pie today, as you are correct, this is something new. In fact, this is exactly what I have been telling you oafs to expect in this new age of enlightenment that we are entering. It will be a time of scientific enlightenment leading the masses forward and not religious dogma or political bullshit. Religion and power are opium of the Dark Ages that still enslaves so many today. Scientists are going to become the leaders of the world. We will be saved by empirical knowledge rather than blind faith to an unseen deity who will not lift a finger to save us from ourselves."

I do hope Georgie is wrong. I do hope there is room in the world for both God and science. The group briefly discussed the moon shot, but once Georgie left to greet a new customer, the discussion shifted to the real interest of the day—sports.

The biggest story in the city was that the New York Jets were in the final football game of the season. A Superbowl they called it. Everyone at the table, along with everyone in New York City, knew in their hearts that the Jets were probably going to lose, but you wouldn't have known it based on the chatter. I know that any American Football League team was no match for any National Football League team, The first and second Superbowls proved that. The NFL teams had nearly tripled the scores of their AFL opponents each time. The facts didn't quell the chatter of these diner idiots.

"If the Jets could beat Baltimore that would be something that just doesn't happen every day," said Sal.

Izzie chimed in next. "The papers are saying that would be biggest upset ever in sports. Even bigger than the Dodgers beating the Yankees in '55. I'm betting on the Jets."

"Me too," added Sal. Everyone agreed. Everyone but me, that was. I sat there quietly and listened. I knew they were suckers to be betting on the home team just because they were the home team. I also knew it was never a good idea to take money from friends. I'll place a bet with Frankie later in the week. I want to see where the odds went. After a while, I went home. I never did get my promised free slice of pie.

Friday, January 10th

Frankie and I are neighbors sharing a backyard fence. His house is only a couple of hundred feet away but the difference between living on 23rd street and 24th is remarkable.

Twenty-third Street residents move about safely, even throughout the night. There are still a few trees lining the street, and whenever it was daylight, children played on the street or in its playground. At night, there are plenty of cars filling nearly every parking spot. Twenty-fourth Street has no trees on it and few houses. It's mostly factories and fenced-in truck parking lots. Only foolish souls walked there at night. It was a place for drug dealers and car-strippers.

There was only one old house remaining in the middle of the street. Sandwiched in between two factories is Frankie's house. It was a two-story, wood-shingled house with an old wooden carriage house that now holds Frankie's Cadillac. Frankie probably bought the house because of its isolation from prying eyes.

On one side of Frankie's house, the roof joins directly with the jelly factory roof next door. On the other side of the house is an alleyway, then another factory wall. I could hop my backyard fence and walk through the alley onto 24th Street without ever being seen because there were no windows on the alley walls. I have never needed to move so secretively but suspect my sons as teenagers probably had.

At night from my kitchen window, I have watched Frankie's houselights going on and off behind the always drawn curtains. I doubt anything good ever happens there. A couple of hundred feet away is not safe for anyone, not even the criminals who walk there.

Saturday, January 11th

Sancho was the perfect addition to our household when I brought him home as a puppy during Marysia's last few months. I named him after the famous squire of a knight who took on impossible tasks.

Marysia thought this was a bad idea to bring a poorly trained mutt home at that time, but she allowed it. I thought I was doing this to make her life easier. Now, I think she allowed it to make my life easier. Sancho did offer comfort and some excitement to both of us. Within weeks of his arrival, Sancho understood his role in his new home. He was another ragamuffin finding a place in the village.

Sancho has now become my only companion. When I could talk aloud, I would hold long conversations with him that he seemingly enjoyed, as he always offered me his undivided attention. I think that people thought I was in denial of Marysia's death when I began speaking in the plural, *we*, whenever asked what I had been doing. "*WE* had a good day today" or "*WE* watched baseball today."

Fathers and Sons and Other Village Idiots

Today, it's Sancho and me still holding lengthy conversations—just without sound. I stare him in the eyes and think my thoughts, and he pays attention as he always did for me. Maybe he thought that odd five years ago, but now that he is deaf, it's perfectly natural for both of us. We had a nice conversation this afternoon, so I thought it belongs in this journal.

Sancho, when I was a boy back in Poland, I often heard the word *vigrish*, so I asked Momma what it meant.

"Kazimierz, it is a Yiddish word that referred to the profit for the money lender from a loan," she said.

Today, Sancho, in Brooklyn, the term has been shortened to vig. The vig is the fee associated with a shyster's loan. The vig was always getting larger until the loan plus the vig was paid in full.

For some reason, Sancho, Frankie is letting me run up a real big tab. I can't bet with Tony anymore because Otto interfered. Did I ever tell you that a few years ago, Otto once paid off my gambling debt to Tony under the condition he stop taking my bets? I didn't expect that little Italian would take this seriously, but he did. It's really Otto's fault that he drove me to Frankie, who has a higher vig and less favorable odds on every bet. This one's not on me. It's Otto's doing.

Anyway, I need to go to Frankie's right now. I'm going to make one big bet that can't lose, and it will wipe out my debt to that shyster. I need to go right now, but I'll be back in about thirty minutes. I know that you don't like the winter. I'll be right back mi amigo.

*

Oooh Sancho, things didn't go well for me this afternoon.

When I arrived, there was a customer there, so I went to the rear of the store and grabbed a stool by the soda fountain. When the customer left, Frankie finally came back and as he poured me a cup of coffee, I handed him my note. It said that I wanted to place a bet on the Super Bowl large enough that if I won, then all my debt to him would be wiped out.

Frankie just looked at the note, then he returned it to me with a shake of his head. He was not going to accept the bet. He explained why.

He said that my debt was never with him. I owed his boss money, not him.

Well, I tell you Sancho, I was mad as hell and banged the counter with my hand. If he was on my side of the counter, I would have grabbed him by his little shirt. But I couldn't. I wrote down to him that my bet was always with him. He shook his head and said it was always with his bosses and added that they came by a few days ago and while reviewing his books, told him to cut me off from any more bets. Frankie also said they wanted their money in full by Monday. When I told him that I didn't have it that SOB said that that was not his problem.

There was no more to say, so I got up and left. I tried others in the neighborhood who I knew took bets, but oooh Sancho, no one will take my bet anymore without money upfront.

I'm in big trouble, Sancho. I have no way to get all that money by Monday.

Sunday, January 12th

Was Joe a Superman? On TV, the Jet Quarterback, Joe Namath, was guaranteeing a win. The Baltimore Colt players didn't like hearing it and said that they intended to bury him for shooting off his mouth so much.

As I read the story in my kitchen, suddenly there was banging coming from the front door. When I opened it, a cold wind blew Frankie through it. He tossed his coat over the stair post like he owned the place and continued back into my kitchen. Instead of sitting down at the table, he walked over to the window and stared out into the backyard.

"I didn't realize you had such a good view of my house over there. Seems like you have a very good view of those factory roofs too."

Fathers and Sons and Other Village Idiots

"So what," I thought. Frankie finally sat down and gestured for me to do the same across from him to get to the purpose of his visit.

"Kaz, you currently owe my boss quite a lot and, by the way, his flunkies were asking me again whether I thought that you could ever pay. I said no. Tomorrow, they will deal with you."

I wrote on a piece of paper. "When I win my bet today, I'm clear."

"And what if you lose?" We both left that remark sit on the table between us.

"Here's my proposition. I didn't put your bet into my book yet, but I could. I will or won't depending on what you want me to do. This is what I can do for you Kaz because you are my friend and a good customer." What bullshit, I thought.

"I can leave your bet off the books and pay them the money you owe. If the Colts win by 22 points or more, you are correct in that you will no longer owe anybody anything. I like you and this is a good thing for me to do for a friend."

"The betting line is 15 points," I wrote.

"My offer is 22. If you want 15, bet with my boss.

"But if you lose, you owe me quite a bit more than double your existing debt. Frankly, I don't think you will ever be able to pay me back." He looked around my kitchen as if to confirm his point of view.

"If I put the bet on the books, you owe them. If you lose today, do you want to owe me or to owe them? They want their money tomorrow. I don't." Frankie was quite right. I could never pay back either him or his boss.

"If you lose, you start to do some jobs for me."

"What kind of jobs?" I knew he used young men who owed him, to run bags of money back to the boss. I could do that.

Frankie answered quickly, "I don't even know right now." He turned away from me and started to stare out to the back of his house. "To start with, you can keep an eye on my house from here. If you ever see anyone on that roof, you call me straight away with that telephone of yours over there. You don't call the police. You call me. If you grunt a few times, I'll

23

know it's you and that someone is coming. You watch my back, so to speak. I can then protect myself." With that, he showed a handgun hidden under his sweater.

"I could do that," I wrote back. "How long would I owe you?"

"Kaz, you are not a young man. If you want me to hold your debt, consider that you will be owing me until the day one of us dies. When you die, your debt is clear, and I won't go after your sons for it. It's a better deal than my bosses will give you or your boys.

"Of course, I'd let you buy yourself out of it if you ever had enough cash, but I ain't holding my breath on that one and remember the vig is always growing."

I tried to delay but he stood up and said, "Take it or leave it. My boss will be sending a runner over just before game time. They'll review my book to see who is betting on what. I need to know now, whether you want to bet with them or me."

I had only seconds to decide because he was nearly out the front door. From the foyer through the open door, I grunted a YOU at him. When he turned back, I was pointing at him.

"Good," then he added, "and maybe your bad luck will finally change. The Jets will probably lose big anyway. I mean, buddy, this is a good bet for you even with that point spread. This will all be over in a few hours." With that he walked out the door and onto the cold street.

I knew the odds were good that the Jets would lose, but a 22 point-spread was a lot to cover. I also wondered why should my luck change now. Twenty-two points! Were the Jets really that bad?

*

C razed Jets fans were already in the Eagle when I arrived just before six. Many were already more than half drunk.

Otto's color TV and cheap beer packed them in. I staked out a stool at the end of the bar. Frankie had come early as well and set up his operations in a booth at the opposite end from the TV.

I looked up to the clocks on the wall behind the bar. Because Otto was obsessively punctual, it was impossible to

Fathers and Sons and Other Village Idiots

not know what time it was in the Eagle, since one would see a clock on every wall. A Rheingold beer clock, a Ballentine's clock, and a half a dozen cuckoo clocks covered the walls in the bar. They showed the same time, and eventually they showed kickoff time.

Behind the bar, Otto, Anthony, and his backup bartender, Alphonso, drew beers from the taps as quickly as the taps allowed. Henry was waiting tables. My thoughts flashed on some family members missing from this spectacle. Duke was still away at college. Louise, Henry's ex, was of course not invited, and Nelson, Otto's gay son, wasn't allowed in the bar, or for that matter, in the neighborhood.

In the first half, the game was closer than anyone expected, and some were beginning to think the Jets might even win without any point spread. More bets came in at even worse odds. Frankie sat smiling throughout it all.

The surreal part was that all this illegal betting was being done in plain sight. A beat cop walked in to check on the score and noticed Frankie doing business in his booth. He never said a word and after drinking a few beers, just left. He also 'forgot' to pay Otto for his beers. The price of looking the other way. The cop would collect something directly from Frankie later.

The 3rd quarter ended with the Jets winning 13-0. With the point spread of my bet, the Colts would need to score five touchdowns in one quarter for me to win. My luck hadn't changed. I'm going to die with it that way. The Jet defense kept holding the line and getting the ball back into the hands of Broadway Joe. Finally, I couldn't take it anymore, so I went home.

Monday January 13th

It was a day for underdogs, or so the papers said. While the city fell into euphoria, my mood was far from it. The radio DJs were already saying that maybe the Mets could be next.

Henry walked Sancho for me before leaving me alone once more. In my mind I heard Ivan.

How's one to know what one doesn't know?

25

I doubt anyone at the Melting Pot even noticed my absence this morning. I'm as alone today as I was some 60 years ago on that Manhattan dock, when the predators swooped in to steal what little I had.

Wednesday January 15th

Otto greeted me a "What the hell did you do?" as I walked into the Eagle this morning. I shrugged a "what" with my shoulders.

"On Sunday, I saw you ducking out of here with a long stare over to Frankie in the corner. Whenever a big game is ending around here, I always watch to see who may be slipping out without paying. I saw you leave. A sign of a loser. Then you have not been around in days. What did you do, goddammit?"

I pointed to a beer tap, but Otto shoved a cup of coffee and a half eaten piece of pastry over to me. I was hungry. Eventually, I wrote about my bet to end all bets, the meeting with Frankie, and the deal I had made.

Otto's gaze went down. Without looking up to me, he started talking.

"Dad, I can't stand it anymore. I just can't seem to protect anyone. I told you to stop gambling and you didn't. Now, you old fool, you have really made things worse. We're just a pair of stooges around here. With our wives gone, nobody's watching out for us anymore. The goddamn police won't protect us from criminals. Even our so-called god won't protect us from evil. This time, Dad, you really screwed up." He let his word sink into my stupid brain.

"Frankie is far more dangerous a bookie than Tony. Tony's a nice guy who just got caught up in things, and his boss is making him pay. Frankie, on the other hand, sought out the mob. He wanted to bring the mob into our neighborhood for him to make money.

"In this city, everybody thinks of a bookie as just a neighbor providing a service to the neighborhood much like a banker, but Dad, you gotta remember these guys are the mob and if you're working for them, you're in the mob."

"Maybe I should go to the cops," I wrote.

"Frankie would know about it before we got home and that's if we got home.

"Bookies have two important functions: covering bets and paying off cops. Not all cops are on the take, but only the bookie knows who is and who isn't. It's no coincidence that bookie territories map exactly to police precincts. It's us against them and we don't even know who them is. The reason our neighborhood has two bookies is because the neighborhood is in dispute between two crime families.

"Frankie's the kinda guy who has been getting many of the kids in the neighborhood into trouble. I think that this was how Tony was entrapped by his own gang. He started making bets and got in over his head. Frankie's bag boys come in here, and some drink too much and talk too much. It's how I know all this shit.

"Smart bookies, like Frankie, never touched anything incriminating. If you searched their store or house, you wouldn't find anything. The only incriminating item always nearby is his book. If that book with all the debts and payouts were to become public, heads would roll. Frankie's book, where all his transactions are written down, is his greatest asset, but that book could also get him killed and he knows it. He's careful as hell.

"Dad, Frankie's boss didn't come down here to look at his book. He was lying about that. Twenty-third is the slums to them. If they wanted to see the books, he'd get a copy to them with a runner. He's always maintaining two sets of records. They didn't come down unless they had serious business to deal with.

"As long as Frankie sends his bag boys with enough money each week, they don't care much if he skimmed some off the top. Frankie had his own side hustles going on and it probably doesn't concern them. He's a golden goose for them and for the people he pays off. Frankie's bosses hadn't been calling your debt to due on Monday. You were baited and you bit.

"How much do you now owe him?" I pulled the note that was in my newspaper this morning. Otto looked at it and then we both sat in silence for minutes.

Otto finally spoke. "Okay, for now just do what he asks you to do. If you see anyone on the roof near his house, call his number. Maybe be a little slow about it." At first, I thought he was kidding. He wasn't smiling.

"If he comes back to you asking to do more, you tell just me first. No one else. Not Henry. Not anybody else. Dad, you got that?" I nodded.

I came home after that. I knew that Otto was right. If he or I made one mistake in who to trust, it could be our last.

Friday January 17th

H iding forever was not going to be possible. I needed a few groceries and had to go out to get them.

While passing the Melting Pot, I stopped in and listened to everyone still gloating about the game. Eventually the topic changed. The world's news was no better.

In Paris, they continue to argue about the shape of the peace talks table. While America was calling itself the world's greatest superpower, Soviet cosmonauts were boarding a rocket in preparation for their own moon landing. The paper speculated about who was going to win the race to the moon.

In the national news section, Sal read an article about a new train called the Metroliner. It could travel from New York to Washington, D.C. in less than 3 hours. Georgie was especially excited about this engineering achievement.

Locally, it was cloudy and freezing again. The winter going to be a long cold one to live through. I sat with my friends at the table in silence and just listened. No one seemed to notice. I had become an insignificant fly on the wall.

Initially, when Little Prick cut out what I call my voice box, I was mad as hell when people began to ignore me. I know my debility made them uncomfortable, and they just wanted me to be quiet. I no longer have the energy to fight it.

Oddly, I have begun to enjoy being this invisible fly. Without the burden of participation, I can listen. All I needed now was to hear something worthwhile.

David said, "A police station got bombed and cops ambushed the other day. Boys, this war has reached our home front."

"We need to start shooting these protestors," responded Sal.

"Those protestors are fighting for our freedom," countered Georgie from behind his cash register. "We're in this war because the country is being led by religious and nationalistic zealots and not men of reason."

"Did you see the prayer that LBJ wrote for his last day in the White House? The president wrote a prayer that the *Daily News* published this morning. A president of the United States is openly praying in the newspapers. Jesus Christ! This is bad." I noted the irony of an atheist swearing. David read on.

"Deliver us from the follies of power and pride. Show us the uses of our strengths that will make life better on this earth for all Thy children. In season and out, help us to hold to the purposes Thou has taught us, feeding the hungry, healing the sick, caring for the needy, trusting our young, training them up in the way they should go."

Sal added, "Feeding the hungry, healing the sick. I wonder what Jesus thought when he read that over his morning coffee."

David jumped in, "Think of all he killed with his bombs. Hey Sal, with you being religious, is being a hypocrite a sin? LBJ may be sitting in hell soon."

Time to bring in the next liar."

Tuesday January 21ˢᵗ

Nixon stated that his quest was for peace abroad and unity at home. Time to bring in the next liar.

Wednesday, January 22nd

I hoped that today would be better for me, but it wasn't. This morning, I walked into the Eagle, only to find Otto and Anthony arguing. I never found out what they were fighting about, so just had a cup of coffee then went home to stare at Sancho and think about my family.

Henry and Duke have been fighting each other for years too. I can't seem to stop any of them. It's all just so stupid. Fathers and sons are all such idiots.

Thinking of Duke does remind me that I need to remember to stop calling him Duke. He prefers William, his baptismal name. Henry was stupid to start calling the boy Duke after his favorite Dodger. Louise should never have allowed it.

William has grown to hate his father for many expectations that fathers can put on their sons. Fathers truly are a pretty stupid lot, and there seems to be no exception to this rule. Fathers place many expectations on their sons, which contributes to our becoming raving lunatics. There is no escape from this village idiot merry-go-round.

Wednesday, January 29th

Dear Marysia,
Sorry that I have not written to you lately. I haven't written in a week. You know how I can get in winter. It's been hard to just get out of bed, but today I did go outside.

Despite the freezing cold, Henry forced me to spend the day with him and Otto in the Eagle. Sancho sat with me in the booth as I read a book. I can't say that anything interesting happened there today, but it was kinda good to get out. I will try to get out more and resume writing daily. Writing to you seems to lift my spirits.

Your sad sack of a husband,
Kaz

Thursday, January 30th

The winter skies were once again gray, and the winds continued to blow off the harbor. I knew there wouldn't be many in the Eagle with that weather, so I thought that I'd venture out. Otto served me up some potato and sausage in my booth, then abandoned me to return his sanctuary behind his bar barrier. Henry sat before him nursing a beer. I just listened in.

"Where's Anthony today?" asked Henry.

"He's in the cellar getting a shovel and the ice chopper. I told him to get the ice off the sidewalk. Of course, he argued about it. He only wanted to toss sand."

"I didn't notice much out there. Maybe it doesn't need it."

"I own this place, not you or him. If someone falls in front of your house, they just pick themselves up off their dupas and keep walking. If someone falls in front of a business, someone gets sued for their doctor bills." Henry seemed to be thinking of a retort then changed the subject.

"What's Anthony's plans for his future? Does he have any yet?" I know what Henry was doing and probably so did Otto, but he answered anyway.

"He probably thinks he can run this place. Beyond that, I don't think he has any. He didn't get much of an education like your boy is doing. He got through the Army okay but didn't want a career there. He's probably right that he'll get this place. I've got no one else to give it to."

"What about Nelson?" Henry knew the unlikeliness of that. It was just a brother poking at a brother's open wound. Otto didn't take a moment to respond back.

"Do you want Nelson to turn this place into a gay bar like the ones he goes to in the Village? Over my dead body will Nelson get to run this place. I'll burn it down first."

When it was discovered that Nelson was gay, Otto literally ran him out of the neighborhood. Nelson has been living over in Greenwich Village since.

Nelson had been Otto's true pride and hope. He easily let it be known that he thought that Nelson was the smarter son. According to Otto, the smartest kid in the school, best athlete on the street, the funniest kid in the family. He excelled at anything he set his mind to. This was all according to Otto back then.

Nelson had been heading towards college just like William, but those dreams died when Otto threw him out of the house. I see Nelson now and then in the Village, but Nelson never comes around the street anymore. Henry probably realized he'd gone far enough with Otto for today and returned to the original discussion.

"Do you think Anthony can handle running the Eagle?"

Otto showed that he had been considering this question and quickly replied with an emphatic no. "Anthony's world is too black and white. He sees everything in terms of right and wrong and never understands that there are gray areas where compromise is needed. I think his mother influenced him too much with her religion.

"And he pisses off customers as well because he is too quick to tell them they're full of shit. Even when they are, you can't say that and keep them as customers.

"I've had to kick him out of here a few nights because of the arguments he started. Those customers rarely come back, but he does. He makes life hard on himself with his opinions. When he is the only boss around here, he's going to be sitting here alone. No, I don't think he can run the place, which is why I can't retire until I am dead, and I don't need money anymore. He'll run this place into the ground.

"Now your boy is making something of himself. He'll get out of college, serve in the military as an officer, and get a good job. He's got a shot of getting off this street alive. Twenty-third ain't safe no more, for any of us. The goddamm gangs own the streets with those bastard cops who are always shaking me down. It's great that Duke is gonna to be able to get out. Those immigrants keep flooding in too." I smirked at that last comment. Apparently, Otto forgot his father was the immigrant in the neighborhood some 60 years ago.

"Yeah, I guess I am lucky, but I'm not so sure about Duke becoming an officer," said Henry. "I do wish he had come home more often these last two years. He said that his friend's family sets him up with a place to live in the summer and a good summer job. Duke's a hard worker and he is putting himself through college with his scholarship and the money he makes. Yeah, he's going to do well, but I wish I saw more of him. I don't feel like I know him anymore." Otto just nodded.

"I know that my divorce was hard on him. He probably doesn't want to be here to need to be choosing between his mom and me."

"Hank, you really screwed up with Louise. She was something special."

"You know," answered Henry, "even though I have Linda in my life now, I still think of Louise every day. Is that screwed up or what?"

"Does Duke know about Linda?"

"No, not yet. I figure I'll introduce them to each other if she and I are still together in May." Otto had no response to that.

"Have you heard anything from Louise since she moved in with her mother in Staten Island?"

"Nope," he said, as he shook his head, then he turned and called over to me. "Hey Dad, you hear from Louise?" I just shook my head and pretended I hadn't been listening in.

At that point, Anthony came up from the cellar. He made a point of saying the little bit of ice that was there, had been chopped out. When nobody said anything, he grabbed a broom and started sweeping. Some family I got.

Monday, February 10ᵗʰ

Snow drifts impaired my journey to the Melting Pot this morning. Eventually, I got there to take a seat next to Sal, whose face was buried in his newspapers. Georgie stood behind the counter pouring free coffee to three striking dock workers sitting on the stools. The Brooklyn docks had been shut down for months. The silence was deafening until stupid Sal shattered it.

"Shit. It looks like the baseball players are going to strike." The lack of any response from anybody in the room furthered deadened it. The one man at the counter looked over towards Sal with no small amount of disgust. Before he could get up, I hit Sal in the back of the head with my newspaper to try to avoid a confrontation. I gestured to the men at the counter. Sal looked over then said no more.

Maybe someday these unions will become as powerful as the corporations they try to resist, but that day isn't here yet. Outside of the diner window, the snow continued to pile up. The schools and airports were closing. Highways too. The city was shutting down.

*

Once back at home, Sancho limped up to me for a scratch behind his ear. Later, Sancho tried to get comfortable by my feet, but with each move he groaned. I was beginning to consider whether it was time to put him down, then words from Ivan came to mind.

Death doesn't come running, but you can't run away from it, neither; nor must you be helping it along.

"Sancho, that is from Kasyan from the Beautiful Lands.

"What shall we do my furry little friend? Shall we try to run anyway?

"You probably don't fear death like I do. How could you when you don't understand the permanence of it? Your only awareness is life, so you have no fear. Lucky you.

"I don't really understand death any better than you, yet I have such fear of it. Religion makes us think we understand death, but we just don't. They're full of shit and so am I for hoping they are right.

"Anyway, Sancho, for now, let's live with our pains until we find some answers. Maybe we cannot run faster than death, but we can keep running to buy more time for our quest.

"For now, Sancho, we are two old dogs running as hard as our timeworn bodies allow. We'll run until we cannot and that will be that."

He licked my hand then returned to his nap on a comfortable mat near the radiator.

Friday, February 14ᵗʰ

My happiness today cannot be deterred by the snowbanks on 23rd Street, the student protests occurring at City College, nor the raging war in faraway Asia.

Regardless of these burdens, I have one thing that always makes me happy, the thought of you, Marysia. I cannot let my sadness with life deter me from saying what I feel on this Valentine's Day.

My Beloved Marysia,

You have always been in the joyous seasons of my heart. For all future seasons, it will always be so. Before you in my life, there was only winter's lonely darkness. My cold existence had no reason for it. All the depths of my experiences from my life before you are trivial by comparison. You gave my existence warmth and purpose.

Our marriage vow to each other was to be loving hearts enriching the world. My life flowered with this expectation. This started our seemingly endless summers of happiness. We enjoyed the passions of love and emotion; bore our ecstasies and hardships together; raised two boys into men; and built a family from where there was none.

Fall's splashy colors rejuvenated our love for each other. We strived to sustain our wedding promise. We never expected death would kill off our celebratory autumn.

Winter's darkness has been in my heart since you left, but this year I have resolved to seek my light to be with you this time forever. You left for what you said would be another place for us to love each other. Through your loving heart, you have fulfilled your wedding promise to me by enriching me beyond my expectations. I cherish that you spent your lifetime with me.

Your loving Kazimierz

Wednesday, February 19th

B erkeley student protests were once again in the news. This is where William studies. He is supposed to graduate in May. Of course, Uncle Sam will want to send his poor white ass to fight some poor yellow ass until one or both of them are dead. His own father, who went to war in Europe, does not think fighting in a war is such a bad thing for the boy. He expects his son to do the same. I don't think it is a good idea. All wars are not all necessary.

Even in the world wars, for every rich kid, there were dozens of poor kids going through the breach. Disproportionately, the poor are sacrificing all to protect the rich's way of life because the poor are certainly not fighting to protect their way of life. I no longer trust my country to be doing the right thing. I trust it now as little as my father trusted the tsars of Europe.

But I have no say on this matter. I came of soldiering age between wars, so my voice does not seem to count to anyone but me. Even my sons don't want to listen to my dissent.

Henry expects William to enlist this summer after college to become an officer, but I know the boy better and that he will not enlist nor allow himself to be drafted. He had told me as much in his occasional letters to me. I was hoping for a peace before he graduated, but it doesn't seem likely. Maybe I should have prayed.

Rational leaders, like Kennedy and Eisenhower, who fought for the good of the country, have now gone away. My only remaining hope seems to come from these student protesters. I don't like putting all my hope in them alone, but they seem to be the only ones speaking out. Blacks and women are protesting, but only for themselves. Some say they cannot afford to align with those other causes. Selfishly, we all look out only for our clan. Nelson told me once of the gay groups that were fighting for their rights, but no one wants to support them and be thought to be gay. Imagine if all the protestors could unite. But they will not and divided they each will fail.

William has no rich family to protect him, and he is not likely to take a defense job. After college is finished, he will be the first that Uncle Sam takes, while the rich kids go back home to their families to make more money. The serfs are still the warriors who die for the rich. Nothing has changed. These next few months are going to pass quickly. I cannot trust even God to save William. We poor seem forsaken by all.

Thursday, February 20th

Mad people all live a long time—you know, every grief has its good side.

Yes, Ivan, I am surrounded by madmen and idiots. Sadly, I am related to a few and have always been one myself. The madness helps us all to survive.

I hate my father and would still do anything to hurt him wherever his soul may be. One of the last things he knew of me was that I wanted to be a writer. He took that away from me, just as Otto has taken college away from Nelson. For no other reason than simply to torment my father in hell, I think that today I shall write in poetic metaphors. While I realize I am using verse as a weapon of hate, hating him does help me survive. Yes, I am mad, and it is my good side. With madness, I survive another day.

Billy Warren

My Village Idiots

I am like a pathetic old dog who does not know when it is
time to die
My squat little Sancho remains a faithful servant to his
imprudent knight
Bless him that he still walks alongside me and teaches me
how to joust with death
My sons, Otto and Henry, have been both shields of protection
for their country but are also swords that slash at the flesh of
their own offspring
William does not endure his father's lightning bolts
temperately but revolts back as a raging storm
Otto's now favorite son, Anthony, smells only wickedness
wherever he looks
His righteousness makes it hard for him to understand
goodness
Otto's vanquished son, Nelson, is the lion who stands for
truth to self, regardless of the fief to pay
My ex-daughter-in-law, Louise, is a maelstrom of reasonable
unreasonableness
For her to be happy, she needs to pick between those two
opposing realities
Edward, my lighthouse, shines no more for me
With him in my sights, I could hear my way through
darkness
If I would allow, he would protect me, even from myself
The last idiot in this village is a cancer
Ever present, ever growing

My Queen

Marysia you of course were none of these things and
all of these things to me
beloved queen of the realm
heroic protector from my depressions
righteous lioness shielding her cubs
conflicted enigma of contrary passions
emotional compass through darkness

You are the malady that will forever enrich
all seasons of my soul.
You must nurse my madness along a path to my redemption.

Friday, February 21ˢᵗ

The baseball strike seems to upset more people than the students getting hurt at Berkeley or City College. I am giving up on this day.

Wednesday, February 26ᵗʰ

Baseball peace. People do seem to need it now. I confess that I can't bear any more bad news. I need the pastime to sooth my mind. Georgie calls religion an opium. Maybe my religion and drug have become baseball to quiet my mind. I cannot disagree. Baseball peace is wonderful.

I found a letter on the vestibule floor this afternoon. It was for me from William. Even though Henry had picked up the other mail, he left that letter on the floor. He no longer gets letters from his only child. William's letter was a thoughtful one, so I will staple it into this journal.

Dear Grandpa,

Thank you for writing to me. It was good to hear from you, but you asked many questions of me without telling me how you were.

I hope you are well and if you are not, please let me know immediately. Family and friends are always needed to support one another during bad times. I have a close friend here, who I can share my thoughts. I was wondering who your close friends might be these days.

Bazarov is my friend's name, but I usually call him Balzie. My being a history major and he a political science major, we have been in many classes over the years. Politically, we are aligned against the war, though we have our differences too. He believes that people don't follow socialism because they are uninformed, while I believe people prefer capitalism because they are self-interested and inherently greedy. Our debates do help me formulate my points of view.

Last Thursday, we went to an anti-war demonstration on campus. It was sad to see it end in a riot. I am still not sure how that happened. Most protesters were content to march and shout, but then others arrived whose only intent was to incite both sides. They taunted those on the one side of barriers as they also incited those on the other side to react. A few wore helmets and when I saw one pull a brick from a backpack, Balzie and I decided to leave. We were not hurt, but we did need to move quickly to escape the riot as well as the police, who also seemed to have come for the same purpose—violence.

Again, I am fine, just disappointed. While I confess that I am afraid, I will be as brave as I can be, and continue to go to peace marches, but I will keep a greater awareness of those around me.

I recently read a letter in the New York Times in which the writer wrote of Americans' disenfranchisement with government. He cited that we were abdicating too much authority to a single man who can keep a whole nation in war.

I do agree with this notion that presidents have become too powerful, which is why I will continue to protest despite the dangers to me. I do this not only because my student deferment will end when I graduate, but also because I believe this war is immoral. It does not fit with American values of justice for all. Capitalist greed and nationalist pride are driving this war, not America's value of freedom and human rights for all.

Take care of yourself and please write again.

Love,
William

I feel ashamed that William's protesting and not me. He has so more to lose than I do. Am I a coward to not stand up for what is right?

I am afraid that at my age, I will be hurt if I protest. When I was a young man, I thought it would be bad for my family if I got arrested. Now, these protests seem dangerous to me. I am afraid. Once again, I am silenced.

It makes me angry to think that both the agitators and the police want the riot to make these protests unsafe. It scares people like me away from participating. I am afraid for myself, and this makes me selfish. I am afraid that if I am hurt or even killed right now, I would have failed in my quest. It's only about me and I am ashamed.

Now it seems my quest, which I had thought was good, is having me value my life too much. Life is precious, but I might be better off without this quest. It is preventing me from doing the right things.

Tuesday, March 4th

Apollo 9 launched yesterday. I imagine that Georgios must be very excited today. Maybe I'll drop in to see him tomorrow. Today's not the right day. In truth, I haven't been outside in nearly a week.

What got me out today was that I needed to go over the hospital where I had my throat surgery five years ago. I heard that Terence was back in. He too has begun his 5th year, but he's not doing so well.

After our surgeries, he'd come over to the Eagle now and then, or I'd go over to see him at his local bar. What I remember most about him was how alone he seemed. Even in his local bar, no one knew who he was.

Today, I sat for a few hours by his hospital bed, but he's already in a deep sleep. A nurse told me that he won't be waking up. In all the hours I sat there, few came. One orderlie asked me if I was family and I shook my head. "Too bad. I heard that nobody else has been in since he arrived."

"What'll happen to him when he goes?" I wrote.

Fathers and Sons and Other Village Idiots

"Don't know. Social worker takes care of that." With that said, he pushed his cart out of the room and turned down the hall.

Dying alone sucks. Only thing worse is being alone when still alive. Terence had both happen to him.

I have written about 23rd Street as my little Polish village, but lately I see it more like a rowboat in vast sea. I see groups of us are adrift in our little boats. Some of the boats adrift with a whole family in them. Others may have only one soul in them. No one talking from boat to boat. Us and them, even when the us may be only one.

Across the street from my house, is an eight-family four-story walk-up. There are people living in that building who I have seen for many years. Despite being so close for so long, I hardly know them at all. Many seem so isolated, living in that big, red brick building.

It was actually Father Ed who introduced me to Margaret the prostitute. He, of course, does not call her that, but that is her profession. She lives on the first floor with two small children, a boy and a girl. She is from the Dominican Republic and attends OLC church. Maybe Our Lady is saving her as she saved me. From my window, I can see the men who come and go throughout the day and night, even when the children were home. During the summer months, she'd come over and sit with me on my stoop. She knew that I can't talk, yet she was always willing to read my notes. Sometimes we would converse about the weather, our children, or how hard it can be to live in this country. Other times, we would just sit. I have enjoyed it when she came. She is such a lonely young girl, fighting to keep her children alive.

Tony, the bookie, used to have his own house up the street. Somehow his fortunes changed. Now, he rents an apartment in the big brick building. He's close to my age and has daughters and a son somewhere in New Jersey, however no family live on the 23rd anymore. He always makes a point of saying it was temporary, but he has been there alone for years. He says that when he closes his barber shop, he'll move closer to his children. I can see that Tony doesn't seem to have much fight left in him.

Eugene is a black man who lives alone on the top floor. He's a factory evening shift worker, so he is often around during the mornings and comes home after midnight. Occasionally, I'd see him in the Eagle for a nightcap near closing time. He once mentioned to Otto that he had an ex-wife and children elsewhere. He used to attend Father Ed's annual friendship party when it was held at the Eagle. That party hasn't happened in years. Not since I threw Ed out of my life.

Wilfredo, the Puerto Rican, owns the grocery store across 5th Avenue from Frankie's. I know Wilfredo and his family pretty well. I shop at his store when I don't want to walk seven blocks to the A&P. I've never seen him in at the Eagle except at Father Ed's parties. Wilfredo's sons are getting older. He's more worried for them now. Felix joined the Navy and is in the war somewhere. Hector, the younger son, is in and out of high school.

All of us in our little rowboats, not tossing a lifeline to anyone. Ed's party used to toss lifelines to those willing to catch them.

I wish that I could wake up Terence to tell him that I'll miss him.

Wednesday, March 5th

Henry has never called William by phone since he went to university four years ago. For some reason, he called California today. Linda had just left the apartment.

Because Henry's extension of the house phone line is near the top of the stairs, I could hear only one side of this conversation and it sorta went like this.

"Hi Duke, it's your Dad." Henry waited for a response.

"Yeah, I saw you wrote Grandpa last week, but you and I can talk out loud which is better. Right?

"Yeah son, it's good to hear your voice too.

Fathers and Sons and Other Village Idiots

"So, I'd been wondering when you'd be home after graduation and what your plans were. I want to have a party back here at the Eagle to celebrate. You know you're the first in the family to get a college degree.

"No, I want to. Everyone here wants to see you. This way, you can see them all at once.

"Okay, sometime in late May. Can you pin that down?

"Well okay, that's fine. Will you be flying or taking a train?

"Driving? How can you do that?

"Oh, with that friend of yours. Well good, I guess. Good for you and him to see the country to see what you're fighting for when you enlist.

"What do you mean, you want to talk about a few things when you get here? If you don't enlist, you're gonna get drafted into the Army as a private. That might get yourself killed. Use your education, Duke, to get into officer training school. You'll be fine there.

"Okay, okay. We'll talk when you get here.

"How 'bout this? Try and call me a few days out and let me know when you will be here. I'll book Uncle Otto's hall for the night.

"Okay, okay, we won't have it that night, but will you call a few days out anyway?

"Good. Thanks.

"Oh, about the party, I think it might be best if you don't invite your mom. She and I don't speak anymore, and I think it would be awkward for her to be here. You can see her later and she can do her own thing and then you could see Grandma

45

too. Her mother's nice and I know that she would like to see you.

"She died last fall. No one told me. Well, I guess we won't be seeing her. You know that old line, "I have a great mother-in-law, she's dead.

"Okay. Okay. Bad joke. Sorry. Just again, I don't think you should invite your mom here. I am sorry too that your mom is alone over there. I didn't know and guess I'm kinda got surprised with this news.

"Okay, thanks. Well, talk to you soon. It's okay to call collect here if you need me. Just talk fast, these calls cost a lot.

"Yes, good to talk to you too Duke. So long."
And with a click of the phone, the call was over in less than three minutes. What wasn't said on that call was, of course, all the important stuff that fathers and sons should talk about. I'm the pot calling the kettle black on this. I was a failed son in my father's eyes and he in mine as a father. Why should this be different for my son and grandson?
Here's another worry I have after listening to this call. Given Henry's reactions, I know that William never mentioned his recent political activism, and Henry forgot to mention he had a live-in girlfriend here. The fireworks of summer are coming.

Thursday, March 6ᵗʰ

Marysia, please forgive me.

Henry's deceitful conversation with William yesterday made me realize I should be more truthful to you and to reveal an awkward secret. I feel I must be honest if I am to achieve honest redemption. There is someone other than you, who lives irrationally within my heart and one who I also can never seem to vanquish from it. While my love for you has never and will never waiver, there is another I love, but I love in a much different way.

My other love hugged me and maybe she even kissed me. I really cannot remember a kiss. I only remember I cried in her arms on the day you died.

Then one day came and she, too, was no longer in my life. The night she told me goodbye, tears rolled down my cheeks as I walked up the snow-covered sidewalk away from her new home. I guess I was going back to Brooklyn, but it was not important where I was going. She and I had just said goodbye. I was truly alone again in the world.

I was lost because she would no longer be a part of my life. I didn't fully realize how absolute that would be. I truly believed she loved me then, but her mind could not allow me in her future. While you have passed on to a better place, she still walks this earth, but not with me even as a friend. My only remaining hope is that someday, I can just know that she is fine. I know all this is irrational and this is all about my needs not hers, but I remain in love with the memories of her.

Of course, Marysia, you can guess who I miss. I can never forgive her for so completely leaving my life so easily. Nevertheless, I cannot vanquish her from my thoughts and heart either.

Your irrationally stupid husband,
Kazimierz

Saturday, March 8th

The Melting Pot was where I had my breakfast today, and I was pleasantly surprised to see Sal there as well. It was nice to sit with him reading at our table rather than being alone in my kitchen. Georgios sat nearby daydreaming. Few customers visited his diner on Saturdays.

"Two days ago, the spacewalk was canceled due to illness," Sal said. "Today, a rocket failed to fire. Perhaps my God is not so happy with your Aquarians stepping into his stars."

"That's exactly the fears your religion has strewn upon humanity for centuries. We Aquarians will continue to rise into your god's stars and beyond, and he'd better not stand in our way."

I sat there wondering who will prevail in the escalating tension between man and God. Is there no room for both in this world? I want science to provide reasonable answers to our challenges, but for Marysia's sake, I do so want for there to be a god and a heaven.

Monday, March 10th

A fly on the wall was again what I became at the Eagle. After coffee with all the boys at Georgie's, I went directly over to the Eagle for a lunch.

Otto was behind the bar getting ready for his day of business. Henry sat across from him drinking his early lunch. Other than us, the bar was empty again. Business hadn't been good lately, so Otto had time to listen to his brother.

"Otto, he just does not really understand how hard life really is," started Henry.

"His life was going where Louise and I wanted it to go. He studied hard. He got a scholarship to a big school out west. This spring, he is going to become the first in our family to graduate college. How about that? I am sure Louise is very proud of him too. At least, I think Louise is proud of him."

Otto's heard all this before and just played his part as a listening bartender. Letting the customer talk until they paused and were looking for some response. Henry hadn't yet reached his pause.

"I am not so sure we made the right choice for him. I am not so sure that he is prepared for real life. Life's hard, and he does not understand this." Otto managed a grunt at this point but still said nothing. He might not have been listening at all.

"The divorce was hard on the boy. I know that. I really messed up when I lost her. I think of her every day—almost every minute. When is she ever going to leave my mind?" Finally, he paused and looked up from his beer to his brother. Otto finally noticed the pause and spoke.

"Yeah, Henry, Louise was a blessing to you, and you pissed off a great gal. I'm not sure how you could have made such a wonderful person like her hate you so much, but you did. You won't even tell me what you did."

"You want to know what I did. Well, I'll tell you. I just hit the boy when he was talking nonsense. I hit him in the face and blooded his nose, and she left me for it." Otto said nothing. I too absorbed the revelation. I never knew what had happened after I left the house that night. Thoughts of my dad hitting me, returned to me.

"She was right to leave me and I'm sorry for what I did. I'm sorry she left. I can't change any of that. She won't talk to me. I've tried. She won't even stay on the line. She just hangs up each time."

"Stop trying Hank. Leave her alone and move on. You owe her that much."

"But I can't stop thinking about her. When is that going to end? It's been over two years."

Otto didn't answer immediately. "Maybe it won't. Maybe this is your penance."

"Otto, I am not old yet, but I can't keep thinking about her all the time." This time, Otto was quick to respond.

"Wake up Hank! Look in the mirror. We're both nearly 50 and neither of us are going to be young again. Our sons, they are the young men now. Now it's their turn to screw up. Step aside. Dad did to let us screw up, so it's their turn. We're three old drunks pissing away our lives." I stopped writing and

49

looked up to Otto. He noticed me looking and shut up. He had never called me a drunk before. I had thought only I knew that.

He continued to stare at me, then finally back to Henry. Abruptly, he ripped off his apron and turned to walk away. "I've got to get some stuff from the loft for tonight's hall party. Maybe see you both later."

Henry asked, "Ya need any help? I could use some cash."

As Otto continued to walk away, he answered, "Yeah, sure, tonight. Be here at four to help setup the hall. I need you after midnight to clean up. I got a funeral lunch tomorrow afternoon, so the hall has to be cleaned tonight. Come back sober or don't come at all." Otto just walked away.

And that was it. Henry swallowed his last gulp of beer and left too. I'm just a fly on the wall that everyone forgets is even still alive. Fine family that we have collapsed into. Three old drunks pissing away our lives.

Wednesday, March 12th

F rankie showed up at my doorway this morning. Fortunately, Henry was not home.

The scum didn't come in. He just handed me a piece of paper and said, "I haven't seen you in a few days. You need to go see someone and tell him his debt is due on Friday. Here's his name and the address. It's his restaurant, so go a little before noon tomorrow and he'll be there. On the back of the paper is my message."

This seemed safe enough as it was in a pretty good neighborhood and during the day. I decided to not tell Otto about it.

Thursday, March 13th

T he breach was what I walked through today. About 11, I got on the 5th Avenue bus towards Bay Ridge then transferred at 86th Street to make my way up to Bensonhurst. The place wasn't really a restaurant at all, it was a pizzeria bar under the el. I walked in through the door. In the vestibule to

Fathers and Sons and Other Village Idiots

the left were stairs going up to the apartments above. To the right was a blacked-out glass door to the bar. I went right through the darkened door. After the door closed behind me, I could barely see the bartender standing behind the bar.

"I need to give the owner a message," I wrote on a note that I pushed over to him.

"Don't you talk?" I shook my head. I mimicked taking a pull on a cigarette then pointed to the scar on my neck from Little Prick's surgery.

"That sucks for you. Okay, then what message ya got?"

"Are you Green?" I wrote.

"No, but I know him personally. Just give me the message."

I passed him Frankie's note and he read it loudly enough that he could be heard throughout the bar. "If you don't pay up on your debt by Friday, we might be having some problems."

"That's it?" He started looking over my shoulder to see if I was really alone or not. I was very alone, and both he and I were very aware of that fact.

"Are you making a threat, old man, to my friend?

I wrote quickly, "I was just told to bring your boss this note. I don't know anything more than that."

As he started to come around the bar he said, "I told you, old man, that I am more than an employee of Mr. Green, I am a close friend who watches out for him. You can take that f-in message and shove it up your . . ." A voice from the back interrupted.

"Bring this man over here, Johnny. Let me see his face."

Johnny pulled me by my arm to the rear, and this obese old guy looked up from his spaghetti. This was like out of a two-bit mobster movie from the '30s. We both just looked at each other, then he said, "You know what this is all about?" I shook my head.

"I can tell you, Mr. Delivery Boy. Those goddamn Jets that's what." He was getting angry now and with only me in the bar, I didn't like being the delivery boy in this room. I could see why Frankie didn't do this call himself. I was the poor bastard sent into the breach.

51

"Who told you to give me this goddamn message?"

"Frankie, a bookie down on 23rd," I wrote, then added, "I lost on that game too. That's why I'm here working off what I owe."

"Frankie?"

"Frankie is now collecting debts for Joey," he said in somewhat disbelief.

"And they both sent you. An old man. Are they dreaming, old man?"

He stared into my eyes. I could not tell which way this was going to go for me. All this time, the bartender stood directly behind me with his left hand still on the scruff of my jacket and his right hand curled into a fist. Finally, the big man spoke again.

"This guy is a dreamer. Let go of him." With that, the bartender released me with a push towards the front. I moved as fast as I could out the door into the light of day.

Once back in the neighborhood, I went to Frankie's store and wrote that it didn't sound like Mr. Green was going to pay. Frankie didn't seem surprised. Finally, he said, "That was sort of an obligatory notification. He has until Friday to pay. After that, it will all be rectified.

"The funny thing is he has the goddamn money, but he is testing authority here. It's too bad that this has become a pissing contest between the two men." With that, he turned away.

I always feel that the less I know, the better for me, so I went home. I can't tell Otto about this yet. He can't do anything anyway.

Saturday, March 15th

Stan the cop stopped by the Eagle tonight and mentioned that last night up on 86th Street, a bartender got tossed through a glass door. Stan heard from a fellow cop that the bartender had been worked over pretty badly before he was tossed. The police responded, but the bar owner quickly said that the employee tripped coming down the stairs and tumbled through the glass door. It made no sense to the police on the scene, but without a complaint from anyone, they were happy to walk away.

"Looks like someone picked yesterday to settle an old debt. Let's hope that ends it and settles that matter, whatever it was." Stan finished his beer, paid his tab, and left.

Sunday, March 16th

I went to church. I can't really believe it myself. Georgie would be ashamed of me, but I'm not here to make him happy.

After the last Mass of the day, when nearly all had left the church, I moved forward to kneel before my Black Madonna. There I wrote my prayer on a piece of paper. Writing it down seemed to make praying more real for me than just thinking it.

Dear Holy Mother,

I have sinned in doing wrong for Frankie.

I have also risked all that is left of importance to me, my quest.

I need strength to fight my fears and depressions.

I pray for you to send me an angel to guide me to my next step.

Kazimierz

Then from behind, I heard a voice speak. "Well, I thought I spotted you in that back pew, but I couldn't really believe it to be true. A heathen in my church." I turned.

I was hoping to see a glowing angel hovering above, but I knew the voice. I looked into the fat old face of Father Ed. When did he get so old and so fat? Ed was a few years older than me, but since I last saw him, he had aged a lot. He now needs a cane to move his fat dupa around. Nevertheless, Ed's over six feet tall and I'd bet those arms could still lift me over his head and toss me as my father once did.

"I had been waiting outside for you on 24th street and thought you had slipped away from me. What brings you here today?" I gestured with my head to the painting and raised the paper in my hand.

"Oh." He responded with a nod. "May I read what you have been discussing with our Madonna?" Strangely, I didn't hesitate. At that moment, I almost felt compelled to show him. He read my note slowly and considered it. Maybe I saw a slight upturn to a corner of his lips.

"So, you are seeking to know what your next step should be in this mysterious quest of yours. Well, perhaps I am already too late to answer that one as I think you have already taken several steps today.

"First, you are here in a church on a fine Sunday afternoon when I suspect there is some ballgame on your TV. Second, you are seeking help from our Madonna. And third, you are even talking to me again."

I wrote, "Don't tell me that you are the best angel that she could come up with on short notice."

As he laughed, he answered, "I am quite sure I have not been sent to be your guardian angel, but you could do worse. Frankly, they don't pay me enough and I'm not that holy to be an angel.

"I can say that if you let me hang around with you again, together we can find your angels and mine. Perhaps you can complete your quest, and I will get to see the once-in-a-lifetime miracle I have always wanted to see. I am getting old, so it needs to happen soon. Perhaps none of this will happen, but at least we might have a laugh or two looking for angels in all places—South Brooklyn."

"When did you get back to OLC?" I wrote.

"Well, you know the diocese. They kept transferring me to other parishes. After a few years, I got to come back here. This neighborhood is my only home. The bishop has finally agreed that I may retire here and live in the cottage behind the rectory. I got back last year."

He continued, "I have missed you, my friend. I have missed you not only as a parishioner of the church, but also as my friend. You know better than anyone I have never had very many close friends in life. It has been difficult for me knowing you didn't want to see me after Marysia left us."

"She was taken from us by him," I said as I gestured to the crucifix above us.

"Left or taken as you say. What would she want us to be doing until we can be with her again?"

I had never realized until then that I had done to Ed, what Louise had done to me. Louise and I abandoned the ones who love us even though it was not their fault.

Ed and I hugged before our Madonna, then walked out of the church together. It felt like a good day today. Winter thawed just a bit and hope was warming. Maybe this could still be a good final spring for me.

Monday, March 17th

Everyone is Irish on Saint Patrick's Day. The parade was this afternoon in the city. As a result, the Eagle was packed this evening with all sorts of people. We might not have as many real Irish in the Eagle as in the Irish pub up the avenue, but we did have more people tonight because we had us Poles, the Italians, the Greeks, some Jews, and even a few Irish as well.

Otto was putting green food dye in the beers and wore his green bartender's apron. Anthony had changed all the lightbulbs to green bulbs. In the dark green light, we all looked the same. Tonight, we all melted into one Irish village and got drunk together.

Father Ed, who hadn't been at the Eagle for St. Pat's Day in quite some time, entered it, greeting the crowd with a "Beannachtaí na Féile Pádraig oraibh!" He later wrote that down for me. It means *a St Patrick's Day blessings to you all*. Because of his long absence from the Eagle, he was continually toasted by everyone he bumped into. I doubt that he bought any drinks tonight.

Last week, I mentioned that Stan the cop was a regular patron of the Eagle. Despite his being Irish, he, too, chose to celebrate with us in the Eagle. When Stan saw Ed, he greeted him with a "Sláinte mhaith," which Ed responded with "Sláinte agatsa." Ed told me later the greeting meant *Good health* and the response meant *To your health as well*.

Ed drank for good health with so many that my dear priest was not in a decent condition to go near his rectory. Tonight, he sleeps in my spare bedroom. It would not be good for his Polish Monsignor—and now his landlord—to see his Irish Priest was once again drunk on the streets. Despite the facts that Ed was Irish and a priest as well, it is good it to have my companion back again.

Tuesday, March 18th

Saint Patrick's Day parades in New York are the largest anywhere. I, myself, have marched in it three times, which is more than the times I have marched in the Pulaski Day Parade in the fall.

Living here on 23rd Street has exposed me to more cultures than I would have encountered in my little Polish village. Even if I had succeeded in reaching university in Warsaw or Moscow, I would not have experienced the same diversities. Nevertheless, we are not the wonderful melting pot as politicians like to tout as their accomplishment. We are more like a stew with battling chunks of differing flavors.

Within this stew are different vegetables and meat, all of which soften differently in America. I see some chunks holding tightly together and others seem less banded together. Poles are the latter. The Irish, Greeks, Italians, and our newly arrived neighbors, the Puerto Ricans, all seem to have sense of large extended family that they hold together very clannishly. Poles here don't seem to want to unite as tightly, beyond immediate family. Poland was one of the last groups of European kingdoms to unite into a country. History shows that made them vulnerable to outside attacks. It hasn't been an easy time for Poland. At least, since the end of World War I, we are a country again. Maybe someday she will be a free country again.

Which is better or which is worse? I don't know, but I am uncomfortable with strong clannish behavior. Excessive nationalism, religion, politics. They all seem to lead to war. It's white man verses black man verses yellow man and so on. All this "us and them" talk will get us all killed, and these days, we now have the big bombs to do it so well.

I started this day so happy, yet St. Patrick's Day always ends, and we return to "us and them". My gloominess is trying to seep in. I need to fight it off. I need to be in a better frame of mind tomorrow because I plan to see Ed again. He's become that lighthouse in my sights again, trying to keep me on course.

Wednesday, March 19th

Ed never ceases to amaze me. With the final piles of snow gone, we went down to Coney Island for a lunch at Nathan's. Rather than take his Buick, we decided to use the subway. With waiting for trains that time of day, the ride took us about an hour.

As we approached our final stop, the train emerged from the tunnel into the Coney Island trainyard. The trainyard could be seen through the left-side windows of the train. On our right, a red brick wall zoomed by the windows. Seeing the wall awakened a memory in me.

"Basil once took a bunch of us up there one night," I wrote as I pointed up the wall.

"Really," said Ed, "tell me about it." Ed, the true friend that he is, sat patiently as I wrote down this story.

"One night, a bunch of us were sitting around the Eagle wondering about all the graffiti on the subway cars. Basil offered to show us where it happened, so we piled into his Olds and drove to a street up there." I pointed up and over the brick wall on our right.

"He couldn't get us into yard, but there's an abandoned terrace over that ledge on top. To get on the terrace, there's a hole in a fence up off a nearby street.

Ed squeezed closer to the window to look up the wall to see a ledge about 20 feet up.

"I wonder if we could get in now?" Ed wondered out loud.

I shrugged an "I don't know."

Our train continued to skirt the perimeter of the trainyard, and within a few minutes, reached the Stillwell Avenue Terminal. As planned, we walked over to Nathan's and ordered our food, then took our meals over to the chevron-planked boardwalk about a block away. No problem finding an open bench this time of year. Facing the ocean, we chowed down on our hot dogs and fries.

When the boardwalk opened in the 1920s, Marysia and I would spend the day just walking, talking, laughing, and even dancing when we felt like it. Before the boardwalk was built, all we were able to do was look through wire fences to watch the surf. Building the boardwalk made it the best public park in the city. That was when Coney was a wonderful new place to be. Now, the wooden benches facing the sea are splintered and uncomfortable to sit on, even in winter clothing. The metal railings before us were showing spots of rust, and graffiti covered everything else. Coney Island used to be the best amusement area in the country, maybe the world. Nothing is forever.

After lunch, Ed and I walked over to where Steeplechase Park was. The entrance was now all boarded up. Another sign that just like us, this city was dying. We didn't linger there. Not much to see. We probably walked about a mile and reminisced about our many adventures together. He also told me an interesting story. One I never heard before. It has been his secret of the heart.

He told me of a time when he fell in love with a woman. Already being a priest, he never revealed these feelings to her or to anyone. He referred to this woman as being a saint not only to him, but an honest-to-god saint. He mentioned that someone once called her that, and she quickly retorted she was no saint. Then she would add that she didn't want to be dismissed that easily. Clearly to him, she was more than a saint. I never thought of him as being capable of such emotions.

We circled around to where our visit began at the terminal and were about to go up the stairs to our elevated train station when Ed turned to me. "Kaz, today has been good for me. Let's continue our little adventure."

I gestured to a tavern across the street.

"No, let's walk over to where Basil showed you the train yard. Perhaps the fence hole is still there, and we can get in."

"We might get caught," I wrote.

Fathers and Sons and Other Village Idiots

"So what! We both need to start to take more chances to find out angels."

"Might be over a half a mile away."

"We'll go slow and be there in no time. Shall we?" And we did.

We walked up Stillwell to Avenue Z, turned right, then left on the dead-end street of West 13th. Abandoned warehouses and empty lots lined one side, and just as I remembered, there was a hole in the fence across the street from the last warehouse on the street. If I didn't know where to look, I never would have found that hole.

We held the fence hole open wider for each other and were soon walking across the broken glass covered terrace above the trainyard. We carefully leaned over and peered down to the tracks some 20 feet below. Just then a West End train popped out of the tunnel and within moments was passing beneath us. We watched trainyard activities for a while, but the sun was going down. We still had little bit of a walk back to the nearest subway station.

As I write up today's adventure tonight, I'm happy to have had some mischief with my old buddy again. It resurrected the boys in both of us.

Thursday, March 20th

I am not a minion of the stars and refuse to march lockstep to their celestial procession. The stars may say it is time for spring, but Mother Nature and I have our own free will. Nevertheless, I concede that this year here in Brooklyn, the stars, nature, and I choose to begin springtime on the very same day.

Marysia, here's another haiku for you.

spring rings in color
for a village idiot
sweet taste of a hope

The snow piles are gone, the crocuses have emerged in the backyard, and the New York Mets—if only temporarily— are in first place in the pre-season. In the beginning of anything, there is always hope for an underdog.

I have been rereading Ivan's *Spring Torrents* and he offered me this thought to consider today.

If you have succeeded in doing something you wanted to do, something that seemed impossible—well, then, make the most of it, with all your heart, to the very brim. This is the only thing that makes life worth living.

Have I succeeded in doing something I wanted to do? I have always wanted to write. Maybe I should relish this moment. Now redemption may truly be something that seems impossible. I would savor achieving that.

The seasons of nature and man don't necessarily comply with the drumming of the stars in the sky, but today I consent that the torrents of my spring may commence.

Fathers and Sons and Other Village Idiots

Friday, March 21st

*W*e sit in the mud, my friend, and reach for the stars.
— Ivan T.

Here on earth, I read this morning that the U.S. war toll reached 33,063. Since the Paris Peace Talks began ten months ago, over 10,000 people died. We sit in mud. In the heavens, Apollo 9 mission successfully put the lunar module in Earth orbit.

I went to church on this Friday morning and there knelt Father Ed in his usual rear pew. As I joined him, he exclaimed, "Twice in one week?"

"Yes," I wrote on my pad, "Things seem to be changing for me in odd ways." He remained silent, so I wrote further. "I hadn't seen you for a long time in the Eagle on a Saint Patty's Day, yet there you were this year. I know why I have not been here in church, but why have you been away from the Eagle?" He smirked as he read this.

He gathered his words carefully and spoke softly.

"Other than the fact you and your son threw me out, I've had other reasons.

"After Marysia passed on and you banished me, I began to drink even more heavily. The Monsignor had been advising me that if I wanted to keep my pension, it would be best for me to not drink regularly in public anymore. Seeing you again last week, gave me some courage to disregard his advice."

"The Monsignor? You have outlasted many of those. What has changed?"

He turned his gaze from the quiet altar before us towards my eyes. In a still lower voice he said, "This one has been able to beat an old man into submission. This one holds my rectory cottage and my pension papers like he is holding my balls." His eyes looked away and down.

He added, "He could not have done this when I was a young man, but now, I am too old to start again. I need to submit to his rules, or I will be transferred out of the neighborhood I love. Right now, only the bishop protects me from my monsignor and my bishop is old and this monsignor is not so."

61

Finally, I wrote, "I am sorry that I had abandoned you, my friend."

"Yes, you did," he quickly retorted, "as had all others. I am viewed by many as the drunken Irish priest. I need an old friend right now who will not judge me. I reserve the right of judgment only to God, my father."

We resumed looking forward in silence. I never imagined he would need me when he had a god. After a long while he said, "Let's go to my apartment while I still have it and have a drink."

"But it is still just morning."

He looked to whisper, "it's not too early for either of us when the need is there. You would not be here if you didn't have a great need."

I gestured for him to lead the way.

His apartment was a stand-alone cottage on 25th Street next to the rectory. There was a little driveway in front of it where he parked his old black Buick. His cottage was actually a converted carriage house. It was the breadcrumb that the diocese provided him for his controlled conduct. Even the bishop probably conceded that they could control Ed better here than if he were reassigned elsewhere in the diocese. In his home, we laughed some, we ate all day, and we drank a bit. At dinnertime, we parted as he had a parish commitment.

As I write now at the end of my day, I can't see how this day helped me much with my burdens. In truth, they made my load heavier. Ed's sadness is for me another example of my unsuccessful life.

Sunday, March 23rd

After Sunday Mass today, Ed and I sat in the front pew near the altar. There he told me more about the story of the Black Madonna painting before us.

He explained to me that the Black Virgin Mary was an essential part of Polish Catholicism. The painting before us in Brooklyn was a replica. The original painting had been painted on wood by Luke the Evangelist himself on a table supposedly built by Jesus himself. Nice story but I don't really believe it and indicated as much. This didn't keep Ed from telling me more.

He said that in about the year 300 AD, St. Helena, the mother of Emperor Constantine, found the painting in the Holy Lands and brought it back to Constantinople where it stayed for 500 years. The painting was highly prized and often gifted between nobility. Over the centuries, the painting moved about Europe. During one such journey in Poland, when traveling through the town of Czestochowa, the then owner was confronted with an impasse. His horses refused to go further. He told everyone that he was advised in a dream to leave the paintings there at the Monastery of Jasna Góra.

More centuries passed and the Swedes invaded Poland. Their first objective was to capture the monastery. The legend went a hundred Polish monks held off four thousand Swedes and stalled the invasion into Poland. Due to this pivotal victory that stopped the invasion, King Kazimierz made an oath proclaiming the icon to be the Queen of Poland forever. I was named after King Kazimierz, so in a way, the lady of Czestochowa is also my queen.

I wrote Ed that this painting had guided me in life since the very first day I stepped into America. When I needed to decide, I came to the church and discussed my options with her. Once before her, usually I could figure out what was the right thing to do. The difficulty was more when I didn't want to do it. Ed reflected on my writings.

"I have had a guide of my own these many years, but it was not this painting. My inspiration is a living person." I recalled his story of the woman he loved, and wrote, "Does this person have a name?"

"Oh yes. Dorothy Day." I was startled.

"Dorothy Day the communist?"

"NO," he yelled when he read my note. His voice echoed throughout the church.

In a softer tone, "Well, yes and no. Yes, that Dorothy Day, but no, she is not a communist. That is just a slur used by those trying to diminish her by putting an unpopular label of today on her. I would call her a radical Catholic.

"She cared for the weak and sacrificed her few belongings for anyone in poverty. She fought against the powerful even when the powerful beat her down over and over again. Her early life was not angelic by any standards, but after she embraced Catholicism, she became vocal about some shortcomings of organized religion in not truly supporting the poor enough. The church itself didn't welcome all the views she expounded in her newspaper, *The Catholic Worker*. To the poor of the depression, she offered an alternative to communism thorough the teaching of Christ. She was an anarchist in that she didn't recognize organized authority, so the church didn't welcome her.

"The example she set for me with her actions has guided me though my life, but sometimes I also don't want to follow her guidance. Now that I am old, I am too afraid. I am afraid of the prick that holds my pension."

I wrote, "We all have little pricks that we are afraid of."

"Yes, I imagine we do."

"Maybe it is time for us to stand up to the pricks and return to listening to our guiding angels. At least your guide speaks. Mine just sits up there," I wrote and as he read, he chuckled.

"You should go see her to talk to your angel," I wrote.

"I doubt she would even remember me. She serves many and of all those who need her help, I am the least needy of them all. My burdens are really not so bad. They're only about my happiness and not about survival of my spirit."

"Survival of one's happiness is important too. Go see her."

Fathers and Sons and Other Village Idiots

"She herself is getting old as well, so I cannot trouble her. Last I heard about her was that she was carrying on her communal work from Vermont."

"Well maybe someday you will see her again."

"Perhaps, but you know what? That's really not so important anymore. It's like this painting here before you. She does not speak to you, but you can still be guided in your thoughts and actions. From knowing what these women profess to be Truth, we already know our answers. Then we make our choices."

I expected him to continue, but he stopped abruptly. We had no more to say of any consequence, so we parted. Tonight, here I sit writing all this down. I wonder what does have any consequence for me anymore.

Monday, March 24th

The Melting Pot didn't disappoint me today.

"Did you hear that the New York University president declared that the federal government has no right to interfere with universities?" exclaimed Georgie to me as I was the first to walk into the Melting Pot this morning. "Finally, a scholar is assuming the role of a leader." I did agree it was good to read that adults were finally trying to oppose America's authorities. The seed of resistance has sprouted outside of the students.

As Georgie went to get me my cup of coffee, I quickly looked over my paper. The frontpage headline was the one that worried me. "Ike growing weaker." Soon Sal, Izzie, and David had joined me with a coffee. I show the headline to the table and wrote, "Sad." Sal reacted first to this.

"Are you saying that you voted for him? A Republican?"

I replied. "Sal, Ike was the last Republican I ever will vote for. I was angry with Truman for letting Poland fall behind the iron curtain and could not vote for him."

"Now, I agree Ike was a great general," said Georgie, "but Kaz, his policies and actions as president were not progressive for us minorities in America."

65

I disagreed but could never write as fast as the debate grew around the table. It didn't matter. The fact was that we are losing him—a reasonable voice during times of madness. We need more sanity today.

Wednesday, March 26th

*S*o long as one's just dreaming about what to do, one can soar like an eagle and move mountains, it seems, but as soon as one starts doing it, one gets worn out and tired. - Ivan T.

After reading that Ike was in critical condition, I found little energy to do more than ponder Ivan's words. Everything seems so hopeless right now. There is so much wrong in the world. There must be something I can do about it. When I sit in the Melting Pot on Mondays, I get so stirred up on what needs to be done, but by the time I get home to start, I become lost as to where to start. I am so tired these days. It's even hard to go outside with Sancho. Even Ivan cannot inspire me to think any further on these days.

Monday, March 31st

My fellow villagers showed up to kick me in my dupa today. At about nine, Ed banged on my door until I opened it and demanded that I get dressed. Once dressed, he wrestled a coat on my back and smacked a hat on top of my head, then thrusted me through the front door and down the stoop steps. With his arm around my shoulders, we walked up 23rd Street to the Melting Pot. To my surprise, everyone was already sitting at the front table with an empty chair ready for me. While looking at all their faces, Ed spoke from behind.

"Kazimierz, we, your friends for so many years, are aware that today is a very important anniversary for you. Do you even remember what it is?"

I didn't have a clue and shook my head.

"Well old friend, you once told me that on March 31, 1910, the *SS Graf Waldersee* steamed into New York Harbor and brought you to America. Fifty-nine years ago on this very day, you also met both Lady Liberty and Our Lady of Czestochowa. What a good day for you and one you should never forget again."

Georgios then placed babka, a Polish bread, before me. He had baked it just for me. In its center, it had a lit wax candle in the shape of the Statue of Liberty. As Ed stabbed in a tiny flag of Poland into one side of the bread, David stabbed in a stars and stripes in the other. Then Sal shoved in a tiny crucifix into it. I blew out the burning torch of my Mother of Exiles as everyone sang a modified version of "Jolly Good Fellow." I was both literally and figuratively speechless.

As I think tonight about this morning, I am also reflecting on the fact that a few short years after my arrival in America, I would meet my Marysia, and a year after that we'd be married in OLC by my lifelong friend, under the gaze of my Lady Liberty. My fellow villagers guided me through my darkness today as did my Ladies so many years ago. I have a lot to be thankful for and think it time for me to get something off my chest.

Dear God,

I know that I am not one of your most obedient of children and I am not asking you for your forgiveness without earning it. Of course, I have been the SOB, not you.

I would be a far worse and an ungrateful SOB if I didn't acknowledge that you have given me so much that I am thankful for.

Thank you for placing many angels in my life.

Not to be too greedy, but I could still use one more.

Kazimierz

Friday, April 4th

E d ranted to me, "He used me like his little errand boy. He sent me all the way to Buffalo to deliver a little package to some fat ass up there. It made that guy seem important and me inconsequential."

Apparently, last Tuesday, Ed's little prick sent him out of town on this task for a few days. He just got back late last night. This morning, he was making his neighborhood rounds and discovered that no one had seen me at my usual places since my Monday cake. He came here straight away, and we sat and drank coffee in my kitchen.

"Monsignor knows I have a car, so he tells me to pack a bag and drive to Buffalo with a package that he hands to me. I didn't know what was inside until I get there as this guy opens it in front of me. It was OLC holy water for his grandson's baptism. Four hundred miles to make this guy seem like a big shot in his Polish church up there. They even have an OLC of their own in Buffalo."

I wrote, "You should've spit in it." That did get a smirk out of Ed, and it seemed to calm him down.

"So, what's going on with you, Kaz? Your sons said they hadn't seen you in a few days."

"You mean they noticed?"

He replied, "Do you want to know the truth?" I nodded.

"Well, no. I asked if you had been in today, they realized that no one had seen you in a few days. Has your sadness returned?"

I stared down at my pen and paper, then wrote.

"After our cake at the Melting Pot the other day, I actually reached out to God. This made me realize I have a big problem and maybe you can help me."

"I am back now. What can I do?"

"I want a better understanding of confession." He considered my statement before answering.

"I am not sure what you want to know, Kaz. Are we talking friend to friend or priest to parishioner?

"Priest, and I want you to explain to me, the Seal of Confession."

Fathers and Sons and Other Village Idiots

"The Seal of Confession?" I nod.

"Can you narrow this down for me as to what you want to know?" I shook my head.

"Well, without knowing what you are looking for, this is going to be a basic catechism lesson like I give to the kids on Wednesday afternoons." I nod that I understood. This was what I wanted.

"Well, let me start with some fundamentals, but you will need to ask questions in your little notepad there in order for me to address what you need to know." Again, I nod.

"In Catholicism, when you confess to a priest, you are no longer talking to a man—you are talking to God Himself and God alone.

"When a priest listens to a confession, he is bound by a Seal of Confession. It would be a grave sin for him to reveal anything to another person. The punishment would be both immediate from the Church but also eternal from God. Saint Thomas Aquinas clarified this with his writings that the priest knows the confession not as a man, but as God knows it."

I wrote a question. "What if police asked you for information about a certain individual?"

"When a priest says, 'I do not know' to anyone, it is meant to be understood that they do not know with knowledge outside the Seal of the Confessional.

"Now, if I saw you commit a crime, then you came and confessed it to me, I have this knowledge of the crime from outside of the confessional, I could talk to the police about what I saw. If I only have knowledge from within the confessional, I could not speak."

He continued. "When you say out loud your sins, you are telling only God because he is the only one who has a right to judge you. You can confess to God right here and now."

"No, this is not a church."

"That really does not matter."

"It does to me."

"Then when?

"Saturday."

"Tomorrow? Why wait to remove this burden and set things right again in the eyes of the Lord?"

69

"Tomorrow is Saturday? Yes, tomorrow."

"Okay, then tomorrow it is and just in time for Easter."

"Easter is this Sunday?"

"Yes, it is—our glorious Feast of the Resurrection"

"Well perhaps my soul will be resurrected as well by Sunday."

"Perhaps you will."

And after this exchange was over, in my mind, I was back to talking with my friend, Ed, and the priest was gone. Eventually, he left for the day.

My heart is telling me that I need to confess things that I have done and some that I am thinking of doing. They must be sins, but I don't want to have others hurt if my sins were known. I at least need to confess to God what I have done and repent for them. Marysia would want me to do this. So would Our Lady. In order to relieve these pressures on my brain, I must. I have too much to do and so little time.

With the help of God, I need to shut off these crippling thoughts that disable me. I do need a god to help me.

Saturday, April 5th

Catholic confession is an odd experience. On a clear, beautiful spring day with birds singing outside, it seemed wrong to go into a dark, morbidly silent dank church. It seems hard to believe that this dark place would brighten my soul. I was right in that skepticism.

The confessionals sit along the aisles on each side of the nave. Each confessional booth consists of a wooden door in the middle where the priest would enter and sit down. On either side of the door were curtained doorways to the sinner's booths. Sinners speak to the priest from their sinner booth through a small metal grating, which has a sliding wooden panel to open or close the passageway.

Today, being the day before Easter, there were a great many people lined up outside each sinner's booth. This was going to take some time. Some sinners might pick the shorter line while others might select by which priest was sitting inside.

Fathers and Sons and Other Village Idiots

The line to Father Ed's confessional was shorter than most. He had a reputation for tougher penances.

To start, the priest would slide open the wooden panel to a sinner booth and the confession would commence. Yes, I call it the sinner booth because if you weren't a sinner, what the hell would you be doing there.

Inside a sinner booth was where the sinner knelt in darkness awaiting the slamming open of their wooden panel. Each booth smelled of old wood and musty curtains. As you knelt in the dark with your nose close to the grating, you might hear two muffled voices from the other side. One you'd recognize as the priest you picked, and the other was another sinner. It's rare to understand any words by the sinner, who probably spoke in soft tones. Occasionally, one might hear the priest exclaim, 'What?' or 'Excuse me, please repeat that?' You wait in the dark and maybe you sweat. Then without warning, there is a loud slam of wood on wood from the other side and a moment later, your panel slams open to reveal a sitting priest in a dim backlight. One's heart might skip a beat with the bang and the brightness of the light now in one's face. If it wasn't so serious in there, it would almost be like being in a carnival spook house. I got a "Welcome child" and there before me was the silhouette of Father Ed.

I tore a small bit of paper from my pad. Previously, I had wrote, "Bless me Father, for I have sinned. It has been many years since my last confession." I slipped it through a slot in the grating.

"It is good that you have returned before God to confess your sins, my son."

Ed plays his part with such a straight face. As he has done this thousands of times. he leaned in toward my grate to listen as he waited for me to continue. It's just a habit to him, as I wasn't whispering today and won't be any future day either.

Today, I hadn't completely separated in my mind that this was God alone and not Ed before me. It was still Ed to me. This was not a good start, and I was beginning to think this whole matter was not a good idea.

I wrote him that I felt responsible for my father's death some half a century ago and hadn't mentioned that in all my previous confessions. I somehow felt guiltier about that more recently. I told him I have hated God for taking my Marysia, and I have been calling God names to belittle his status to me. I told him I was doing illegal tasks for a bookie. I rambled on more trivial stuff and finally I thought that I was finished.

"Do you intend to stop all these things?"

We both sat quietly for quite some time. I knew I couldn't stop working for Frankie. Ed stated a different question. He probably was going to come back to the other one later.

"Do you have any other sins you wish to confess?"

I wasn't expecting that one either. Did protocol change for confession in the last years? In all my years, I don't remember priests probing. I felt angry, but this time, not at God. I was angry at Ed.

"NO," I scribbled out in larger letters.

"Are you sure, my son? You know, even sins of intent are sins. Confess all to God and he will absolve you."

This was not fair in my mind. If Priest Ed cannot tell the world about my sins, then it should also be true that Friend Ed should not tell the priest what I have not yet revealed. I finally chose to respond. "I have nothing further I choose to confess."

Ed considered my response. "But you have other sins?"

I nodded.

The Father Ed was not prepared for that frank admission. I created a dilemma for him. Finally, he answered.

"I cannot absolve you for your sins if you have not confessed them all."

"I understand," I wrote on my last note, and with that, I got up and left.

On reflecting on the events of this day, I feel I did the right thing. I was not going to lie in a confessional booth anymore. I did realize that I might need to commit a grave future sin and right at this moment, I would do it if I had to do it.

Somehow, the outcome of the day didn't depress me as I thought it might. I confronted God himself and as I walked down the street to return home, he didn't smite me down. I feel that I am on the right path and that God was going to allow me to discover it.

Fathers and Sons and Other Village Idiots

Overall, this was a good day with God, and maybe I will go to church tomorrow to celebrate Easter and the miracle of his son's resurrection. Of course, my unwillingness to confess all makes me ineligible for communion, but I understand the consequences of my actions. I have maintained my free will for now, but I am not yet in a state of grace to reach heaven.

Sunday, April 6th

Seventy thousand people marched to Central Park yesterday to protest the war. I remain too afraid to join a peace protest myself, but there is new hope for peace.

This prospect of peace so uplifted me that I did get to church for Easter Sunday Mass. After that, Ed came along with me for an Easter Sunday dinner at Stella's house. Stella's connection to our family is a bit confusing. Suffice to say she married into the family and never left, even after her husband passed away.

Stella and her husband, Stanley, bought a beautiful big house on 93rd Street very near to the Verrazano Bridge, with the intent of raising a large family in it. Sadly, God didn't provide one. In many ways, God hasn't been kind to my family. Within one year, He took my Marysia, Otto's Gloria, and Stella's Stanley. It's no wonder we found we could no longer worship such a God.

Nevertheless, all the large family gatherings continue to be held at Stella's house because her dining room could accommodate all of us. Before our great year of sorrow, Ed was always welcomed by Stella. Time does heal old wounds and today, Ed, the man not the priest, was welcomed back. Perhaps God can learn benevolence from my family.

The fact that Ed was available on such short notice on Easter of all days was not a surprise to me. He really has no other family or close friends in life. Of course, he was very happy to be invited back. Because parking in Stella's affluent Bay Ridge neighborhood was always a problem, we took the subway.

Lunch was a wonderful lamb roast with all the possible sides, so we ate until we could eat no more. It was a beautiful day with temperatures in the 70s, so after we cleaned up the dishes, we all decided to take a stroll along Shore Road. Upon reaching the water's edge, we stared across the Narrows waterway to Staten Island. It's been 50 years since I sailed through the Narrows. Now spanning it was the newly built Verrazano Bridge. The papers say it is the longest span in the world. Another monument of science and engineering. Georgios would be proud. We all marveled at this newer colossus of New York Harbor. It was fun to take that walk today. For tonight, I will accept this little happiness that the day has brought me.

Tuesday, April 8th

P lay Ball. Today is opening day for baseball.
     I, as King Kazimierz of Brooklyn, proclaim it to be the *Feast Day of the Underdog*. For this one day, despite all odds, every team has a chance to win the World Series. By June, these hopes are gone for most teams and fans.

A few years after I arrived in Brooklyn, I'd walk over to Ebbets Field to watch the Dodgers play. On some Sundays, I'd sit and watch a doubleheader and be at the ballpark all day. I'd bring my pretzels and sandwiches in a bag and buy my beer there to just sit and scream at anything. In Brooklyn, especially with those Dodgers, one screamed if they won, but more often, we screamed as they lost. It was a pastime.

Since Henry and Otto could walk, I took them to games. Henry especially loved *Dem Bums*. He loved them so much that he nicknamed his son after their star centerfielder, the Duke of Flatbush. My son was an idiot to do this. Later in life, it just pissed the boy off on his dad's expectations of him.

I always rooted for the Dodgers, but as I said, they rarely won. Once they did win the World Series, then the next year the SOBs moved to L.A. I felt betrayed by those underdogs, for deserting us when they became great. In '58, the Dodgers left and took the Duke with them. Brooklyn has not been the same. Now, the field is a housing project.

In 1962, New York was given the Metropolitans to replace both the Dodgers and Giants, who also left us. They brought in Casey Stengel, a former Yankee great and funny old guy, to manage them. The Mets immediately broke a 100-year-old baseball record for being the worst team ever in a single year. Eventually, they brought *The Duke* back from L.A. to play one year here before he retired. Old timers and has-beens. The team was so bad that Casey once asked his players if anyone actually knew how to play the game. The Mets have become the perfect replacement for Dem Bums.

Last year, the Mets finished in 9th place, 24 games out of first place. Their new manager, Gil Hodges, said in the newspaper that, just once, he would be happy for the team to win more than they lose. He does not seem to have high expectations for the team, but he's probably being very realistic. In their first seven seasons, the Mets have never been able to win half their games. This is my hope for them for this year, just not lose more than they win. Eighty-two wins will do it. If they can win that many, then maybe I, too, can achieve an impossible task.

Here in Brooklyn, it does make sense to root for an underdog because Brooklyn is filled with downtrodden underdogs. I now feel that there is honor to root for the underdog. For them to win is extraordinary and by picking a loser to win and they do, I become extraordinary.

Today is opening day, my feast day of hopeless causes. Let's go Mets!

Wednesday, April 9th

Many years ago, I met an artist on the Coney Island boardwalk. He stood by the railing with his easel, painting a pleasant scene of colorful umbrellas and blankets dotting the sandy beach. A gentle surf rolled in from the left edge of the painting, while children splashed into it.

I asked him if he sold many of his works and his eyes looked down and a frown appeared across his face.

"Yes," he said. "I have and am sorry for that. I need to eat occasionally, and paints and canvases are expensive. I have painted things that others would buy. I can only comfort myself by thinking that those paintings were not my children, only the product of an occupation. To others, my paintings are an entertainment, a decoration, or a novelty to possess. My best works are my children and not for sale.

"My paintings are my only family. They give me purpose. They make me look at the world and notice the beauty always there.

"Did you notice that little cloud over there near the horizon?" he said as he pointed with his brush. "My eyes have been enjoying it for 20 minutes as it grows and moves. Before I started painting, I would not have noticed it going by. Over there is a child who is walking cautiously into the little waves as his nearby mother watches him. All priceless and all beautiful.

"I am better because of my children. They make me a part of the world in which I walk." The painter then sighed and said that he lost the light he desired. He began to pack up his things. Before he left, I asked one final question.

"What will happen to your paintings when you are gone?"

"I cannot say because I don't know, but I also don't worry about that. I can only control what I can control. No parents truly knows what will happen to their children after the parents are gone." After that statement, we went our separate ways.

My daily writings are beginning to be my children too. They make me a part of something. I thought of Ivan's words again.

That's what children are for—that their parents may not be bored.

My writing has enabled a better attitude in me. Nothing may become of my writings after I am gone, but I hope that God finds them a good home. I also hope he finds a good home for my soul as well. Hopefully, my writings will also enrich someone else's spirit. If so, that's gravy. They have already enriched my soul.

Fathers and Sons and Other Village Idiots

Sunday, April 13th

I zzie was in the Eagle this Sunday evening. He took his cap off his bald head and sat down at the end of the bar next to Ed, who had also joined us tonight. He waited quietly until there was a lull in the conversation then jumped in.

"If no one would object, I have something that I'd like to discuss, and it seems fitting to do it in a Polish bar," he said in his heavy Jewish accent.

Ed injected before anyone else could, "Of course, you are welcome to speak here Izzie. What do you have on your mind?"

"I am here to buy drinks for anyone willing to drink with me to honor the memory of the family I lost on this day in 1943." After a moment, Ed's face revealed that he had figured out what the topic was. Ed noticed that no one else did.

"Izzie, tell my friends here what happened in Warsaw in 1943."

"Priest Edward, this is exactly my problem," said Izzie, "and why I am out tonight. We here all know about the holocaust, but there were many sad events of the war that many Polish Americans have forgotten. Today is the 26th anniversary of the weeklong Warsaw Ghetto Uprising. I was there and lost my parents and many other relatives and friends that week. I can never bring them back, but at least I can assist today's memory of them.

"I will buy a beer for anyone willing to listen to me." With a few empty beer mugs being pushed across the bar, the attention turned back to Izzie. Up and down the bar, mugs were refilled, as Izzie continued.

"The Warsaw Uprising was the largest uprising by Jews during World War II. Over 13,000 Polish Jews died in Warsaw that week. We had no hope of escaping and no chance for pushing the Nazis out, but we chose to revolt anyway.

"Each day, we watched the Nazis taking Jews away who would never come back. We heard rumors of what might be happening to them.

"My people made the decision to not let them pick the time and place of our deaths. The men and women took to the

77

streets to resist. My mother would not let my father take me along as I was only ten at the time. One night, I was left with an elder. Both my parents never returned that night.

"I have always felt guilty for not joining them and dying alongside them. I cannot change that feeling of guilt. What I can do today is to honor them and all the others by reminding the world of what happened. My purpose is to keep the memory of them alive."

Izzie then proceeded to call out a name then told us a little story about each. Somberly, we drank.

After his last story, which was about this father, Izzie found out who in the bar had gone to Europe to fight the Nazis. After he gave them each a robust hug, he toasted them as well.

Izzie ran out of people to toast and took out his wallet to settle his bar tab. Otto pushed back his money and told him he needed to come back here each year on April 13th to remind all of the bravery of those Polish Jews. Izzie smiled at him, got up and stepped toward the door. There he turned and said one more thing to us.

"Thank you all for honoring my family tonight. In doing so, you have honored yourselves. Good people drink here. Thank you." With that, he turned and left.

Tonight, I write in my journal again and I think about what I wrote last week about underdogs. Being an underdog is not just about sports. During this year of my quest, I am remembering stories of many oppressed underdogs. Stories I should never have forgotten.

I was ashamed that I had forgotten about the Poles of the Warsaw Riots. For them, it was never about winning. Maybe I should look at my quest that way. Maybe I don't really have a chance, but I do still have my free will to fight. I don't need to play by the rules of Little Prick, or the church, or Frankie, or anyone. Maybe I can't beat any of them, but I can die honorably fighting. I will not be extorted by them to do what's right for them.

Monday, April 14th

I skipped the Melting Pot again this morning. It appears to be another beautiful day outside, but no matter how hard I try, I am barely able to move.

I should be happy right now, but I am not. I don't understand why. Sometimes I feel that this sadness in my head is not my fault. At times, this melancholy seems far worse a burden than my cancer ever was.

Thursday, April 24th

Shore Road was beautiful today. After two weeks of not getting out of the house, I had to make a money bag drop for Frankie. Before I came home, I took a walk under the bridge. It was a picturesque afternoon.

The days are getting longer, and yesterday I went into the backyard and reviewed my journal there. I am surprised by some of what I wrote. I keep rethinking Ivan's quote.

If we wait for the moment when everything, absolutely everything is ready, we shall never begin.

I have wasted many weeks. Maybe young men can waste time, but the old cannot. Ivan is right. I need to begin.

Saturday, April 26th

Time has been such a burden lately and is passing slowly. One day, I'm good. The next, not so. I have been thinking more and more of Ivan and his writings.

As we all know, time sometimes flies like a bird, and sometimes crawls like a worm, but people may be unusually happy when they do not even notice whether time has passed quickly or slowly.

While minutes and hours crawl during my times of sadnesses, days and weeks seem to be flying by. This makes me even sadder. Daylight saving starts at 2 a.m. tonight. I sat this evening in my booth at the Eagle. It was a quiet night with few in the bar for a Saturday night.

A customer, who had glanced up at a clock, asked, "Otto, is that the right time or is that already tomorrow's time?" In the fall, in order for customers to stay longer and drink more, Otto always turned the clocks back the Saturday evening before daylight savings time ended.

Years ago, on that fall Saturday night, Father Ed often organized an annual community party at the Eagle. A gathering of the various ethnic groups to sit together and drink with each other. Since Marysia's death, he has not used the Eagle for his party. I made it clear that a priest was no longer welcomed.

But this evening in April is a night that is shorter, so Otto would never turn the clocks forward early in the spring to shorten the drinking. He retorted back.

"Do you have anywhere to go in your miserable life." The man just shrugged.

"Then don't bother to look at clocks. Just drink."

The customer tipped his mug slightly in Otto's direction and then took another gulp. I went home early as it seemed like there was nothing for me there tonight.

Almost a third of this year has flown by since my quest started, but with no progress that I can perceive. I must take control. I must.

Monday, May 12th

Ed got my dupa out of the house this morning, and we went up to the Melting Pot. As we sat down with our coffee and pastries, David asked, "Father, what do you think of the church taking away the feast days of hundreds of saints?"

"I hadn't heard about this, but I knew the Vatican has been considering these actions all year."

"Sure, sure. It was in yesterday's *Times*," David added.

"Well, I hope that Saint Edward the Confessor is still on the list," said Ed, "as I really don't want my namesake to become Saint Edward the Martyr."

"I don't recall those names," said Georgios, missing Ed's jest, "but St. Christopher and St. Nick are out of your club." Ed smiled.

"Well, these were still great people and much closer to saintliness than I. We should still honor them and what good they did during their lives. As for the Catholic Church being a club, I can't agree with that at all." No one responded, so he changed the subject.

"I am actually more concerned about what I read in the news today." I looked up from my paper to listen.

"I read that a Long Island draft board is denying conscientious objector status to Jews, contending that Judaism is not a pacifist religion. Goddamn rich WASPs on the island just out to take another swat at Jews." I think that Ed always did like to jolt those around him with an occasional vulgarity. I've seen him do this on many occasions.

"Conscientious objector status is not about religion. It is about morality. An atheist could be as much of a CO as any Christian.

"It's all about our free will. Now, if we do what is right in our conscience, God will be pleased with us. If we do what we know is wrong, he will not reward us."

Ed paused, hoping someone would agree or even disagree with him, but there was only silence at the table. Given this lack of interest, he yielded. "Gentlemen, what else is in the news today?"

I wrote, "Did anyone read that story on Nixon urging colleges to display backbone against dissidents."

"I did," answered David. "On the same day, there were riots at Queens College, and a professor at Columbia was clubbed by radicals as they seized halls. I don't support the war, but this is becoming a real problem. I can't support students beating up professors. Maybe we do need some backbone with these kids."

"Who is actually doing those beating, that's what I what to know," said Ed. "Both sides seem to be getting infiltrated by extremists who only want to incite violence. Both sides need to be accountable for the actions of their people and denounce the agitators."

For a while, we all argued back and forth about the protesters and the protests, while finishing our pastries and coffee. Nothing was resolved other than some old men just clearing their pipes.

I noticed one more story from the other day that I didn't bring up. *The Times* reported that the city had lifted a job curb for homosexuals. With everything else going on in my life and with William coming home soon, I had completely forgot about Nelson. I wonder how he is doing these days. He lives only a short subway ride away, yet he seems even farther than William.

Monday, May 19th

Another week has passed and I haven't been out of the house or even written.

By telephone, Henry and Otto argued yesterday about scheduling William's graduation party. Otto and Anthony nearly came to blows last weekend after Anthony showed up for work drunk or high on something. This morning, Henry and his girlfriend, Linda, were yelling about his drinking. I can't seem to stop any of this bickering. I escaped to the Melting Pot, but there, it was more of the same old shit.

Sal read from an article. "Shotguns and tear gas were used to disperse rioters at Berkeley." He looked up and asked me if that was where William was. I just nodded.

The table's readings continued around me, but I didn't hear much else. I became lost in my own thoughts once again.

I can't wait for William to be out of Berkeley and back home. I will admit that I am afraid for him. I am afraid for all my family. Worrying about my sons and grandsons is going to be the death of me yet.

I had been thinking about ditching this journal but can't seem to stop. When I write, my mood does seem to find some peace. Like my artist friend from the boardwalk, my writings, for better or worse, are my children. I need support from somewhere.

Tuesday, May 20th

Apollo 10 was halfway to the moon. This mission is meant to be a flyby rehearsal for the actual July landing. There is no turning back now.

I'm in the Eagle tonight awaiting William's return. Henry had pulled together quite a crowd for the party, however the guest of honor was missing.

Henry had been overplanning for this night and spent quite a lot of money on it. I do understand why he's so proud. I am too. William is the very first in the family to graduate from university. Marysia and I never got our boys to even attempt it. A truth is we needed for them to start bringing in some cash.

William called last week and told Henry that he would be arriving today. He was driving across the country with his college friend, but Henry didn't mention the party. I'm beginning to think it was a mistake to make this a surprise party.

Four years ago, William went to California. In the beginning, when Henry and Louise were still married, he came home for Christmas and summers but not since the divorce. Divorce was another first in this family.

For the last few summers, William worked in California in jobs secured for him by his friend's family. Just as well, since Henry could not afford to bring him home. The geographic distance between father and son may have helped to mend their relationship, but this distance will soon dissolve. I worry that their relationship will lapse back to the arguing that often happened between them. They seem to be able to argue about anything. Politics. The war. Even baseball. It wore everyone out, including Louise. Then came the big fight in the living room. I walked out in the middle before Henry punched him in the face. I haven't seen William since that night. Louise left the next day as well.

For the past year, William did start to call again on birthdays and holidays, but those calls were always very short. I did get letters. I know that Henry didn't.

Since William was last here, much has happened. I suspect from the undertones of his letters, much has been changed in him as well. Back in Poland, by my teenage years, the differences between my father and me become readily apparent. I didn't understand then that these differences were universal between father and son. The best advice that I can now offer parents is to ride out those rough times. Both sides will eventually grow up. Sadly, nobody wants my advice.

Me? I do love my sons, but it is because they are my sons.

Louise, of course, was under no such obligation to Henry or, for that matter, me. It would have been a point of friction if she tried to stay in touch with me after the divorce. While I may understand it, I still don't like it. Louise is never coming back. With Linda in the picture, Louise and Henry's marriage seems to be a forgotten thing. Out of sight and out of mind.

All night long, Henry kept stepping outside every few minutes to look down 23rd street. People in the Eagle were starting to go home. Otto eventually announced it was closing time. William never arrived.

Wednesday, May 21st

Early this morning, William arrived with his luggage in hand and a friend by his side. Because I live on the ground floor, I was the first to reach the door. It was so good to see the boy again.

I only had a few seconds on the stoop step before Henry descended the stairs yelling, "Duke." His embrace of William was more robust than what William offered in return.

The last time they had seen each other was the scene in the living room. While they reconciled by telephone long ago, it took Henry a few moments to realize, from the awkwardness of the hug, that all was not forgotten by William. Henry released him and backed away.

William said that he had been calling the house all yesterday evening. He explained that they arrived late in the city and stopped in Staten Island to spend the night with his mom. Introductions were done and it was explained by Henry that William and his friend, Balzie, would be staying in my apartment and not upstairs.

Fathers and Sons and Other Village Idiots

I heard some footsteps in the apartment up above us and remembered that Henry had still not told William about Linda. Almost on cue, she came bounding down the stairs.

William was speechless seeing a woman coming down the stairs from his dad's apartment so early in the morning. I, being always speechless, remained so. It was Balzie and Linda who broke the silence with some hellos and handshakes.

At first, one might write off Balzie as just a shabby hippie, but his ring and wristwatch gave him away. Even his shoes were not discount sandals that one could get at Kovette's. His physical presence was also enhanced by his chatting ease. In no time at all, Balzie and Linda seemed to be hitting it off just fine.

Tonight, we did have a small gathering in the Eagle. Henry was buying rounds of drinks to show off to his friends his college graduate. William shared stories of California with us. Balzie spoke to anyone who would talk about anything but especially about politics. He seemed to have a strong socialistic point of view. He pissed off quite a few people in the bar when he spoke about it.

One customer attending this little shindig called William "Duke" and, with no hesitation, William immediately corrected him on his real name. Henry overheard and turned his back.

To anyone walking in, it would seem to be a nice gathering. Stella attended. Frankie was there with his girlfriend, Betty. Anthony stopped by on his night off to say hi too. Even Father Ed made an appearance. A nice party on the surface.

What was not happening was William ever talking to either his father or Linda. On the other hand, Balzie and Linda never stopped talking. Henry stayed away from both boys and also it seemed, Linda. He seemed happier talking about his son rather than being with him.

I think that William, who had just seen his mother last night, was unprepared for the presence of Linda. Henry was unprepared for Balzie the hippie. I'm sure he was worried whether his son had also become one too. Up until tonight, Henry was probably dismissing his son's long hair as being the expense of haircuts in California. Had his own son become a hippie socialist?

85

This may be quite an interesting summer around here. All the village idiots have been assembled. Time for me to take a short walk with Sancho before we go to bed for the night.

Thursday, May 22nd

The death of Little Eddie was the topic of the table today at the Melting Pot. Eddie was a kid who came home in a box last week. Earlier this spring, he was playing stickball on the street. A poor boy from a poor family. Another one tossed into the breach. We talked and talked and talked. In the end, nothing came of our idle chatter.

A family legacy was resurrected at the Eagle tonight. Just after World War II, Otto and I built a long mahogany table for the Eagle. *The Table*, as I like to refer to it, usually resides between the bar and the booths. On special occasions, it has been used in the social hall.

It was my and Otto's idea to create a communal spot where ideas of mutual concern could be discussed. Whoever climbed up onto a chair before it, could become the recognized leader of the evening's discussion.

The Table could be a podium, a soapbox, or maybe a pulpit. Originally, The Table was a local Polish forum. In the late hours of the night, after all points of view were expressed at least once, the leader might call for a vote on the topic. Frequently nothing of consequence was resolved other than a healthy exchange of opposing points of view.

Over time, meeting rules evolved and, when necessary, were physically enforced by Otto, master of the house. In my younger days, I helped Otto heave violators out onto the street when they refused to yield to opposing voices. Physical fighting was never allowed in the Eagle, but no one minded if the two parties took an argument into the back alleyway that led to 24th Street.

Being forcefully cast out of the Eagle for fighting inside also entailed at least a week exclusion. Since the Eagle served the cheapest beer around, expulsion was never taken lightly. When it came to enforcing any rules of conduct in the Eagle, Otto was fair but unyielding. In his well-honed role as bartender, he himself rarely voiced an opinion during a debate, but even when he did, he likewise yielded to the speaker of the table.

For many years, the meeting was conducted in Polish. That practice stopped in the late '50s when other nationalities started to come into the Eagle.

The process would begin with someone standing up on a chair before the head of the table. When Otto and the crowd took notice, it was Otto's responsibility as gatekeeper to respond. First, he needed to decide whether he wanted the Eagle to host a discussion that evening or whether there was more money to be had selling beer. If the crowd was small enough, he would lower or turn off the radio or TV, then pose a question to the speaker. "What have you to discuss?"

At this point, the room was usually silent and awaited a topic.

One would not necessarily know the speaker's position on the question, though one could usually guess. I rarely saw Otto reject a topic at this point regardless of his own views on the matter. He would let the crowd decide with another question. "Who here has reasons to discuss such an issue?"

If at least four hands were raised, mugs were refilled, and the speaker stepped down to prepare their thoughts. Only once did I observe Otto veto the topic before it started. He knew the speaker and the four raised hands were in conspiracy with him to stage a revolt. It was five 18-year-olds who wanted to discuss the idea that price of beer should be set by the wages of the drinker. Otto would not sanction the debate and when they refused to yield, they were banished for a month. Stan was there that night and happily assisted Otto with the forceful removal of the youths onto the street.

If there was going to be a discussion, procedurally, Otto would then pose another question to the speaker and to all the participants who gathered around.

"Do you all understand the rules of debate at this Table?" His emphasis was always on the word of Table, as if it were a sacred altar. I always loved the solemness of that moment. If a newcomer didn't, they were enlightened. More beer was purchased, and the speaker could begin.

The reason I was reminded of this history was because this evening, I sat in a booth with William and Balzie. William was telling him the history of the tavern and eventually got to the Table. Balzie's face instantly showed his socialist delight.

"Do you think that your uncle would allow me to speak?"

"I really don't know. Grandpa, has anyone spoken recently?"

I wrote, "Not in many years."

"Well then, let me go ask Uncle Otto," but Balzie grabbed his arm.

"No, not yet. Let me formulate my issue and let's say next week. I will follow protocol and go stand on a chair. Let the master of the house and the crowd decide if I can be allowed to speak." The two of them laughed like giddy little boys who just discovered where the cookie jar was hidden.

I thought the evening was already eventful enough, but Balzie was so excited by the Eagle that he went around the room asking William about the significance of everything in it. I followed along to fill in gaps in Williams's knowledge. "How old was this?" "What type of wood was used in the table?" "What's with all the clocks all over the place?" "What's with the White Eagle over the bar?" "Who are all these people in these old photos on the wall?" Eventually, he came to Crazy Henry's photo. Not my Henry, but Henry Krajewski's. William told the story of Krajewski.

In New York/New Jersey Polish circles, Henry Krajewski was a celebrity of sorts, who continually ran for public office. In the newspapers, he was known as the "Pig Farmer of Secaucus," which was where he owned his pig farm and a tavern of his own. He was on the New York and New Jersey ballets for President of the United States in 1952 and '56. William explained that he ran on either the Poor Man's Party or American Third Party tickets. He had slogans like *A pig in every pot* and *Free milk to every child and free beer to every grownup.*

"Was he a communist?" asked Balzie.

Fathers and Sons and Other Village Idiots

"Oh no, far from it. He once planned to ride horseback across the nation to warn the country of the dangers of communism. He was a capitalist with some socialist ideas, but he was both of those things because it played well with blue collar workers."

"Did he ever make that ride?"

"Not to my knowledge. Ultimately, he was a PT Barnum-like showman always promoting himself and his bar. He would stage political rallies with real elephants and donkeys to symbolize he represented both democratic and republican interests. His campaign button read, *I like Ike. I like Adlai. But Vote for Krajewski.* I don't think he ever won any election for anything. Fittingly, he died on an Election Day just a few years ago.

"He had an aunt who lived on 23rd street. His cousins said that he said anything to get noticed and ran for everything from president to governor to dogcatcher. He wanted to get people worked up and to come and see Crazy Henry in his bar. They even wrote a polka for him. The chorus went something like, 'Hey Hey Hey Krajewski. Hey Krajewski, Hey Hey!' I'd bet that record is on Uncle Otto's jukebox over there," said William, as he pointed across the room.

"He did know how to pack in the crowds and was popular to some, but his cousins here disliked him. Especially in 1956 when he showed up to their mother's funeral in a red, white, and blue campaign car. They say that everything he did was just a publicity stunt. He never had a chance to win, but he spouted off on social welfare because he knew that was what the impoverished wanted to hear."

"A socialist platform then?"

"Well, traditional labels don't fit him well, but yeah, his political platform aimed at the working man. That's what the Polish neighborhoods were, blue collar families. He had a few drinks in the Eagle, and this is a picture of him in here during a campaign."

"What happened to him after '56?"

"He died around maybe 1966, but rumor had it he had even wrote a letter to LBJ in '64 pitching himself as a good running mate. He never stopped drumming up interest in

89

himself. He was a politician who never seemed to get elected but who still made money at it."

Balzie was so excited that I thought he was going to wet his trousers. I wondered if I should warn Otto of the impending request for the Table next week, but I needed to go to home. There's plenty of time before next week to tell Otto.

Friday, May 23rd

I rediscovered a forgotten jewel of the neighborhood, and it was Balzie who helped me do it. Just after I finished reading my morning paper, Balzie was asking me about where the nearest library was. I told him there was a one nearby on 9th Street. The main branch was a bit farther at Grand Army Plaza. He insisted that I take him to 9th Street that very morning. William had other plans for the day, so, after coffee, Balzie and I set out.

Balzie's not a bad boy, but I believe that he was brought up in sheltered privilege until he reached university. Walking past all the ethnic storefronts on 5th Avenue was thrilling for the socialist in him. His comments were about the working classes living closely together with little visible social advantages seen. To him, everyone seemed like everyone else. I could see why William enjoyed his company. He looked at life through a different lens and speak easily about what he saw. I better appreciate the uniqueness of my home. We reached 9th Street and 6th Avenue and entered the Park Slope Library.

As we entered, Balzie was in awe of the splendor of entrance in, what he called, "this workingman neighborhood." The librarian picked up on his enthusiasm and offered to give us a tour. I had been going there for decades but never really looked closely at its features. The stained-glass archways. The vaulted ceilings. The tiled fireplace.

The librarian told us that it was built in 1906 using an Andrew Carnegie grant. She felt it was an imposing presence on the neighborhood and called it, "a jewel in the crown of Carnegie libraries."

Eventually, Balzie remembered why he so urgently needed to seek out a library, to prepare for his debate. In a low voice that I could not hear, he told her the subject of his research. She led him into the Reference section. I didn't follow. I knew where I wanted to go, to visit Ivan.

I pulled out all the books they had by Turgenev that I didn't already own. I piled them onto a table and began to read. It was early afternoon before Balzie returned. He said he needed to walk over to the main branch at Grand Army Plaza to do more research. While it was only a mile away, it would take a couple of buses for me to get there. I decided to not go, so he left on his own. I checked out some books and walked home. I spent the afternoon and evening reading the musings of an old friend.

Late in the evening, William and I were beginning to be concerned for Balzie, but we had no way to find him. We never thought to give him the house phone telephone number. Finally, about 10 p.m., Balzie bounded in, still full of enthusiasm. He was thrilled with the library's main branch, and the Brooklyn Museum next to it. He met some fellow socialists distributing flyers in Grand Army Plaza, and they all had dinner together. He learned of a war protest the next day and wanted William to join him. Of course, William accepted and asked me if I wanted to come along. I said that I was busy with something important, which was not true. What could actually be more important than stopping this war, but I remain a coward.

I was glad that Henry was not around to hear of their plans. There will be a conflict here soon.

Balzie has a great love for stating his convictions. He also has a deep love of self, and I wondered if he ever needed to reconcile between the two. For tonight, none of us needed to make any reconciliations. I wanted to go to bed, and these two boys were going into Greenwich Village in the City to meet up with Nelson. I thought they would take the subway but watched them get into Balzie's car and drive away. This worried me, but then again everything does.

It's now 4 a.m. and I hear them coming in. At last, I can go to sleep. I heard footsteps on the floor above. I was not the only one waiting for the boys' return. Again, I recalled Ivan's *That's what children are for—that their parents may not be bored.*

Saturday, May 24th

The Mets have won only 18 games so far this year. A far cry from the 82 wins I am hoping for.

This afternoon, after attending a peaceful peace protest, William and Balzie left to visit Louise in Staten Island. The boys intended to stay the weekend and return on Monday. I'm anxious to hear from William on how his mother was. I am resigned to not seeing her anymore, but knowing she was okay would comfort me.

Sunday, May 25th

Berkeley professors accused California Governor Ronald Reagan of precipitating the violence at the school by his use of national guardsmen against student demonstrators. I'm glad William is here now. I might be the only one.

Since his arrival, Henry has been out of sorts. His anger finally surfaced into another heated argument with Linda. From my apartment, I heard their yelling at each other for over an hour. Then it stopped.

I was about to go up to the Eagle when I heard heavy steps coming down the stairs. As Linda went past my open door, I noticed that she carried a suitcase. I wondered if she would not be returning as Louise never did. I continued on to the Eagle anyway.

I wondered if I was being a terrible father to not go up to check on my son. No matter. I did leave. Henry joined me in the Eagle a few hours later but didn't come over to my booth. I eventually left. It's now past 1 a.m. and he's still not home.

I can't solve all his problems when I have my own. He didn't even notice that I was out of sorts last month. Same as me, Henry's an adult and needs to figure out things for himself.

Monday, May 26th

I was sitting on the stoop this morning, when I heard Henry yell, "I don't know what your mother is saying about me, but she walked out of here. I didn't kick her out. And she insisted on the divorce too."

William shouted back, "She told me it was her idea to leave, and now that she is knows about Linda, she said she made the right choice."

"Then what are you complaining about? She's happy with her choice. I'm happy with mine. Just grow up and accept it. We have."

There was a slam of the apartment door above, and I turned to see who was coming out. It was Henry. He paused at the sidewalk to consider where he was going then went down the street. Balzie came out next and sat down next to me.

"Vocal family you have here, Kaz. This weekend in Staten Island was not much quieter."

I knew that Louise had as much piss and vinegar in her veins as Henry, but it never occurred to me that the weekend visit went badly in Staten Island. Next, William appeared on the stoop.

"Balzie, perhaps we should plan to leave on our trip sooner than we planned."

"Whatever you want, Will."

I gestured that I didn't understand what they were talking about. Balzie immediately looked at William to let him handle this.

"Grandpa, Balzie and I are going to take a road trip up to Canada to check things out." I wrote down a question. "What kind of things?"

"He and I don't support the war, and now that we are out of college, we will be losing our student deferments. I was hoping this war would be over by now. We feel this war is wrong. I will not be drafted into it. I'm sorry if this disappoints you, but I can't support the war and possibly need to kill people who are just fighting to stay alive.

"Last week, Ottawa announced that Canadian immigration officials would not ask US immigrants their military status if they showed up at the border seeking residence. We will be welcomed there."

I thought about how to respond. Clearly, Henry does not yet know about these plans, and it would be best to get William out of here before he does. I stood up and walked over to William, who was still standing in the doorway, and I hugged him. I shook my head and patted him on the back of his head. While still holding him, I cried into his shoulder.

I finally wrote, "It would be best for you to go and not tell your father where you are going. Stay a few more days, then leave on some excuse or other. Make something up. He does love you, but he will never understand or accept this."

We all contemplated our next decisions. Eventually, I indicated that I needed to leave for a while to go down to OLC. I first wanted to talk to Our Lady, then I wanted to talk to Ed.

We all agreed to keep these plans to ourselves and not tell Henry.

Possibly to reassure me as I got ready to leave, Balzie spoke up. "Yeah, Will and I just finished a great adventure in college. Canada will be our next."

William seemed taken back by his comment. He told me later that he was not viewing moving to Canada as an adventure, and that he was taking this seriously.

For me, Our Lady was as mute as ever. This time, I don't know what she would want me to do. Ed was even less help than Our Lady. I'd like to call Louise but know I can't. I felt alone again. Ivan has gone silent. I don't want to weather this storm alone, but I fear I must.

Fathers and Sons and Other Village Idiots

Tuesday, May 27th

Everyone kept their distances around here today and I was glad. I needed a break from the yelling.

In the news, NASA gave the go ahead for Apollo 11. My country is going to the moon soon.

To make things a little better this evening, at the Eagle, there was a great resurrection of the Table. Tonight, I am transcribing my notes into this journal.

There may have been about a dozen or so patrons in the Eagle. They were all conversing in their own small groups or watching the Mets losing another game on the TV. I sat with Ed in a booth and occasionally, he would make a comment to me, and I'd write down a response. Mostly, we sat and drank beer. William and Balzie walked in about nine. I noticed Henry look away when they walked in.

William walked over to me and sat in my booth, while Balzie found a loose chair and brought it to the head of the Table. He stood up on the chair, and there he waited to be recognized.

Otto was busy behind the bar, but finally turned around when he noticed the room had gone quiet. I had mentioned to him of Balzie's plans to speak, so he was ready.

"What sir do you have to discuss on this fine evening?"

"I wish to offer my point of view on a question and to possibly correct a misunderstanding of terms."

"What is your question?"

"I ask whether those here are really capitalists and if not, what were they?"

Otto hesitated for a moment, then responded, "Well, that is two questions but related enough, so your issues can be entertained if there is any interest. Who here wishes to listen and consider these matters?"

People were bored with the Mets and had a need for some entertainment. A few hands were quickly raised, including William's. I and Ed had no reason to raise ours since there were already more than four willing to engage. The Eagle was, as NASA would say, *Go for a launch.*

95

"All right then. Please clear the Table for the participants. Others can sit elsewhere. Anthony, please shut off that miserable Mets' game for as long as this is less painful.

"We will allow the speaker to speak for a reasonable amount of time. I will determine if it gets too excessive. Then we will have a discussion. Anyone who gets physical with another will be tossed and banished for a while. There is no one in the funeral pallor or the hall tonight, so you can raise your voices all you want. Does anyone here not understand the rules here?"

No one said a word.

"Order whatever you want to keep you all in good voice and settle up your tabs as they are now. This is just in case I need to quickly toss you out on your dupa later." A few laughed.

As we all settled in, Otto left for a minute to do something in the loft. I knew what he was doing, but no one other than immediate family would. Otto had purchased a tape recorder in the '50s and had set it up in the loft. The microphone was hidden in the chandelier. My advance warning to Otto had allowed him to set everything up again. He had purchased the tape recorder years ago to record formal sessions of the Table. Balzie was sitting down as Otto returned to the room. William brought Balzie a beer and then rejoined me. Balzie gathered his thoughts for a moment then stood up and began.

"Who here was not born in America?" I, Ed and a few others raised our hands, including two of the Puerto Ricans sitting in the corner booth. They raised their hands but much more slowly than I and Ed. They might have thought it was a trick question as Wilfredo once told me he felt that Puerto Rico was already part of America. Balzie continued with his questioning.

"Who here had a parent who was not born here, but you yourself were?" Otto, Henry, and most of the bar raised their hands.

"Well good, you are what I would call first-generation Americans.

Fathers and Sons and Other Village Idiots

"And who here had grandparents not born here, but your parents were?" And there were fewer hands that included William and Anthony.

"Congratulations to you. You are second-generation Americans.

"Is there anyone who has not raise yet their hands?" No one moved.

"Too bad, but apparently tonight we have no native Americans. This means all our ancestors immigrated to this great nation, and probably in this century.

"These labels of first or second or native or immigrant should be meaningless in a fair democratic society. There should be no extra status or pecking order because of who got here first or last in America, but alas, there surely is. Native Americans, in fact, do say it is we who don't belong here and that they should have the highest status."

Someone at the table yelled out, "What about you? You didn't raise your hand at all."

"That's a reasonable question. I am second-generation American. Balzie paused for any more questions then proceeded.

"Is anyone here part of the upper class?" A few laughed, but no one spoke. It was William who broke that silence.

"Other than you. I have seen your family's home. I doubt there are any others here tonight."

"I confess that no one readily admits he is upper class, especially when in a bar in South Brooklyn, but in all honesty, I think of myself and my family as middle class and working middle class to be sure. We have been blessed with good fortunes for our hard work and we have fared better than most newcomers to this land of plenty. Nevertheless, we are far from the non-working upper-class capitalists of whom I will speak." He paused then continued.

"And there is the label I wish to consider with you all. Capitalism. I also want you to consider the labels of socialism and communism because in truth all three are very different.

"These terms are just labeling for types of government and economics, that is all. They are not religions or philosophies of life, just different socioeconomic systems. They are not about

97

human rights, but in practice, they definitely impact them." He paused a moment then took a deep breath in order to proclaim his next sentence in an even louder voice.

"We hold these truths to be self-evident, that all men are created equal, that they are endowed by their Creator with certain unalienable rights, that among these are life, liberty and the pursuit of happiness. All men.

"Now, perhaps it was an oversight, or thought it was implied, but the founders did forget to include women. An even worse error was not protecting the rights of people of color. Mistakes that our nation is only beginning to address some 200 years later. I am not here tonight to rail for those noble causes, but indeed they are vital to the continued success of our republic. I'm here tonight to discuss economics.

"Our Declaration of Independence does not promise that we will all be wealthy. It only promises all men have rights to life, liberty and happiness.

"But we here live in a capitalist society where the worker does not have the ability to say no to the boss and still be able to eat. He no longer has liberty and free will. It is difficult to stay alive when one does not have enough food or decent shelter or enough medicine to even live another day. It is difficult to be happy when you don't have a choice."

A "Hear, Hear" was voiced from someone at the Table. Balzie continued.

"In America, the rich hire the poor to do the things that the rich don't want to do. You there," he said while pointing a finger at a man, "go into that coal mine.

"Or you there," with another point, "clean the asbestos out of that basement for me. Or you there, go to war for me." With that Balzie pointed at William.

"I was here on Thursday when you all got word of Little Eddie dying in Nam. I'm sorry for your community's loss. Let's drink to his memory and acknowledge his family's great loss." And we all drank up.

"I have heard that there have been many other families on this street who have lost their boys. Do you think there are as many dead boy families on Park Avenue?" The room was silence.

Fathers and Sons and Other Village Idiots

"Yes, I realize that many of you here fought for our country in World War Two, but many of you also realize that this war today is a different war.

"In World War Two, rich and poor served side by side and saved our freedoms from a powerful fascist threat. Let's drink to all of you who did that for those of us who were not yet even born." And we drank some more, but Balzie was only getting started.

"Capitalistic system is a system based on private ownership and personal economic freedom. Ownership and freedom are good, right?"

A "Damn right," came angerly from Otto who might have been concerned where this was going. He lived through a decade of Joe McCarthy and didn't need the Eagle labeled as a communist bar. Balzie ignored him for the moment. He turned his attention to those at the table who were quick to agree with him. "Do you or you, own very much? And do you or you or you enjoy personal economic freedom?" he said as he pointed around the room.

A "No," came from one of them. Otto kept an uncomfortable quiet. The boy continued.

"Well, why is that? Don't you work hard enough to earn that?"

More muttering and uneasy shifting of bodies at the table. Many probably wondered where this was all going. Ed seemed very engaged with everything that Balzie was saying.

"Yes, there are a few here tonight that do own a house or a business or a car, but in truth even those very few don't have a complete sense of personal economic freedom. Even the owner of this fine establishment who built this wonderful community table with his father is working for others who are making excessive amounts of money on his hard work. He buys their beers at the price they set, he buys their whiskey, and he pays more taxes than rich men do, but he makes much less than them. Uncle Otto is definitely working class just like the rest of us. He, too, is working for a few big businessmen who make as much on his hard work as he does.

"But this big businessman also makes money from your work and your work and your work. A few men own most of

99

the big businesses, while others cannot afford to buy even a small one. They have locked us out of their playground. Do you think any of you will ever catch up to these big businessmen?" The room was quiet.

"Then there is the socioeconomic system of communism, as those poor souls in USSR or Red China live under. There is no private property there. There is no personal wealth. There is no freedom to choose one's life. You do what you are told by the state. In theory, there is no rich or poor and there is perfect economic equality. No matter how hard you work or how smart you are, everyone gets paid the same amount.

This is a fantasy and in practice, these countries operate very much under a small ruling class living off a large poor working class.

"But communism is not socialism as many believe to be true. Don't be fooled by thinking that USSR has socialist in its name that they are socialists, they are not." He let that sink in. Maybe he was expecting debate on that, but there wasn't any. Ed was now listening even more intently.

"Years ago, at this very table, you had Henry Krajewski speak to some of you about a pig in every pot and working man's rights. These are not capitalist ideas nor are they communist. In fact, *Crazy Henry*, as I've heard him be called, hated communism and campaigned against it. He ran for president of our great United States on the Poor Man's Ticket.

"A few of you may remember him and may not think fondly of him. In truth, what little I could find out about him didn't uncover much as to how he helped anyone but himself. This does not mean that his worker welfare platform was wrong. He was saying the right things, but many still doubt where his heart was. No matter to us tonight.

"But how is real socialism different from communism. Well, for one, socialism is not advocating for violent overthrow of capitalist governments, as communists are.

"With socialism, you can still have private property and wealth, but socialists only want a fair playing field to narrow the gap between rich and poor. In a socialist society, it is the government's job to make things fair for all men and not just the rich. A society guided by socialist values will protect all men's interest and not always send just the poor into coal mines. Maybe some of you are more socialist than capitalist."

There was some silence after Balzie stopped talking. Many faces showed some relief he had stopped talking as they stood up to buy another beer, and others were mulling over his words. No one was walking out yet. The silence continued until William broke into it.

"Well, Bazarov, you make many good points and thank you for presenting them for discussion this evening. You and I have discussed these matters at great length before, but the one thing you refuse to concede is man's desire for his own well-being and not the greater society's welfare. People are inherently greedy and self-serving. Working men want more economic equality, maybe even to the point of communism that everyone gets the same. They do want equality but only to a point.

"Until they have more than most, then they don't want to get pulled down to the average. They want more wealth, more privilege, more freedom than would be possible to give to all and share with the masses.

"When this happens, they want to be little capitalists again. They don't need to be as rich as Rockefeller, but they want more than their share and they are willing to work harder or steal better to get it. They want the better doctor, not the state assigned one. They want the Cadillac, not the Beetle. They want more than their share."

Balzie quickly continued. "But socialism does not take that away. What it does do is to provide a minimum, those inalienable rights for all. Beyond that, we are free to earn more. The government's job would be to protect the weak and poor from complete destitution. With that Ed voiced a "Hear! Hear!" I could see that Balzie took note of it and moved on.

"As children, we are taught by our parents and our church to share and play nice. But as we turn into adults, these same parents push for their family first. The church, I just don't know where they stand on all this.

"The Church. Yes. The Church. Catholicism, Christianity, all religions. What do benevolent religions think?

"Father Ed, what do you think on this matter? Would Jesus Christ be a capitalist or a socialist?"

Ed was not going to get manipulated by letting Balzie phrase the answer by how he posed the question. As a professional speaker, he knew how to gather his thoughts and took a few moments, then he answered. Balzie was about to be surprised by his response.

"I speak only for myself and do not represent all religions or Christianity or all of Catholicism. I speak as an individual whose thinking happens to be consistent with the Catholic doctrine, but I am an individual soul in the eyes of God and that is where all this discussion of which system is better or worse, is flawed.

"Jesus Christ would not be a socialist." he proclaimed.

"A primary tenant of the Catholic Church is that each individual is just that, an individual, and he or she has free will to make their own choices. Socialism relies on group thinking and group policies and does not recognize this individuality of choice. "If I could pick which economic system we lived in, I would pick distributism." From the blank stares that Ed received from everyone including Balzie, it was clear that no one here ever heard of distributism. Ed continued.

"This system worked for a thousand years in Europe. Under distributism, property ownership is an essential right for the individual, but property ownership must be possible for all," he paused again, "and not just in the hands of a privileged few. We do not have a Distributionist society in America today. Ownership is in the hands of the few and the poor suffer horribly for it. You only need to walk this city to see this is so in capitalist America.

"No, Jesus Christ could not have been a socialist because he taught of man's free will to make choices no matter what his society demanded of him. A man who makes the free choice to do the right thing will be saved. You cannot have group think to achieve a personal redemption." Ed stopped talking and, after a moment, the room exploded. Some applauded. Others got off their stools and chairs to come and pat Ed on his back or shake his hand. I think part of this was

Fathers and Sons and Other Village Idiots

that some didn't want the rich snot hippie to have the last word.

Balzie didn't seem to mind that he had lost control of the discussion. People argued with Balzie. They argued with each other. One man got into the face of Ed, and Ed stood his ground and yelled back until he became red in the face, but Ed's eyes revealed to me, he was enjoying himself.

From behind the bar, Otto observed the crowd and seemed ready to end the arguments if he needed to, but no one was getting physical with others. There was only loud discussion. Many were still buying beer, so Otto was happy. The Eagle was alive once again. There was also no motion from the table leader for a vote on any matter. The verbal freedom for all, joyously continued.

The discussion was bringing back memories to me of years gone by. Now, decades later, I am proud I had a hand in the building the Table with Otto. I am proud that he preserves the tradition to this day.

Otto remained behind the bar and continued to observe. His presence there with his arms folded seemed to be enough to keep everything civilized. William and Balzie engaged and debated anyone who came near them. Anthony seemed quite stimulated and engaged in many of the arguments that were flying about the room. The boy actually had opinions. Only Henry seemed to be uncomfortable with the moment.

The discussion had ended without any need for a vote on any issue. Balzie did what he set out to do, to have people reconsider their beliefs. He, too, seemed very excited. And so it went.

After a while, Ed, Henry, and I left for the evening. We walked down the street in silence. I brought back Otto's tape recorder to help me recreate the events in this journal.

It was a wonderful night, but a question came to my mind. So what?

I continue to think of my immediate quest and can't seem to focus on others right now. I want to enjoy what was good about tonight, and I do. I also feel that I need to be greedy and only worry about my needs. Being selfless is not something I can do easily. I would have made a bad priest or bartender. I

103

am ashamed that I am so selfish yet continue to think about what's my next step. Nothing short of my redemption will make me happy.

Thursday, May 29th

Expected temperature and humidity would be in the mid 90s today. We were all sweating in our tee-shirts as we sat around the breakfast table.

The boys came up with a story of leaving to do some New England camping and visit a fellow student up there. William went upstairs to feed Henry this story. Unfortunately, within minutes, they were yelling at each other. Then I heard William blurt out he was going to Canada to "dodge the draft."

Henry yelled back some obscenity, and I realized that I needed to get up there as fast as I could. As I went up the stairs, Balzie came down. I entered Henry's kitchen with the two of them being only an arm's length apart, when Henry stepped even closer. In mid step, William pushed him back hard on his left shoulder. Henry lost his balance and grabbed the back of a chair to avoid falling. I got between them before Henry could recover.

Fortunately, nether tried to get more physical. I could not have stopped them if they had. Balzie then apparently reappeared.

Henry looked over to Balzie, then back to William. "Get out you ungrateful bastard." William stepped forward, but Balzie got his arms around the boy and turned him towards the door. William took the shove through the doorway, and they went back down to my apartment. Henry stormed down the stairs after them, but instead of pursuing them, went out the front door.

Within 20 minutes, William and Balzie had gathered all their things and walked out, too. William turned to me from the stoop.

"Sorry, Grandpa."

Without giving me a chance to write anything down, he stepped back in, grabbed me by the shoulders and hugged me, then within moment, he, too, was gone. I stood alone on the stoop. No grandson. No son. No angel. No god. Nobody to help me stop the madness.

Henry never returned today. Don't know where he found to hide from himself. Probably the bottom of a bottle in some park somewhere. Idiots just pissing their lives away. At three a.m., I write and wonder why my life went so wrong.

Friday, May 30th

Memorial Day was celebrated by many today, however there wasn't any celebrating in our house. Henry was still gone. My family is dying, and I don't know how to save it.

Saturday, May 31st

Henry returned sometime last night. Early this afternoon, I heard the doorbell ring. When I opened the front door, I saw Linda standing on the stoop. She had a piece of luggage with her but left it by the door in the foyer as she entered. She told me that yesterday, Henry and she had been talking on the phone and she decided to return. Upstairs, we both heard Henry was on the phone with Louise in a heated discussion. She decided to stay downstairs with me. We both sat uncomfortably still and listened to one side of the conversation.

"This is not my fault, you bitch. This has nothing to do with Linda. She is just my friend." I looked over to Linda, but her stare was looking down at her lap. While the yelling continued upstairs, downstairs Linda got up and left. As she walked out, Henry's yelling continued.

"If you think that I don't care about William dying in Nam, then why do you think I'd want him to be an officer in the Navy or Air Force." Louise was probably yelling back a retort.

"He made his choice and he's gone. We really have no way to contact him even if we wanted to and I don't want to."

"I don't really care. I don't love anyone right now. Not you. Not him. Not anyone."

Billy Warren

"From now on, don't bother to call here. You're not part of this family anymore anyway." With that, the call was over.

I never told him that Linda had been there. I'm sure later he saw a key she placed on hallway table. Henry's my son, but I don't have to like him right now nor do I want to comfort him. Let him suffer alone.

Sunday, June 1st

T he phone rang. Being alone in the house, I picked up the receiver and gave a grunt into it.

"Hi Grandpa, it's Nelson. Is that you?"

I made another grunt. There was traffic noise in the background and guessed that he was calling from a street corner phone booth.

"Let's use our tapping code like we'd done before. One tap for yes and two for no. Is that you Grandpa?" In response to the question, I tapped on the mouthpiece once with a nearby pencil.

"I was calling for William. Is he home right now?" Two taps.

"Will he be home soon?" No.

"Oh. Okay then. Can you give him a message?" No.

"Is everything there, okay?" No.

"Oh. I see." Then he added, "Might he be at his mom's?" No.

"Really. Oh, okay. I was expecting to see him last night and when he didn't show, I thought that I'd call." There was a pause.

"Did he go on his trip?" Yes. "Up north?" Yes.

At first, there was only the street noise coming over the line.

"I see. Then you now know where he was heading?" Yes.

"Well okay. That's good, I think, that someone there knows where he went." Another pause. "Are you all right?" I had no response to that. The truth was I wasn't all right, but a no might worry the boy and there was nothing he could do anyway. With the prolonged silence from me, he continued.

106

Fathers and Sons and Other Village Idiots

"Tell you what. I'd like to see you. How about getting together tomorrow? I can't come over there, but I haven't seen you lately." I thought about it then I tapped once.

"Great. Well, where should we meet? How about Juniors? 11:30?" Yes.

"Okay, see you then" and with another tap from me to confirm, we hung up.

Nelson's call today made me feel nice. Nice is the only word that comes to my mind right now. I feel slightly better than I did before.

Ed always harped on me about the unknown comforts that can come from a simple act. Nelson's simple call and the prospect of seeing him soon put me in a better mood. Later in the day, I resumed reading my *Daily News*. I hadn't been touching it lately. Today's sports stories did distract me for an hour, even though the sports news was not all that good.

The Yankees were 11 games back from first place, and Mets were nine in their league. There will be no pennant in New York this year. The Mets didn't get any better. The Yankees just got worse. It's only June 1st, but this season is already over.

After finishing the entire paper back to front, I sat alone again in a quiet apartment with only my thoughts. My accounting of the events of the day in this journal are over for today and I am ready for bed. Maybe seeing Nelson tomorrow will be good.

Monday, June 2nd

J uniors is a Brooklyn institution. It's a deli on the corner of Flatbush and DeKalb. The décor was typical diner with bright lighting, shiny chrome ornamentation, and an eating area of tightly packed tables and chairs. I always thought the light fixtures looked like flying saucers. Each wall had some sort of theme, from sports to celebrities, and two chairs from the old Ebbits Field hung on a column. As always, it was noisy and alive with activity. A heavyset waiter waddled over to our table to take our orders.

107

After ordering, I finally got to look into the face of the boy. He looked a little lean to me but okay, I guess. Given how fast he ate, I doubt he had eaten today.

During lunch, he asked about everyone, including his dad and Anthony. I wrote down what I knew, which wasn't good. He seemed to perk up when I mentioned that his brother was thinking of junior college in the fall. I did mention the resurrection of the Table and he seemed genuinely happy with that and said that he's wished he was there that night. My thought then was how Otto was being such a dupa to this boy. The whole family was. Just because he was gay.

I asked about what he was doing in the City and what his plans were, but he was vague about everything. He seemed very uncomfortable discussing his life. He said he had a boyfriend for a while, but they broke up a few months ago. That was the most he revealed, which really wasn't very much.

I can't say that I communicated anything deeply personal about the state of my life either. I did mention that Ed and I were talking again, and that Sancho was probably in his last year. I omitted that I expected the same for myself. With my cancer surgery being five years ago, no one ever thinks to ask about it anymore. I see Little Prick in a few weeks. It's on my mind, but no one else's.

Our lunchtime flew by, and it was already 1 p.m. when our overweight waiter returned.

"What are you having with your cheesecake," he asked.

"How do you know that we're having cheesecake?" asked Nelson.

"You're not a regular."

"No, but an irregular."

"Only the regulars might not order the cheesecake because they probably already had it five times this week. All the out-of-towners always order cheesecake."

"But we're not from out of town."

"Hey, I'm not here to entertain you. Do you want the cheesecake or not and are you having coffee with it?" Nelson ordered the cheesecake and a regular coffee. I gestured to give me the same. With that exchange, he turned and waddled away. When he returned with two plates of cheesecake in one hand

Fathers and Sons and Other Village Idiots

and two cups of coffee in the other, he also brought the check. When he slapped in down, I quickly grabbed from the table.

Nelson started to protest until I raised a finger to my lips while writing with the other hand that this was a belated birthday present. He consented with a thank you.

As we exited Juniors, we turned together to walk towards the DeKalb Avenue station. After we went through the turnstile, we hugged a goodbye. As we embraced, I shoved a five into his hand. He doesn't seem to be thriving in his new life in the Village.

Overall, it was a good visit for both of us. I think that Nelson enjoyed it more than he was expecting. My bottom line was that I think he knows that I still love him, and I want him in my life, despite his father's wishes to expel him from his world. I wrote down that he was always welcome in my house and that his father could go to hell if he didn't like it.

We said that we would see each other again next month. He wrote down a post office box address if I ever needed to reach him since he had no phone. He turned and headed down the stairs for the subway track back to Manhattan. I went down the stairs to the southbound platforms heading towards South Brooklyn.

Wednesday, June 4th

Montreal Expos took a major league record away from the Mets, the longest losing streak ever. Montreal has now lost 17 games in a row. The Mets set the record of 16 in 1962. The Mets can't even be the best at being the worst.

Baseball is not such a useless diversion of time as some people think it is. It is like a medication that continues to help me forget. Reading about the losing Mets each day not only diverts my attention, but it also gives me a cause, the lost cause of rooting for probably the best underdog team of all times.

I did have a reasonable expectation this year. I just want them to not lose more than they win. Today, they're back up to 24-23. Next month is the middle of the season already and it's gonna be close, but I still have a hope. Eighty-two wins is my magic number.

109

Friday, June 6th

D-Day happened 25 years ago today. Otto and Henry went through those Normandy beaches a few days after the initial landing. Marysia and I received letters from them now and then, but neither boy could say much. After they returned, we learned they were both in the Battle of the Bulge. I remember when news of the beach landings started to hit our papers, we were fearful that they might be in those first waves. We were always dreading when the black sedan with military license plates would show up on 23rd Street.

Our ignorance of where the boys were, made our imaginations go wild. Marysia cried every night. It was the first time I remember sinking into my depressions. There were things in the world that I could not control to protect my family. I feel helpless now that I still cannot protect them. If I were a rich man, I could. I would have hired better doctors for Marysia. Money could protect my family.

Everything is ultimately my fault. I didn't do everything possible to protect my family. Decades later, I would lose Marysia. I think that I should have done more to placate God. He punished me and took her. Today, he tortures my sons and grandsons.

After my sons did return from the war, they never spoke much about it. They were changed by it. Marysia and I noticed the difference but were thankful that they got back safely. We saw those black sedans stopping on 23rd Street. Selfishly, we were thankful it wasn't for our sons, but those cars came for other boys. Poor boys sent into the breach for the interests of the rich.

Eddie's only the latest to die for his country's wars. He will not be the last. Sadly, now that military car comes and goes, and few of us on the street even notice. We are not aware of the grief just across the street. It's not like World War II. There is less shared sorrow with this Vietnam war. There may be much grief so nearby that I am unaware of. We have become isolated from each other. My village is falling apart.

Thursday, June 12th

Little Prick saw me this afternoon and ordered up more tests. He wants to take the time to review the test results carefully with me in person and not by telephone. He scheduled my next appointment on Saturday the 21st because he felt this could not wait until his next weekday opening. He seemed to already know what the results will be. Now, he's got my attention and I'm sure I should be worried too.

He will want me to be prepared to do the treatments and maybe more surgeries all over again. I just can't and told him so. He said that if the tests were not good, I'd die without the treatments. I told him that cancer will not kill me. I will not allow it to define my demise. He answered this with a "let's see what the results were first."

He asked if I might want to bring a family member or friend. I wrote NO in big letters. No one was to know. I've got more to worry about than this cancer or about how people will treat me different because of it. I did the tests he ordered, then went home to a quiet house.

Saturday, June 21st

The longest day of my life happened today. Little Prick was the one person I didn't want to see but did.

Alone, I saw him, and alone I was not surprised by his news. Without treatment, he gave me six months. Alone, I rode the subway back home.

At first, I was unaware that there were others sitting near me in the subway car. Then I became very aware of them.

Everyone in the car seemed to know what the old man had again. The well-dressed white woman glanced with indifference at me. The old black woman with her own problems just turned her eyes away from me. The little Puerto Rican punk looked through me as if I already didn't exist. I felt naked. Everyone somehow knew I have it again.

Of course, only I and the Little Prick knew because no one else really cared. Henry and Otto never ask about it anymore. William used to occasionally ask, but now he does not even call. I have heard nothing from Nelson since Juniors. Maybe it's because I can't talk to anyone. I am silent, therefore, invisible.

All this summer, people may talk at me, and I will listen to them, but they don't really want to read my replies. I can only curse to myself. This is my last summer with everyone, but no one knows or cares. My final season approaches. I will die during the cold months and be forgotten by all by next summer.

I reached 25th Street Station and the car doors slid open with a jolt. Those left in the subway car didn't even look up to see me walk out. I stared up the station's stairs leading from this hole. I climbed those steep stairs, and, once on top, looked around the neighborhood. Who here in the village could help me? Lady Liberty stands only miles away in the harbor, but today she seems so far. Closer was OLC. I walked up her stone stairs and stepped inside. I looked up to my silent Black Madonna. I heard a sound from behind me and turned towards it. It was the custodian asking me to leave. The church needed to be locked up.

In the fading sunlight from the west, I walked up 23rd Street and my long shadow on the sidewalk ran away from me. I think I just need to accept that it is time for me to die. There is no one here for me and no one needs me to be here anymore.

spring offered hope
summer light reveals demons
time to confront them

Thursday, June 26th

Self-imposed censorship is what a newspaper really is. It's just pieces of paper with some information that has been censored for me by someone who does not know me. It's all the news that someone thinks I should hear, and that I am willing to pay them for their suppression.

The mayor declared *Daily News* Day in honor of the 50th anniversary of the paper. Fifty years of pushing their propaganda.

All the news that's fit to print is the *Times* slogan. Each day, they're basically saying on their front page, We are not telling you everything. Trust us. It's not fit. Why don't all newspapers just say, We are only telling you what we want you to pay attention to.

Sunday, June 29th

Nelson may be in danger tonight, but I still have no way to reach him. There was nothing in the *News* this morning, but tonight in the Eagle, I overheard Rocco, a local cabdriver, saying he drove by a riot in Greenwich Village. According to him, riot police were teargassing and beating the gays.

Otto once told me that the mobsters owned most gay bars in the Village because the police needed to be paid off to not raid them. Sounds like someone missed a payment and the police moved in.

Nelson once told me that this did happen frequently at gay bars, but he had been lucky so far and got out before being hurt or arrested. His father didn't seem to realize that his son was in great danger.

Rocco said he saw police raids in the Village before, but this time the gays fought back. At first, the surprised police pulled back until the riot police showed up, then, he told us, "they started breaking heads." As he spoke of all this, it reminded me of Izzie's story of the Warsaw Ghetto. These gay protestors never had a chance to win but they resisted.

I'm praying for Nelson tonight.

Monday, June 30th

Nothing was in either the *Daily News* or *Times* about the riots last night in the city. Apparently, it's not fit news. They don't want people to pay attention to this vulgarity.

These days, I have been worrying more and more about Nelson and William. I once thought it was good that Nelson had found his own village to call his home. I had hope that Canada might be a safe place for William. I wonder what William and Balzie walked into up there. I wish my grandsons would call me. Not knowing is hurting me.

"Did you hear about the suicide on the Verrazano this weekend?" asked David as soon as I sat down at the Melting Pot. I shook my head.

"Yeah, this guy got all the way to the middle of the bridge and with cars going by him, he just jumped over the rail and plunged into the water 200 feet below. The tide was going out at the time and the current just took his body out to sea."

I sat down at the table and wrote, "I didn't know there was a foot path on the bridge."

"There isn't. He walked out on the 92nd Street onramp to the lower level. They just opened that lower level this weekend. Maybe he wanted to be the first to die from there. Who knows how people are thinking when they're crazy in the head like that?"

'Didn't anyone see him?" I wrote.

"Probably, but would you stop a car on a bridge to try to talk to him? This is New York, Kaz, nobody's going to do that. Papers said that some people did tell the fare collectors at the other side, but by the time the police could get there, he had jumped. Maybe he heard the sirens coming and it rushed him into doing it."

I opened my paper, but I continued to think about this man. What was going on in his mind? He might have thought this was his best option and maybe it was. Why should I judge him?

*

Fathers and Sons and Other Village Idiots

My worst fears were realized this afternoon. As I walked back into the house after writing up the morning at the Melting Pot, the phone was ringing. It was Nelson. He was asking if he could live with me for a few days.

I clicked my yes, and, within an hour, he showed up in a cab. Bandages on his head. A cast on his leg.

It was an effort to get him up the front steps. Under his shirt, I could feel more padding wrapping his torso. He was going to be here more than a few days.

Throughout the afternoon, he told me about the police raids of last weekend. The East Village community was so fed up with both the cops and the mob that they decided to fight back. They made their stand in front of a bar called the Stonewall Inn.

No one had a chance once the riot squads arrived. He felt that the cops almost looked like they were enjoying themselves. He noticed one of the bar owners walk safely through the police lines that then closed behind him. Once closed, no gay escaped without a beating.

Arresting a few was needed, but the beatings seemed to be more of the purpose of the raid. Bleeding on the ground and with a broken leg, Nelson said he was probably too injured to be arrested, so the police left him bleeding on the street. Strangers took him to an ER. In addition to his head and leg injuries, he had broken ribs.

For now, he won't be able to work or care for himself. Whether his father liked it or not. he's going to live with. By five, Henry found out that Nelson was in my apartment and brought the news to Otto in the Eagle. Otto had the chance to come down but never did. Fathers can slash at their sons in so many different ways. Henry helped us by making dinner and lifting Nelson from bed to bathroom when he needed to go.

Again, I could not find anything about the Stonewall Inn riot in the *Daily News* yet. *The Times* printed a short account buried on page 22 with a headline, *Police again Rout 'Village' Youths*. Let's just dismiss this as if it was just a bunch of kids being disobedient to authority. These young men were fighting for their lives against the very police who should have been protecting them.

115

Tuesday, July 1st

Otto still didn't come over this morning, but Anthony did. He had only found out about Nelson last night at closing time. I had finally had enough of Otto. The boy needed his father, and I was going to bring Otto back.

My sons and I often had physical confrontations with each other, but I could no longer be as physical I wanted to. These days, I can't even verbally argue with Otto, as he would turn away and never read what I wrote.

This morning, I decided fighting was once again the right thing to do. When Otto came around the bar to talk to me, he looked at me and said that he knew why I was there and that he was not coming down to the house. With that declaration, he turned away. I had intended to kick him in the ass, but when he saw me moving in behind him, he quickly turned back towards me. It didn't change my mind about the kick. When he stepped towards me and leaned forward to grab my shoulders, I kneed him in the groin. I had always taught my boys to never kick anyone in the balls during a fight, but that was unless they knew it was a fight that they could not win any other way. Though I was really trying my hardest, my kick was not what it could have been fifty years ago, but it was enough to surprise him and for him to fold over. I had made my point and very quickly left. He was already straightening up.

I came back to the apartment to find both Anthony and Henry getting Nelson to the bathroom. While Nelson was in the bathroom, and Anthony and Henry stood together outside the door, I went over and put my arms around them both. The three of us stood quietly in the hallway until Nelson called that he needed help to stand up and pull up his pants. Anthony opened the door before Henry could and he stepped in to take care of his brother.

Anthony stayed with us all day except for a brief time when he left to bring back some clothing. Henry brought down his portable TV and we watched game shows and soap operas all day in the bedroom. Otto worked at the Eagle alone. After all these years, I finally realize that fathers can't and don't control their sons, and sons cannot control their fathers. My father, me, my sons, and my grandsons, we all have no control.

After dinner, Henry called Stella to let her know of recent events. She too had been aware of recent events in the Village. She wanted to drive over, but Henry convinced her that we were all settling in for the night and it was best if she would not. Anthony stayed the night and slept on the couch. He saw how difficult it was for Henry to get Nelson into the bathroom alone. It has been too long since Nelson and Anthony have been in the same room or even on the same street.

It's been a long day here, but Henry and Anthony came through for Nelson today. I feel good about my being here as well. Nelson was able to come to me. Maybe I briefly served a useful purpose today.

Wednesday, July 2nd

S tella was here before breakfast. She drove over then proceeded to take over the household.

Stella was probably close to 60 now and a bit of a pungent personality. She joined our family through marriage, but even though her husband and sister had passed on, she has never left, and no one would have wanted her to move on. Marysia and she had some minor skirmishes over control of holiday meals at our house, but these were more like sisterly squabbles. When Marysia was dying, it was Stella here every day until the end.

Stella's talent was that she could quickly recognize what needed to be done and proceeded to get it done. She walked in this morning and started ordering everyone. She never needed to ask twice. She is not a small woman nor is she weak. Today, she literally lifted Nelson up from the bed and placed him down gently into an easy chair by the bedstand. She saw no need to ask anyone else for help. It just needed to get done and she did it. She's just that way.

She works hard, but also expects the same from each of us. Ed, who arrived mid-morning, was not exempt. After dealing with Nelson's immediate needs, she looked around the apartment and determined it was filthy. When Anthony said that he needed to go to work at the Eagle, she would not allow it.

"You stay here and wash those windows. Otto can go to hell." There was no argument from any of us. Yes, Otto could go to hell. We all felt that today.

We were able to get Nelson into the living room for a few hours, and in between our cleaning assignments, he talked about his life in the Village. It wasn't much about his gay lifestyle. It was more about the unreported war there. Damn those newspapers.

"When I first moved into the Village," he said, "I thought I had reached a sort of heaven for me. There were people being openly gay and talking about it. It didn't take long before I found out that we gays were just money-making opportunities for others, specifically the mob and cops.

"Because it was really hot last week, everyone was on edge when the police moved in once again. I guess more than just a few of us had had enough and started to resist getting pushed about. Others started to join in, and the police shit a brick and immediately dropped back. We thought we might have won a little battle and some space from the neighborhood Nazis. We didn't think that they were calling in riot squads to deal with us. Over the past few months, the riot squads had too much practice at colleges in putting down civil unrest, but the press were present there, so they had to restrain themselves. There was no press covering the Village. The cops had become frustrated with being so restrained, so they unleased on us.

"We knew that most of the gay bar owners were exploiting us. We knew most cops hated us too and used any excuse to intimidate and beat us. Between the cops and the mob, we had no friends. Politicians, even the gay ones who we would see in the clubs, never stood up for us in public.

"I saw how the mob would shakedown Dad for some free booze all the time. I've seen some cops doing it here too. On 23rd Street, it was all done quietly and out of sight of the public. In the Village, it was done in broad daylight, and no one cared. It was always open season on us.

"We started to hope that there were some newspapers and reporters who were starting to take an interest helping us, but over the last few days, I now see that's not true. Even the *Village Voice*, a paper I thought was behind us, referred to us as "the forces of faggotry." This morning, a buddy called to tell me that yesterday, protestors swarmed the paper's offices and were about to burn it down when the police moved in again."

Despite the hopelessness of everything that Nelson was telling us, he himself seemed calm and not defeated. He has the heart of a lion. He commented that he had never seen or heard of such a big resistance by gays before. This was a start, he said, and not an ending. He's still got hope. Me, I don't know what to believe or hope for anymore. I am happy that he's alive. For now, he would not be on the front lines of this war. A war right here in the land of the so-called American dream where everyone should be free to pursue their happiness.

As I write in my journal tonight, I still don't know what Otto is thinking. His silence makes me realize that people can't read other people's minds very well. I think of all the times I stewed in silence. I assumed everyone knew I was pissed off. I have been such an idiot.

Thursday, July 3rd

The *Daily News* described a takeover of a draft center as being raided by a bunch of "peacenik" women. Once again, they were trying to be dismissive. They attempted to demean the protestors further by also calling them "petticoat militants." Still, there was no story anywhere in the *News* on Stonewall.

The Times buried a Stonewall story on page 19. They buried it in an attempt to trivialize it. They probably think that their readers want this story to go away in their wonderful New York City.

Nelson is moving about the apartment with his crutches today. He plans to move over to his brother's apartment soon. With each meal, Nelson is gaining some strength. With each conversation, his emotional strength seems to be growing as well.

While Henry seems genuinely angry with Otto about how he was not coming to care for his own son, he isn't applying this notion to his relationship with William. It's like it's different in his case. Just pig-headed fathers. He has not yet asked me if I had heard from William since he left. I haven't, but he doesn't know that. He's an idiot who could lose his son forever.

Now I do realize that labeling my sons idiots is my way to demean them. I am no better than those newspaper editors. Nevertheless, they are idiots. Fathers never seem to accept the idea that sons have free will to make their own choices. William chose to go to Canada, but Henry may never accept his right to make that choice.

Friday, July 4th

Fly our Flag, Don't Burn it! was on their sign. At Grand Army Plaza, boy scouts staged a reenactment of the raising of the flag on Iwo Jima.

It's a point of view and I am not angered to see it expressed. I don't like seeing the flag burned. What bothers me is neither side is seeking a dialog. They only want to make a statement to start a conflict.

Without dialog, the voices get raised louder to get noticed. The yelling will lead to demonstration, but still, no one may notice if the papers don't report it. Actions become violent. Then you can bet there will be a reaction. For better and worse, violence gets noticed and it gets reported.

Today is Independence Day. We should be gathering in mutual celebration of our personal freedoms. Instead, we are just shouting at each from across protest lines. Angry voices will encourage violent actions.

Tonight, Nelson and I sat on the stoop and watched the fireworks on the street. Firecrackers and penny-rockets were exploding for over five hours. It sounded like a war zone until midnight, when the explosions slowly subsided. By then, all the parked cars were covered in so much firecracker paper and ash that it looked like snow had fallen.

Nelson talked with me and whoever walked by. I wrote notes to Nelson occasionally. Despite all the noise, it was peaceful to sit with him a few hours and not discuss problems.

With all the interest on Nelson these days, I hadn't thought much about my problems. Frankie hasn't asked me to do much lately. No one knows about the return of my cancer yet and even if they did, what could they do? I still don't know what I can do about my quest, but I do know that I am resolved to not do the treatments again and resolved to not let the cancer be the death of me. It will not pick the time of my death.

Saturday, July 5th

I needed to be scarce for a few days. Nelsen climbed a flight of stairs today without help, so it was decided that he'd be better off living in his brother's apartment, which had more space. Stella gave her stamp of approval and said that she would be over to Anthony's on Monday. My plan is to not go near until Stella has a few days to whip it back into some higher state of cleanliness.

Sunday, July 6th

A battlefield for street hoodlums is what my grandsons' childhood playground has become. Nevertheless, after Mass, Ed joined me to sit in it.

Ten years ago, the park was such a pleasant tree-lined oasis to watch the children playing on see-saws or running through the sprinkler. Today, the vandals had broken nearly everything but the handball wall. The looters have stolen all the fences and metal swings for scrap metal. The word on the street was the city wants to close it down and sell the property.

Ed and I found the remnants of a park bench in the shadow of the factory wall. We each had a section of the *Sunday News* open before us when Ed spoke.

"I see the *News* finally made mention of the Stonewall riot. They called the protestors, "Queen Bees." I just shook my head. It took a week, but they could no longer ignore it, so they chose to degrade it with words. Big surprise.

Of course, they wanted to minimize it with their adjectives. Papers are procurers of hate for profit and influence. *The Times* and *Post* are no better. They have divided up the readership like the crime families carved up the city. *The Times* and *Wall Street Journal* took white collar readers, *The News* got blue collars, and *The Village Voice* bohemians. All pandering to their readerships only to sell newspapers. Reporting the news was only the means to make money.

Monday, July 7th

I didn't escape. Before I could get out the door this morning to go to the Melting Pot, the telephone rang. I made the mistake of answering it. A husky female voice barked out, "Get your dupa over here and tell that priestie boyfriend of yours that if he still wants to eat holiday meals with us, he'd better come too." Then, Stella hung up.

Priestie boyfriend. That's a new one. I walked down to the rectory and wrote down Stella's message. My priestie boyfriend and I went over to Anthony's and cleaned it for the rest of the day, which was followed by a wonderful dinner cooked by Stella.

Over dinner, Ed stated to everyone that this was the last Baranski household that he intended to clean. Ed is never one to state a problem without a solution, and this was no exception. He proposed that Henry and Anthony hire a maid to come in once a week to keep things clean. When asked where they would find someone that they could trust and afford, Ed had that solution as well.

"We have a newly arrived Polish immigrant at OLC and she needs a job. I'll bring her over tomorrow for you to negotiate a fair wage and don't you dare Low Ball her." With that, Ed went back to eating his pot roast. No one said a word as they saw that Stella was making an approving nod of the head. With the tiniest of a smile on his face, Nelson kept his eyes down at his plate. It was wonderful to see him back with us once again.

Tuesday, July 8th

"Agnieszka, this is Kazimierz," said Ed in Polish, "and by the way, he is an idiot."

With that, Ed and this young girl stepped into the house. Without any further invitation, he started up my stairs and she quietly followed.

Conveniently for him, Henry had a handyman job somewhere else, so this salary negotiation was going to fall on me. Henry told me that we didn't have any money to pay anyone anything, but Ed already knew that.

Agnieszka is not much older than I was when I walked into OLC and needed a place to sleep. She is maybe 20 years old. The big difference between me and Agnieszka is that she is strikingly attractive, and this was the problem for OLC. Ed was assigned to find a starting suitable place for her that was safe.

Ed marched her up past Henry's apartment door and on to the third floor. I hadn't recently noticed Ed being so agile as he walked up the stairs. I couldn't catch up with him to stop him. When I reached the third floor apartment, which Henry and I used as a storage place, I wrote that we wouldn't be needing the third floor cleaned.

"Of course, it needs cleaning if she's going to live here. For now, we'll only need to clean out this room and the kitchen. Henry has until the fall to fix the heating. Does that stove over there still work?"

Ed walked her through the rest of the house like he was the landlord. Agnieszka opened every closet and cupboard and often made a disagreeable sigh. When we finally reached the front door to the house, we stopped as Ed spoke in Polish to both of us.

"Okay, this is the arrangement. Agnieszka will live upstairs. If the stove and heat are not working properly, Henry will need to get those fixed. I'll get some decent furniture up there. She will get her own key to that door.

123

"For the privilege of living in such accommodations with such wonderful views of South Brooklyn factory rooftops, she will clean yours and Henry's apartments once a week for four hours each apartment. No one goes in her apartment without her permission." Agnieszka looked at me, probably to see if I would object to that last statement. I didn't grunt any objection.

"He," pointing at me, "will teach you how to write in English and you," now pointing at her, "will cook him dinner now and then. You," looking back at me, "will buy the food."

He had already informed her that I couldn't speak but told her the reason was that God took my tongue away for cursing too often. He clearly enjoyed telling her that more than once.

"If we are all agreed to these terms, the two of you can shake hands on it."

I thought this a more than acceptable arrangement and extended my hand. She didn't accept my hand.

"Nie," she said. Ed looked as surprised as I. In Polish, she explained that while she was agreeable with the terms, she first needed to meet this "Henz." Ed accepted this condition. I was guessing that something must have occurred in other homes for her to start to think for herself and not trust people who seem to be her friends.

"Well, okay, then we'll come back after five for Agnieszka to meet Henz, or should I say Agnes to meet Henry."

"Agnieszka, not Agnes, if you please," said Agnieszka in Polish. Ed nodded agreement and turned back to me.

"Agnieszka and I will be back this evening to meet Henz. Now on to Otto's to negotiate a real paying job."

At Otto's, they were equally successful in negotiating a deal to not only clean Otto's house once a week but also work for him at the Eagle five days a week. She and Ed returned to our house at five to meet Henry. Any reluctance from Henry on the arrangements quickly disappeared whenever Ed wondered out loud whether Stella should be consulted on the fairness of the deal for all parties. Apparently, Ed had used the same leverage with Otto. As they left, I heard Agnieszka ask in Polish, "Who is this Stella?"

Agnieszka cooked a stuffed cabbage dish tonight. I hadn't had Golumpki since Marysia got ill. Later, Ed got Agnieszka on the phone with Stella and those two spoke in Polish for over an hour. I heard her laughing repeatedly at whatever Stella was telling her. At least, the two of them liked each other. As I said, Stella is not everyone's cup of tea and often does not hit it off with newcomers. A newcomer would know quickly how Stella felt about them.

I walked with Ed and Agnieszka back down to the OLC convent where she would stay one more night. She would bring her belongs to the house in the morning. I joined Ed in his cottage for a few drinks, then I got myself home.

By the end of this evening, Agnieszka had work, a place to sleep, and a bit of a social support system outside of OLC. The only question that remained was whether she actually knew how to clean.

Wednesday, July 9th

With a single suitcase, Agnieszka arrived this morning at eight. Stella drove over before nine with some pots and dishes, and the two of them stayed up on the third floor for the rest of the day. Even though they were two floors above me, I could hear them kibitzing in Polish like old friends. It reminded me of days long gone for Marysia and Louise.

Ed had arrived by noon along with two boys from the church, who carried up a bed, a kitchen table, and a few chairs.

My big news of the day was that in today's mail was this letter from William.

Dear Grandpa,

I hope everyone is fine there. I first need to ask you if you have heard from Nelson recently. If not, please check on him. I was reading about some rioting in Greenwich Village a week ago. If you somehow can, please check to see if he is okay. Also apologize to him because I left New York so quickly that I had forgotten that I was to see him that weekend. I sent him a letter but never heard back. Right now, I am camping with Balzie on a farm in northern Quebec.

Billy Warren

When we crossed the border, we did not request political asylum. We wanted to go deeper into the country than Montréal to see for ourselves what the Canadian people thought of American war refugees. They viewed Balzie and me more as tourists than immigrants, so people shared their feelings quite readily. Balzie speaks a bit of French, so we have some limited ability to converse in this province.

First, I want to apologize to you, Grandpa, for never asking about your first years as an immigrant in America. This trip has broadened my respect for what you and Grandma must have endured being in a new land with a different language. It would not be easy for immigrants here in Canada and I am sure it must have been even harder for you and Grandma.

I no longer feel Canada is where I should be right now. We learned that the big city anti-draft groups were constantly under surveillance by the RCMP, which is their police. The RCMP are always looking for reasons to deport what they call USA draft dodgers.

And freedom of speech is also defined differently here. It only goes so far before the government may step in to quell whatever they label as hate speech because it is a radically different point of view from the average citizen. From my years at Berkeley, I took for granted all my rights for complete freedom of speech. I don't want to give that up.

I must say that Balzie and I are being treated courteously, but again, I believe it is because we are viewed as tourists only. I am not sure I can endure being treated as a second-class citizen day after day, year after year in this country. I realize that America treats minorities as second-class citizens even though many of them have American roots older than mine. I want to be hopeful that in my lifetime this will all go away in America. I want to be part of that change, so I have decided to return. Balzie is still not sure and wants to stay a bit longer.

We are running out of money, so we started taking odd jobs to make some cash. We found a farmer willing to pay us to paint a barn. What he is paying us is a pittance, but he knows we are desperate. This is how I will be abused here. Very subtlety but I would be a third-class person here who can be taken advantage of, without the protection of the government. I decided I want to come home and effect change in my own country. I won't be able to change much here as an outsider.

We have a lead for a month-long fishing boat job in Nova Scotia. Balzie thinks this will be another adventure. I expect to be back home in August. Tell Father Ed that I want to talk to him about a C.O.

application when I do get back. No need to fill Mom in on me as I have been writing to her.

I love you and hope you are well. When we cross the border, I will call Dad to see if Balzie and I are welcome back there. It is okay to share the letter with Dad if you want to.

Your loving Grandson,
William

I shared the letter with Henry when he got home. He read it very slowly and seemed to be absorbing every sentence, then he returned it to me and left without any discussion. Ed came by later and I shared it with him. Later in the Eagle, both Anthony and Nelson asked to read it. Apparently, Henry was talking about it at the Eagle. It is good to know that William is on his mind.

As Stella was leaving the apartment late afternoon, she handed a note to Henry. It was a list of all the things that he needed to fix before the weekend and she signed it, "With love for now unless you don't do what I tell you, Stella."

Both Stella and Agnieszka then got into Stella's car to have dinner at Stella's. I happened to be sitting at my vanity looking out the window tonight when I noticed that it was Agnieszka who drove the car back. The girl knew how to drive a car, that's got me beat. They were double parked in the middle of a stickball game, so Stella hurried around the car, gave Agnieszka a big hug and kiss on the cheek, then drove off. When Agnieszka came up the stoop steps, the smile on the girl's face warmed my heart. Any melancholy that I might have felt, dissolved with that smile. The day made me happy because I saw happiness in others. Ed always told me happiness brings more happiness. I feel I am once again surrounded by angels who are looking over me.

Thursday, July 10th

My Dearest Marysia,

Today is our Anniversary. This day will be ours forever. I hope our lives together brought you enough happiness. You deserved the world, which I could not provide, but did I bring you enough happiness? I worry I didn't bring enough.

You gave me comfort through my depressions, encouragement to be my best, family to raise, laughter, passion, and always love and hope.

Happy Anniversary, my dearest. I hope my love brought you enough happiness to keep your heart warm for eternity. Your love to me will keep me happy forever.

Love,
Kazimierz

Wednesday, July 16th

Sancho is with me constantly these days and I now let him sleep in my bed. He does need help getting up and down. Lifting him is the least I can do. These days, it is more a comfort for me to feel him there. This is good for both of us.

These days, I read every day. It distracts me from my worries. Here's what I read in the news today.

Apollo 11 will blast off this morning. This is good.

The weather prediction for New York City is to be sunny and breezy. This, too, is good.

How about this? I can buy a Ford Maverick for $1995. I guess that that's good for a car. I don't know as I've never owned one. Probably best, as I don't know how to drive.

In sports, I still have hope that the Mets can win 82 games this year. Being in first place is too tall an expectation from a team who finished in 9th place last year. Right now, they have won 50. The paper said that the Met's star pitcher, Tom Seaver, has been doing so well that he was selected to pitch in the All-Star Game. This is even better.

When the Mets return to town, I think that I'll take Ed and Agnieszka to a game. I haven't been to a game since I took Marysia to a Dodger game at Ebbets Field. The bums lost that day. These Mets will probably do the same, but now I feel there is honor in the fighting a good fight.

Thursday, July 17th

et's have a holiday! was Nixon's quote in the papers. He wants to take credit for the moon launch even though he's only been president six months.

Articles in the papers compared the astronauts with the Mets. They said they were both doing something impossible and giving the downtrodden something to root for. Win or lose, the Mets are putting up the good fight against all odds.

Friday, July 18th

ussians have an unmanned rocket, LUNA, also going to the moon right now. No one seems to know what they are up to. Some say it might be missile. There is worry that this could start a space war. Apollo 11 is only halfway to the moon with a Russian rocket chasing them. Hard to think about anything else right now, even the Mets.

Saturday, July 19th

UNA will not crash into Apollo 11 was the assurance the Russian Space authority made yesterday. Whether we believe them or not, what are we going to do about it? Both spaceships are flying to their destinies.

Sunday, July 20th

agle will land on the moon tonight. Right now, nothing else matters.

129

Monday July 21ˢᵗ

Agnieszka, Henry, and I huddled around the TV last night. It must have been about 3 a.m. before we watched the first man step onto the moon. All that Henry could say through it all was, "Holy Shit," but he said it with such joyful wonderment that Agnieszka wanted to share in the joy. As she cleaned my apartment this morning, she practiced her *Holy Shits.* This afternoon at the Eagle, a customer was watching the moon landing replay on the TV. Agnieszka walked over to him, nudged him with her elbow, and gave him a Holy Shit.

Tonight, Ed walked into the Eagle. Agnieszka greeted him with a Holy Shit, as she pointed to the TV newscast. He first looked over to me, but quickly knew I was innocent of this maleducation. Then he looked over to both my sons who were sitting together at the bar. Henry immediately turned and started to rant and rave over next year's planned subway token rate increase to 30 cents. Otto locked in on his brother's face, preferring to scrutinize every word coming out of Henry's mouth, rather than look over to Ed.

When each new person walked into the Eagle, Agnieszka joyously welcomed them with a Holy Shit. Ed had finally had enough. "You boys will need to fix this and start teaching her some decent English. I'm bringing her to see Monsignor and Mother Superior next week." He then pulled Agnieszka over to a booth to have a discussion in Polish.

Holy Shit! It was a wonderful day to be alive.

Tuesday, July 22ⁿᵈ

We're *100 to 1 shot - like landing on Mars* was Yogi's comment on Mets winning a pennant. 100 to 1 is not impossible. I'll be satisfied with 82 wins.

On a side note, the Soviet LUNA ended with a crash. Thank God. No war starting in space tonight.

Fathers and Sons and Other Village Idiots

Friday, July 25th

My Black Madonna sent me an angel and she is living on the third floor. Agnieszka has quickly become family around here. Everyone from Anthony to Henry to Stella just love her to death. I hope that she is still around when William returns from Canada. I'd like her to meet a more educated member of the family. My hippie grandson is still the most cultured.

Depending on the situation, one can be entertained, befriended, or comforted by Agnieszka. The girl is a rare person who can make everyone she talks to feel important. She seemed to be experiencing a resurrection of her own spirit. She is blossoming before us. She, like me, left some past history back in Poland that she doesn't want to talk about. Our secrets from the world.

Anthony has become smitten, and I've heard both Ed and Otto commenting on this. We're all watching him carefully. For Stella, I think she found a daughter/girlfriend.

Tomorrow is Agnieszka and Ed's day off from their duties. We agreed to go to an afternoon Met game.

Saturday, July 26th

Holy Shit! Let's Go Mets! What a day!

We left 23rd Street about 1:30 today to go to a four o'clock game at Shea Stadium in Queens. We needed to get there early enough to buy general admission tickets before they sold out. These boys were the hot tickets in town.

As we descended down the 25th Street subway stairs, I discovered that this was going to be Agnieszka's first subway ride. Ed purchased the tokens from the booth and handed two each to both of us. Then he demonstrated how to walk through the turnstile. I went next followed much more slowly by Agnieszka. When the wooden turnstile arm spun through behind her, it smacked her little dupcha through with a jolt. As we all walked down the platform to a wooden bench, Ed and I continued to laugh. Agnieszka didn't look happy at all.

131

While we all quietly settled in on our bench, I heard the squeals of an approaching train. Instinctively, I did what all New Yorkers do with that sound; I got up to look down the tunnel, as if it encouraged the train to get there faster. A stupid habit, but all New Yorkers do it. The edge of the platform is where accidents happen. Nevertheless, I even leaned over the edge to further encourage the train along.

The air on the platform started pushing pass us even before the train came out of the tunnel. The breeze felt good as the train finally stopped before us. The graffiti-covered car door slammed open, and we stepped in. I noticed Agnieszka slyly looking around at the filth on the seats and floor and made a disagreeable sniff. Traveling with a newcomer gets you to notice much about the day-to-day shit we walk through.

We switched trains at Pacific Street from that local to the express. At Times Square Station, we traversed what must have seemed to her like an endless maze of passageways to the Queens #7 line. Because it was a Saturday, trains were on a weekend schedule, so we had to wait about ten minutes for the next train. While waiting, Ed stood near the edge of the platform staring down at the tracks.

"Well, would you look at that?" Agnieszka and I got up off her bench to see what he was looking at. There, between the tracks, was a two-foot-wide brick gutter with a trickle of water still running along it. Here and there was a grated drain. What attracted Ed's interest was a family of little mice that had come up from a drain and were looking for candy bar wrappers that had been blown onto the tracks. When the train roared in over them, Agnieszka let out a little moan, but Ed assured her that they were still fine as probably even a person could lie safely in that gutter. We got onboard the #7, which carried us towards Flushing, Queens, the home of the New York Mets.

The train tracks went from being underground in Manhattan to being elevated in Queens. Once above ground, Agnieszka got to see Queens for the first time. Everything was of interest to her. As we approached our station, she pointed to the giant steel globe in the middle of a fountain. She might have recognized it from a magazine photo.

Ed spoke. "That is the Unisphere, and that park was where the 1964 World's Fair was held. It was a wonderful event that last two summers. Countries came to showcase what made their country special.

"Was Poland there?"

"Sadly, no. They initially said they would come but later pulled out. Their official comment was that the Soviet building was going to be so magnificent that anything Poles could build would pale in comparison. They had no choice in the matter.

"My Vatican was there, and they brought with them Michelangelo's *Pieta*, the body of Christ in the arms of Our Lady." We all silently stared at the Unisphere.

It would be wonderful to be as curious about the world again as Agnieszka is about America. I wonder if, in 50 years, she will become as jaded as I have become recently.

At 4:05, Tom Seaver threw the first pitch, and 45,000 people erupted with cheers. We sat high up near the top of the stadium to have a wonderful view of the spectacle of a 20th century colosseum. The battle between the Cincinnati Reds and the New York Mets began. Today's game would become the best game I have ever seen in person. I pulled out my pencil and started to fill in the lineups on my scorecard.

In the second inning, the Reds hit a single followed by double to have runners on second and third. The next batter hit a long fly ball to left field. As Cleon Jones caught the ball, the runner on third tagged up. Jones threw the ball hundreds of feet toward the waiting catcher. Everyone in the stadium stood and watched as the ball soared in. It reached home plate before the runner, but the throw was slightly off target, up the first base line.

The runner saw the catcher moving away from the plate to catch the ball, so he dove out face first with both arms stretching forward towards home plate. When the catcher finally got the ball, he, too, dove face first with an outstretched glove. Two bodies were flying toward home plate. It was going to be close.

The catcher's glove tagged the runner on his left arm. Then their bodies collided into each other. The umpire strained to see where the ball was. If the catcher had dropped the ball, then the runner would be safe. He finally saw it and made the call. "Yer Out!"

As the crowd roared around us, Agnieszka yelled in nearly perfect Brooklynese, "Holy Shit!" Even Ed had to agree. It was an appropriate expression for the moment.

Agnieszka didn't understand the rules of baseball but understood enough to know that the object of the game was to reach home plate. For nearly four innings, the score remained 0-0. Seaver was looking like his terrific self.

The Mets got their first run in the bottom of the 4th, but the Reds came back in the top of the 5th to tie the game. In the bottom of the 5th, the Mets had a single and then a double by Seaver, followed by another single. The Mets were ahead 3-1, but the Reds scored again in the 6th and the score became 3-2.

The papers had been saying that Tom Seaver's arm had been hurting him for weeks, and he had in fact lost his last two games. No one was expecting for him to be pitching in the late inning, but Gil Hodges, the manager, kept him pitching and Seaver kept getting batters out.

During the last few innings, even from the upper deck, I could hear that Seaver's fastball just didn't have much pop in the catcher's glove. We all thought Hodges was making a big mistake leaving his star in, but the 9th inning started with Tom on the mound. All season long, Seaver was striking out the batters because of his fastball and today in the 9th, it just was gone. The scoreboard showed Mets ahead 3 -2, but we still needed three more outs.

The first Reds batter hit a hard ground ball single. Quickly, the tying run was at first base. The next batter also hit a hard line-drive to right field that everyone in the stadium knew would drop in for a hit. The runner on first wanted to get all the way to 3rd base on this hit and was running hard. Gaspar, the right fielder, was not a player known for his great fielding skill, so no one expected him to try to make the catch on the fly. If he missed it that runner would score. Despite the risk, Gaspar tried to catch the ball on the fly.

He was nearly falling forward as he lowered his glove to be an inch above the grass. His glove opened and the ball disappeared inside it as he stumbled forward. If he fell, the

Fathers and Sons and Other Village Idiots

runner probably could get back to first safely. One step, then another, then another. Gaspar struggled to stay on his feet and did. He reached into the glove and easily tossed in the ball to first before the runner could return. Double play.

It's wonderful to be in a stadium with thousands of fans screaming until they were crying. Something magical happened in Queens today. I become a true believer.

After seeing that play, Seaver, himself, summoned something more from his ragged arm and then struck out the last batter. The game was over. The Amazing Mets had done it. A 3-2 win. Better yet, their season record was now 55 wins and 40 loses.

Baseball is so damn great. It was also great to share the game with an old friend and a new one. What a day! As Agnieszka would say, "Holy Shit!"

Sunday, July 27th

A gnieszka and I were both so exhausted from the excitement of yesterday's outing that we just sat around the house and watched the Mets on my TV. In one afternoon, she was hooked on baseball. Two good days in a row for me. It has been a wonderful respite for my mind.

Wednesday, July 30th

O n the back page of the News was a color photo of planet earth with swirling white clouds over her. A world without borderlines.

Thursday, July 31st

S ince last weekend, the Mets have dropped to five games behind first place. Things can change so fast.

Inside the paper, the sports writers were speaking as if it were the beginning of the end. Even though the Mets have been given me a lot of hope, I must also remember underdogs do lose most of the time.

Monday, August 4th

The Melting Pot seemed unusually quiet when I first arrived. After two Puerto Rican men left the diner, I found out why.

Apparently, a Puerto Rican boy was stabbed a few nights ago in the playground by a white kid. Today, there were dozens of Puerto Ricans looking for anyone in that gang. Those little white gangsters seem to have disappeared.

Some at the table mentioned that they have seen people walking along the roof tops across from the playground. Sal said he's heard there were loads of bricks stacked on each roof. If the stabber was ever seen again, it was going to be raining bricks on him and his friends. Clans fighting to protect their clan. These types of wars never seem to end well, as the innocent will also get hurt. The daily news is killing me.

Thursday, August 14th

The Moon Men had a parade on Broadway today, so Ed and I took Agnieszka to it. She thought the crowds were exciting, but I got worn down quickly. I don't know if it just my old age, the heat, or is something else is starting to kick in. Swallowing is getting harder. Over the last two weeks, Little Prick's front office called here a few times. Luckily, I picked up the phone before Henry. Little Prick is hardly of any concern to me anymore.

The Mets were 9½ games behind first place. Worse yet, they only have 65 wins. They probably won't reach 82.

Saturday, August 16th

Agnieszka read about some rock festival in upstate New York. She tried to interpret the meaning of the captions from an adjoining photo. "What is a hippiefest?" she asked. I just shook my head. It was not worth the time to explain the paper's stupidity. I decided then that I needed to get her over to the library and not waste so much time on stupid headlines.

Sunday, August 17th

I read my newspaper in peace today. It was easier to read stupid headlines than to hear them read aloud. The crowd at Woodstock was now estimated at 400,000. The photos were fascinating. There was one thing that the *Daily News* did well, it was photographs.

Monday, August 18th

The *Age of Aquarius* was launched at Woodstock, proclaimed Georgios, as he served us all another round of coffee. A doctor onsite said it was unbelievable. A total absence of hostility and violence.

Tuesday, August 19th

Agnieszka and I had a disturbing encounter today. I had been encouraging her to pick up any book and try to read it. This morning, I found her crying while reading my journal.

I was too upset with her to find out what she had read. I grabbed the book and walked out of the house with it. I didn't see her for the rest of the day. From now on, I am hiding it.

Wednesday, August 20th

I didn't see Agnieszka all day. I now feel bad about how I reacted yesterday. I tried to talk to her several times here and at the Eagle, but she wouldn't.

In early evening, after my walk with Sancho, the house phone rang. Henry and I picked up our separate extensions at the same time, so I just listened in with my hand over the mouthpiece.

"Hello," Henry answered.

"Hi, Dad, it's William."

"Willie. How you doing?" Henry's tired voice didn't really reveal much, but at least he didn't call the boy, Duke.

137

"Well, yeah, I'm fine. I am actually back in New York State and heading back down there."

A corresponding pause for Henry to think then, "Oh, good, I guess. What's your plan then?"

"Well, I guess I was calling to see if Balzie and I were welcome there."

"Well, of course. You left here. I didn't kick you out."

"Dad, actually you did. So, I am calling to find out if I am welcome there."

After a momentary pause, "Of course, you are. This is your home. You belong here if you want to come home. I'm not such an asshole."

"Okay. Good. I was just checking and not assuming anything. We'll probably get there on Friday. The turnpike up here seems to have cars parked all over it, so we started taking some backroads. See you soon Dad. I'm sorry about the way I left. I do love you. You know that don't you?"

"I do now, Willie."

"Well good. It's good you know. I'll see you soon."

"You bet. See you soon, and Willie, I love you too."

"Thanks Dad. That's good to know too. Bye for now."

"Bye."

With two clicks, the phone disconnected.

The call seemed good. They both have seemed to have grown up a bit in the last few months.

I wish that I could talk to my dad again. Maybe we could have worked things out after I'd grown up and knew more about what he was up against. At least some fathers and sons grow up in time. Some never get that second chance.

Thursday, August 21ˢᵗ

To speak with Agnieszka before she slipped away, I woke up earlier than my usual. It was about six o'clock when I walked up the stairs and first listened at her door. Since I heard some stirring inside, I gently knocked on the door. She opened it and stared at me.

"Przepraszam," she said quickly. She was saying sorry to me in Polish, but I knew that I was the one who was wrong

Fathers and Sons and Other Village Idiots

and sorry. As I shook my head, I reached my arms out to her, she reached out to me, and we hugged. She invited me in, and I sat at her kitchen table that looked out over the yard. She poured me a cup of coffee and offered me some fresh bread.

"No, I am sorry," I wrote in Polish. "I was very upset with myself that someone knew my thoughts. I was not ready to share with anyone. Even Father Ed or my sons don't know of these things."

She explained that she was sorry to have continued to read the journal once she knew it was a diary. She quickly promised to never repeat anything that she had read and promised to forget all. She said that she hadn't gotten too far into the year's events.

I wrote that I knew that forgetting was impossible, but I would appreciate it if she never told anyone anything. I underlined *no one*. She nodded her agreement.

We sat quietly at the table and looked out at the rising sun over the Greenwood Cemetery trees in the distance. Her coffee was good, and the bread was better. Just sitting with her was comforting for me. She would have let everything go from that point, but I needed to know something.

"How far did you read?" In order to not be misunderstood, I wrote in Polish, and she answered in Polish as well.

"I didn't read it all, but I read enough to know that you have a great many burdens on you. I knew you were a troubled man on some days, but I never knew how much or why."

'What do you know?"

"I know of your great love for your wife and your noble resolution to be with her. I know of your love for Louise too and I can understand that kind of love completely. I feel that kind of love between you and me.

"I know of your cancer in your body and also that neighborhood cancer who lives over there," as she gestured to Frankie's house.

"I think you are a good writer because your words made me cry and think. I also don't think that you are a selfish man.

"I know you hate the war, and you are very worried about your family being in another one." With that, we both heard a noise on the stairs. We both thought someone was there. She

139

opened the door to see that Sancho had followed me all the way up two flights of stairs.

"I know that you love your loyal Sancho," she said as she lifted him up and gave him a hug.

"I know that you are at war with God and that is when I cried."

I listened in silence until she stopped speaking, We sat at the table with Sancho in her lap. She then had more to say.

"I feel very lucky that I have found this home. My life back in Poland was not so happy or safe. The first house I found here in America was dangerous as well. I was lucky to escape and find Our Lady of Czestochowa and Father Ed. Thank you for taking me in. I am very happy here.

"I am also very happy because I also feel that I am needed here. There is a purpose for me here. I need purpose too and here I feel that I am not a burden. There is a great need for me, but there is a greater need for you, but you don't seem to know it. This makes me sad."

As we both got teary eyed again, I wrote I agreed with nearly everything she had said. Other than the great need for me, she was entirely right.

She looked at the clock on the wall. It was time that she got to the Eagle to start her daily cleaning routine. She knew that William returned tomorrow with Balzie and that my apartment also needed to be prepared. We parted at the foyer doorway with a big hug.

Friday, August 22nd

William and Balzie walked in about four. They were both unshaved, weather beaten and in truth, a little smelly. Canada might have made them into filthy hippies.

Without saying much, Henry walked up to William in the vestibule and gave him a long hug without words. This time it seemed he got an equal hug in response. Eventually, they released each other. Before he spoke, Henry turned slightly away to wipe his arm across his eyes.

"William, how are you? It is so good to see you." Not knowing everything that had been happening here, William seemed taken back to see this much genuine emotion from his dad. Balzie as well looked surprise.

Henry knew what had been in his thoughts, but even though I had listened in on the call earlier this week, I wasn't sure what to expect today. Bouncing down the stairs from Henry's apartment came Agnieszka to investigate what all the noise was about at the front door. Balzie looked at Agnieszka then looked at William. William looked at Agnieszka, then at me, then at his dad.

"Where's Linda?" he asked.

"Well, err, Linda moved out pretty much the same time you left, but I think that you have a wrong idea here. This is Agnieszka. She is our maid." Agnieszka of course could not understand much of what was being said and was still waiting to be introduced.

"Your maid?"

Henry was genuinely embarrassed by what he thought William and Balzie might be thinking.

"Not my maid. Our maid. And she lives on the third floor. She stays there for free for cleaning my apartment and Dad's. And no, she's not a maid around here. She is family." As he made that declaration, he put his arm around her shoulders.

"She also works for Uncle Otto. She cleans his house and also works at the Eagle. Anthony and Nelson are teaching her English. Dad's been teaching her writing in English."

"Nelson's back and living here too?"

"Not here anymore. He's now living with Anthony, but he lived here awhile."

William could get no words out. Balzie as well, was speechless, but he was smiling more than William, whose face showed how confused he still was. I'm sure he was wondering how so much could have happened in two months, in a place where rarely anything happened.

"Agnieszka," said Henry, "this is my syn, Wilek.

"William, this is Agnieszka. Father Ed and Aunt Stella set this all up, so don't even think of this girl in any way but as your sister or cousin.

"And that goes for you too, mister," gesturing at Balzie.

141

William spoke next. "And Anthony and Nelson are teaching her English? They must be enjoying that."

Balzie added, "Will she teach me Polish? I promise to not miss any classes."

"That's not appreciated, and I won't translate that, and you really better start thinking of her as your sister, or I might need to toss you out of here again. Uncle Otto has already spoken to Anthony about what he expects of him and you'll both do the same." We all considered this momentarily then all laughed. To this laughter, Agnieszka exclaimed, "Holy Shit." This started another burst of laughter and lead to a few hugs. Henry and William held on and didn't let go. After one hug went on unsuitably long, I needed to pull Balzie back from Agnieszka. I wish that Marysia could see all this. Maybe she can, but I also wish that Louise could be here too.

Since William was never taught Polish, it was up to his father to translate quickly to Agnieszka what was happening. The boys then brought their luggage into the house.

Henry and I filled William and Balzie in on the events of the summer. William sat in disbelief with every story.

Quite a day! Thank god that this time all the fireworks were joyous ones.

Saturday, August 23rd

I helped 26thcreate more space in Agnieszka's apartment for the furniture that Ed had found somewhere. Henry and I had so much junk up there, so I was picking through boxes to find items that should be saved or could be tossed. By the end of the day, she had a kitchen, living room and bedroom apartment. More space that she ever had before.

Two floors below, she and I could hear William and Balzie arguing about something. Suddenly the arguing stopped, and then the front door slammed. Agnieszka and I looked at each other, nodded, then rushed to the street window to look down. We could see Balzie walking down the street towards 4th Avenue. I went down alone to talk to William.

"He talked to his parents back in California last night," he said.

Fathers and Sons and Other Village Idiots

"They want him to come home to enlist before he is drafted. They intend to pull strings to get him a safe assignment. This is against everything he ever said was important."

"What about Canada?" I wrote.

"As I said in my last letter, I'd be second-class person up there and a refugee in the eyes of Canadians and their police. I need to deal with life here."

"As a C.O.?" I wrote. I knew he had been talking to Ed about applying for conscientious objector status.

"I will apply, but even if I am denied, I just won't carry a gun to possibly need to shoot someone. I'll go to jail before I do that. I'll stay here.

"I thought Balzie agreed with this, but now he is seriously thinking of enlisting and letting his father fix things." I thought of how Balzie railed about the rich sending the poor to do their dangerous bidding.

William spoke again. "He's selling out on what he said he believed." I sat in silence.

"He'll do what he wants, and I'll do what I want."

I wrote, "The difference is you'll be doing what you know is right. This is your upbringing. Always do what's right and you'll be fine."

"I'm not sure what Bazarov will do, but I am disappointed that he is even considering given up all the things he has said and spoke for. Maybe he never really meant it and Canada was just an adventurous notion for him. It was not really a serious plan for him. He probably always knew that when his plans and adventures fell apart, his rich family would bail him out." I could see William was very upset. In a heartbeat, he just lost all respect for his best friend.

"I need to get out of here. I think that I'll drop in on Nelson and see how he is doing." With that he left.

I heard a little knock on my open door and there stood a bewildered Agnieszka. As best I could, I wrote in Polish what was going on.

She spoke in Polish, "I will go to church tomorrow and pray to Our Lady for peace for your family." I pray tonight that her prayers will be answered.

143

Sunday, August 24th

William went up to Henry's apartment this morning. I heard no screaming, which so often happened in the past. Later, William said to me that he wanted to talk to Father Ed after Mass. When he returned from seeing Ed, he seemed in even better spirits.

He told me that Ed would help him with his C.O. application. Ed had told him of the times he served as a chaplain in the army. Ed said there were many ways to serve one's country without firing a gun. He said it was very possible for a person of conscience to serve God, their country, and themselves. He stressed to the boy that he had free will to make his choices and that he must never be afraid to assert it. With a plan, William seemed calmer.

Tonight, Balzie had still not returned to the house, but his car remained parked on the street.

Sancho was already on my bed. I think that I will join him, hopefully to sleep.

Monday, August 25th

Balzie came back to 23rd Street this morning to collect his car and belongs. Within minutes, William and he were saying goodbye on the stoop. From what I could gather with my eavesdropping, his father had paid for a hotel in Manhattan last night, on the condition he drive home and enlist. His dad would take care of the rest. There was not going to a deadly breach for Balzie to go through.

Balzie didn't want to linger at the door with William. Both boys seemed to be in shock of how their friendship had dissolved so quickly. Balzie said that he felt he had no other choice but to return home. No embrace for the years of friendship they shared, only a simple extension of a hand. After that, he drove away.

I thought to myself this must seem worse than a death of the friend. To me, it would have been the death of a friend's soul.

This evening, Ed joined us for a quiet family dinner, after which Ed left and we went off to our own rooms and thoughts. We all had to think about our futures.

Tuesday, August 26th

Yesterday in Vietnam, some weary GIs defied orders and refused to go out. Maybe some of them figured out that they can't have a war without soldiers. Soldiers have free will too.

Today was also the feast day for Our Lady of Czestochowa. It's kinda like her birthday. Happy Birthday Holy Mother.

Wednesday, August 27th

There oughta be a feast day for underdogs, and God should bless them with some luck.

The Mets swept another series. With only 35 games left in the season, they were only behind the Cubs by 3. When the hell did all that happen. More importantly to me, these boys had now won 73 and were nearly at my 82 win hope. Are they raising my hopes to only be crushed once again? I so want to believe in something.

In Vietnam, the Company A commander was relieved of duty, and his soldiers went out with a new commander. To me, their first commander was a brave man to stand up to power. Ed always says that God gave man a free will if man chooses to use it. A man can't be forced to do something wrong. Nevertheless, the commander couldn't save those poor kids. At least this once, someone fought back. Underdogs may usually lose but at least we can fight back against what is wrong. I must continue my fight.

While I read my newspaper in the kitchen, William was quietly washing some dishes with the radio beside him. With Balzie's desertion, I understand why William is needing some time to sort things out. I didn't know what the right thing was to say to him. We remained in our mutual silences until the radio announcer mentioned that today was the anniversary of the Battle of Long Island. The deejay added to not go out and start celebrating because the battle was a terrible defeat for America.

"That's not quite true," William muttered to himself as he continued to dry the dishes. As some rock and roll started playing. I wanted to encourage him to think about something other than Balzie or his future. I pushed my notepad in front of his face. "Explain what's not true!"

"The DJ's not quite right about that only being a defeat. It wasn't all that simple as a win or a loss. Life's not that simple so why should that day be summed up so neatly." He saw he had my attention, but only added a few more comments.

"We are always wrong to wrap up everything so tidily. Everyone always tries to put nice, neat little labels on everything, either you're a winner or loser with no in-between.

"It has been a few years since I studied the Revolutionary War, so I am not so up on all my exact facts, but it was never so simple. Real men made sacrifices that day even if we did lose that battle. We should still honor them."

After he placed the last dry dish on the shelf, he went to his room. He came back ten minutes later with his leather satchel from university.

"I've got to go out for a while. See you later." Before I could write down a response, the front door slammed closed and through the open window I saw him bounding off the stoop stairs. Before looking down the street for a car, he was already halfway across it. He was nearly in a run by the time he turned the corner up on 5th Avenue. I would not see him all afternoon.

After dinner, I sat with Agnieszka on the stoop, and we watched a stickball game until about seven. Then we made our way to the Eagle for a beer. I was in a booth writing when William walked in. At the bar, Henry and Agnieszka hadn't noticed him and continued their chatting in English. Otto had his back to the crowd and was racking some glasses. Rather than sit at the bar with them or with me at the booth, William pulled up a chair to the end of the Table where he stepped upon his chair to await recognition.

Fathers and Sons and Other Village Idiots

Lately, William has not been very popular with some local patrons in the Eagle due to his and Balzie's previous talks about socialism. He might stand there quite alone for some time. I waited and watched. Patrons continued to ignore him, and Otto hadn't yet noticed him.

William opened his satchel and pulled out his notebook. He was reviewing some notes when a long-time neighbor walked in and noticed him. "Duke, you're home again. It's great to see you, boy." I noticed that William didn't correct him on his name. William simply reached down to shake the man's hand but continued to stand on the chair.

"Otto! You have a speaker. Aren't you going to recognize him?"

Otto turned to see William. He looked over to Henry who also had just taken notice. Anthony stopped his cleaning behind the bar and also waited for his father's response. The crowd wasn't terribly large but there was a ballgame on soon. He finally spoke.

"What say you, young man? What do you wish to discuss with our group?

"I wish to discuss a momentous event that happened on our street that effected every person in his room." Otto frowned.

"I'm afraid I am unaware of any anything of importance happening lately. When did this event happen, sir?"

"Nearly 200 years ago. Perhaps I am misleading in saying it happened on our street. To stand corrected, this event happened on this very slope of rock in 1776 long before there were houses or roads here. American soldiers died on this spot on this date, and they are not being properly honored today."

Otto briefly considered whether to entertain this request, then said, "Who here desires to hear this issue?"

I raised my hand. Many at the bar preferred to watch the ballgame, so there was no help there. The newly arrived neighbor raised his. Anthony raised his. We were at three when the front door opened and in walked Ed. He immediately walked up to William who still stood on the chair in silence. He looked up at him and then around the room at the three raised hands.

147

"I don't know what this boy wants to discuss tonight, but I want to hear it," and Ed raised his hand. When I looked back to Henry, his hand was being raised as well. William also noticed. I saw Otto looking over to Anthony with his raised hand. Otto didn't seem to be frowning, Some family unity for a change. Agnieszka was just returning from the ladies' room and saw all the raised hands. Despite not knowing what was happening, she raised her hand as well along with a loud, "Holy Shit." Which once again broke any tension. Ed and I were now confident that Agnieszka knew exactly what reaction she was looking for whenever she said it. Knowing this, Ed had already told me that he was feeling more at ease with bringing her to dine with the Pastor and Mother Superior soon. Agnieszka winked at me as she took a seat at my booth.

The quorum had been reached, the TV sound was silenced, and the Table cleared. Otto gestured upward with his head to me to go into the loft to turn on the tape recorder. Upon my return, I noticed several patrons had left. Otto nodded for William to proceed.

"Thank you," said William. While he gathered his thoughts, Anthony brought him a beer. After a swallow, my grandson cleared his throat then commenced.

"Today is the 193rd anniversary of the Battle of Long Island."

A man at the bar immediately interrupted. "We lost that battle, so what's to celebrate and don't you mean the Battle of Brooklyn?"

"There is great reason why you should want to celebrate this day in history because you are a free man today because of what happened here those many years ago. You are absolutely right on the other counts, so allow me to explain." William put down his notepad and began to move around the table.

"The Battle of Brooklyn is a far better name for it because it was fought right here in Brooklyn. In fact, right here on this ground before upper New York harbor. The battle was in fact fought all over this neighborhood from Sunset Park to Grand Army Plaza and through the Gowanus swamps.

"Back then there were no streets or neighborhoods, only forests, marshy fields, and this stony hill. Those forests back

Fathers and Sons and Other Village Idiots

then were so thick that there were very limited paths for conventional armies to march through. The Americans created their high ground on this slope to block their advance. It was a terrible battle with a great loss of American lives.

"And yes, my friend you are also right that we could not hold this high ground, and many people in history only sum it up as a defeat." William paused and everyone waited for more.

"But it is not that straightforward. Many brave patriots died here, and we should honor them for the sacrifice of their lives." Otto shut off the TV as William continued. Those who could not hear so well, moved to the long table. Henry joined them at the table as William circled it.

"Just weeks earlier, on July 4, 1776, America signed our Declaration of Independence, but both sides had been anticipating this battle here in New York City for many months and both sides had been getting ready. Washington knew that New York was indefensible because it was an island and America had no navy. Nevertheless, the Congressional Congress ordered Washington to defend it.

"The British were accustomed to putting down rebellions quickly and their strategy was always to hit the opposition hard and terribly, then demand unconditional surrender. By July 4th, there were only a few British ships in New York harbor, but British troops were already encamped on Staten Island and training for an assault. Washington knew British tactics and why they were waiting. The questions that remained were where and when would they march against the colonial forces.

"On July 12, 1776, the British sent two warships up the river and unleashed a bombardment of Manhattan. British officers wrote it was a horrific bombing and one they expected would force immediate surrender. On the 13th, under the white flag of truce, they sent minor officers to offer a pardon to all for complete surrender. Washington replied, "Those who have committed no fault want no pardon. We are only defending what we deem our indisputable rights." The British officers were dumbfounded at what they thought would be Washington's and his army's death sentences.

"Washington was under orders to defend New York. He had no choice but to defend. General Howe, under orders

149

from his King, had no choice but to attack. England had both the largest professional army and navy the world had ever seen. From Manhattan, Washington watched as the rest of the British forces began to arrive.

"By July 25th, there were five ships. Another twenty by the 29th. The temperature soared into the 90s and each day more ships and troops arrived. On August 1, 1776, forty-five more ships were sighted off of Sandy Hook, New Jersey. The professional soldiers and mercenaries of the British drilled on Staten Island to get accustomed to terrain and humidity. British spies were mapping out the terrains of Brooklyn. On August 4th, another 21 ships were counted on the horizon. By August 20, 1776, there were over 400 British ships in the harbor and 75 of them were full modern warships of the day. This amounted to 30,000 troops and another 10,000 sailors, all career professionals trained to fight.

"The American numbers were much harder to count with any accuracy. Most were farmers, who had never been away from home, unaccustomed to following orders, and had never fired a rifle at another human being. At best, they were loyal to their state but had little loyalty yet to our union. In truth, they often thought of troops from other states as foreigners who often spoke a different language from them. Washington's first challenge was to unite them into Americans.

"On August 21st, an American spy reported that the British troops would cross at the Narrows, just below where the Verrazano Bridge is today. Washington moved his troops to Brooklyn and took up the high ground on this stony moraine, the very land we all call home today. Washington himself would come over to stand here alongside his troops.

"On the 22nd, 15,000 British troops and forty pieces of artillery crossed from Staten Island at the Narrows and landed near Gravesend without any opposition. We were probably outnumbered two to one.

"For the next five days, their General Grant and about 5,000 troops moved north against about 1,600 Colonials, but General Howe was a skilled war tactician. British scouts had been surveying out the terrain and perhaps knew it better than the colonials from the other States. Howe sent another 10,000 troops around to Flatbush to attack from the side. More importantly, his troops came around from Jamaica Pass to begin a flanking attack on the American troops. Our troops were being hit from three sides now. The colonials had to break ranks and pull back through the marshes of Gowanus.

"Washington watched as brave Marylanders launched continual counter attacks to slow the British down. They never had much chance. The British were slaughtering anything that moved, but Marylanders continued to fight.

"We here should drink to them." William raised his glass and waited.

No one in the room said a word, but all raised their mugs, clinked a nearby glass, then took a big swallow.

"By the end of August 29th in the midst of a raging storm, the entire, yes, the entire Continental Army and its leader were trapped in Brooklyn Heights with their backs against the swift tidal currents of East River. The British were about to win the war as they had designed, a single battle to end the rebellion with an irresistible show of force. But something happened.

"Some called it "divine intervention," while a historian in the next century would describe it as "miraculous good luck." Really, what's the difference between intervention and luck? Probably just depends on which pew you sit in. Regardless of what you believe, America finally caught a break. In fact, several.

"On that last day of the battle, the fighting was over by late afternoon, but General Howe chose not to finish the war that day. Against the advice of some of his officers, he decided to wait until morning to demand surrender from Washington or face obliteration.

"It had been raining so hard that last day that most soldiers on both sides withdrew into their tents to keep their powder dry and await the final assault. As the rains continued, the humidity climbed to the point that, as night fell, fog settled in heavily over Brooklyn Heights. Washington knew he needed to retreat across the East River.

"Normally in the summer in New York, the prevailing winds came from the southwest. This would have allowed the British ships to sail up the river to seal Washington's fate, but, on this day, the winds came out of the northeast. Ships could not cut off Washington's escape. As luck would also have it, the tide was running hard against the British.

"By the time Washington ordered for an evacuation, the colonials, frontier men accustomed to improvising solutions, had already gathered as many boats as they could. As the fog settled in deeper, all the British could see was the glow of the American campfires. Washington ordered for the campfires to be kept going all night by some troops while others were ordered to silently evacuate by boat. Bad luck struck when a British loyalist found out about the evacuation and sent a slave to warn Howe. Good luck prevailed once again. The slave, who only spoke English, got across the lines, but into a Hessian troop site where no one spoke English. They detained the slave through the night but took no other action.

"The fisherman from Massachusetts navigated the swift currents of the East River and shuttled all the troops across with the legend being that Washington was the last man on the last boat to leave in the early morning. Whether he was the last or one of the last, he risked his life staying so long. Let us drink to George Washington and to our brave Massachusetts' countrymen."

This time there was a robust cheer, downing of beer, and the slamming of empty mugs on the wooden table. As William continued, Otto and Anthony went around the room with pitchers of beer to refill all glasses. I saw Henry pass a ten-dollar bill to Otto with a gesture that he was buying these refills.

"As the fog lifted on the morning of the 30th, the British troops were stunned to find no forces left in Brooklyn Heights.

"Was this battle simply a defeat because America lost control of New York?

"If the battle had ended the evening before, America would have lost its entire army. But it didn't.

"Unified American troops, no longer isolated colonists, held the high ground right here on our very slope of dirt for as long as they could. The brave Marylanders attacked repeatedly from Gowanus as long as there were Marylanders left. The skill of Massachusetts sailors saved our army as well. As united colonies, we thwarted the British superpower. In this battle we became a union of states to be reckoned with. The war didn't end that day. The Continental Army was able to escape to Manhattan, then up the island to eventually cross the Hudson. The British intended to end the American Revolution in the Battle of Brooklyn, but they failed. Instead, the battle marked the start of a great war that has changed the world and every person living in it since.

"All those who died in the battle on this slope are all heroes and should never be remembered as the defeated. Because America would not surrender, the British didn't win the Battle of Brooklyn. Those American underdogs went on to prevail against the greatest superpower on earth.

"The men who died on this land followed what their hearts said they needed to do for the sake of freedom and not for themselves. They resisted tyranny of a king to create a democracy.

"Before I go tonight, let's drink one more time to all our soldiers who choose to fight to resist tyranny. They fought for what their hearts told them was right. Let us honor them."

Everyone raised a glass on his appeal, followed by the stomping of feet on the floor and slapping of hands on the table or bar. We all drank many more rounds, then quickly the night was over. It was time to go home. No one noticed that Nelson had slipped in during William's oration and was sitting in my booth. Otto and Nelson locked gazes but made no move towards the other. Some fathers and sons never cross the gulf between them.

A customer tossed some bills on the counter to settle up, and Otto returned to the running of his bar. His action sent a bitter message across to his son. I got up in a bit of disgust, but I resolved that this was not the time or place to deal with this family tragedy. Tonight was William's great night.

William finished his last beer in a gulp, gathered his notepad and satchel, then came over to me.

"You ready to go home for the night, Grandpa?" I nodded just as Henry came over. "Well done, William. I'm proud of you."

"Thanks Dad, you ready to go home too?" And with that we all stood up to go when I turned to Ed and wrote a note. "Care to come over for a nightcap, it's only nine."

Ed was lost in thought as I shoved my notepad in his face.

"No, I need to see a soul about another problem."

"Right now? Can't it wait until morning?"

"I wish it could, but it can't." With that, Ed did what everyone does to me, when they don't want to talk about something. They turn away and stop reading my notes. Ed hastily left the Eagle using the 5th Avenue door. If he was going home, he would have left in the 23rd Street side entrance with the rest of us. He really was heading somewhere else, and he appeared in a great rush to get there.

When I came home tonight, I immediately started transcribing tonight's events. Once again, I brought home Otto's tape recorder to help transcribe everything that was said. William joined Henry on the second floor, and I heard quiet conversation from them for some time. About 30 minutes after I started writing, I went to the kitchen to grab a snack. As I walked into the room, I looked out the window. In the rear of the yard stood Agnieszka alone. I also heard angry muffled voices coming from somewhere.

I moved as best I could down the cellar stairs, through the cellar, and up into the yard. Unfortunately, by the time I stepped into the yard, she was coming back in. I gestured a "what's going on" to her, but her only reply was a whispered, "It's nothing, I thought I heard something." She then walked past me and went straight to her apartment. Above, I heard William and Henry still talking but unaware of our stirring in the yard below. Theirs weren't the voices I had heard from my window.

I feel so powerless, when even good people like Ed and Agnieszka dismiss me so easily, and I cannot yell for attention. A quote of Ivan's came to my mind.

The sound of one's own voice has a powerful effect on any man.

I'm a man without a voice and feel powerless.

Fathers and Sons and Other Village Idiots

Wednesday, September 3rd

Nelson decided that despite the forecast for heavy rains, he needed to go over to Greenwich Village to retrieve some things he had left there. He called William to ask if he wanted to go. William in turn asked me if I was interested too. I said sure.

We first went over to a lower east side post office to pick up mail from his PO box, then over to his loft apartment on Houston Street. No one was inside at the time, but Nelson still had a key with him. At first, I thought to myself that none of this stuff needed to be locked up. We dumped the few belongings and clothing into three cardboard boxes that we had brought with us. As we left, he left the key, a note, and some cash on the table for whomever had shared this poverty with.

Before we returned home, he wanted to go over to the Stonewall Inn. Every few blocks, he briefly bumped into someone he knew, but the heavy rains kept most people moving along too fast. Some were glad to see that Nelson was okay. He promised most that he would continue to come over to see them but that for now he lived back home in Brooklyn. One said, "Hey man, be thankful for that." Nelson only smiled back. We walked a few blocks and reached the Stonewall Inn, the place of the riots.

The street's filth had quickly concealed any evidence that a riot happened there a few months ago. To put it another way, it was hard to figure out what was already broken before the riot. The street was a slum. Somebody's neighborhood or village, but a slum, nonetheless. We walked in front of the Stonewall Inn and in the window was a sign that read, "We homosexuals plead with our people to please help maintain peaceful and quiet conduct on the streets of the Village - Mattachine."

I wrote, "Who is Mattachine?"

Nelson looked to me then William, but even William's blank stare showed that he, too, didn't know. These two cousins had been living during the same times yet have had very different life experiences.

155

"Well, Grandpa and Will, Mattachine is not a person. I guess you can call it a gay society or gay rights organization.

"A story I heard was that in medieval times, there were these secret societies in France of oppressed unmarried townsmen. These men performed dances of defiance, and you could say rituals, at the Vernal Equinox. Many were peasants protesting against their oppression. To protect their identities, they wore masks during the performances.

"In the 1950s, a local gay rights organization took the name because gay men still needed to remain hidden. We really haven't come very far in the last 20 years. Many around here think that Mattachine has become too cautious and not willing to be more confrontive for gay rights. I think their sign shows they don't support the people who rioted that night. It's like we were the ones doing something wrong." As we continued to walk towards the subway, Nelson withdrew into his own thoughts. He didn't converse much on the way home.

As I write all this down tonight, I realize that while 23rd Street remains my village, it isn't for these two young men. I think William and Nelson are still seeking their village to call home.

Friday, September 5th

O ver six inches of rain in two days. I just wish it would stop. So does Sancho. I think it's going to be a long, quiet weekend for us.

Monday, September 8th

H ow about those Mets," said Sal as I sat down at the Melting Pot table. With my family diversions of late, I hadn't been following the team.

"They're only 2½ games back and this is the closest to first place they've been since the first week of April."

I hadn't picked up my newspapers lately. Frankie was probably holding a bunch of them. Maybe tomorrow I'll go get them.

Tuesday, September 9th

I did pick up all my papers today. Frankie said nothing, so I quickly got away from him.

The Mets are now only 1½ games back of 1st place and have 81 wins.

This is such a stupid and trivial thing to be thinking about, but it seems like the only thing I can now focus on. It's like I can't do anything else until they get 82. It's not my life, yet somehow it is.

Wednesday, September 10th

The Mets won and only trail by a half a game. This win was number 82. Whatever else happens for them, the rest of this season is all gravy on the potatoes for me. Their winning had become a little obsession in my mind. Each win gave me a little spark of electricity through my brain.

Thursday, September 11th

Hell has frozen over and the Mets are in 1st place.

Sunday, September 14th

Ten in a row! When I read this in the paper, I stood up and wanted to hug someone, but no one was here. Everyone was out and about, getting on with their lives.

Sunday, September 21st

A week ago, it was like someone flipped on a switch and I was happy.

Then, the switch was turned off, and my brain is once again in darkness. I should be happy, but I'm not. There's so much good going with the Mets. Even my grandsons are all here now and alive. Time is running out. Even daylight itself is deserting me with each shorter day.

Last night, for the first time in years, I knelt by my bedside and tried to pray but heard nothing back. Maybe, I am not only physically speechless. Perhaps, I am now spiritually mute as well. Neither Ed nor Ivan have offered me any inspiration lately. Even my Black Madonna and Lady Liberty remain silent before me. Only Sancho is near, but his strength seems to be waning faster than mine.

Monday, September 22nd

Autumn started today, and I am alone once again. I need to do something soon because it's gonna take a miracle to turn things around before I die. I think it needs to be something irrational since rationality isn't working. I can't count on God or my Ladies anymore. This is all on me. Egotistical? Yes, but ego is all I've got left.

Agnieszka got me to agree to see Little Prick tomorrow. Maybe if I don't show up, he'll stop calling here.

Anyway, it's autumn. I must do my duty to Marysia and write, even if my thoughts are not happy.

decay in fall
leaves and dreams die so goes hope
redeemer deaf

Tuesday, September 23rd

My closing time is drawing near. I finally got someone to give me advice and I didn't like it. It was from Ivan.

A person who gets angry at his own illness is sure to overcome it.

Ivan, sometimes you are just so full of shit. Maybe all writers are full of shit who are just entertaining their egos.

I didn't go to my appointment with Little Prick. Instead, I took the subway to the St. John's cemetery in Queens to visit Marysia. It might be the last time I ever go there. If I don't achieve redemption, it won't be right for me to be buried there.

At her gravestone, we talked all afternoon. We agreed that there was no point to further surgery or treatment. I can't waste any more time doing treatments for Little Prick. Treatments are his idea of the right thing to do, not mine. With this agreement with Marysia, I returned to 23rd Street.

As I walked up the street, I noticed again the long length of my shadow running away from me again. My days are getting, oh, so short. I turned back to look down to the harbor and to take in the sun setting behind Lady Liberty. She still looks so beautiful in her silhouette.

When I reached the house, I sat down on the stoop to watch my neighbors coming home from work. Women in their dresses. Some men in suits and others in their overalls. All in jackets now that summer has closed, and autumn's chills were sweeping in. Temperatures tonight will be near freezing. Some neighbors waved to me, but no one paused to chat today. Too tired and too hungry to waste time with me. I sat there for an hour as darkness rolled in.

I was still not hungry, so I went back down to visit my Black Madonna. I sat with her in silence for quite some time. She too had nothing to say. Suddenly, there was someone by my side. The caretaker came to tell me it was closing time.

"Closing time this early?" I wrote.

"Yes," he answered. "We've been having more robberies lately, so I need to lock up." Closing time for a church.

I walked back up to 4th avenue and paused in front of the butcher shop. One housewife was completing her selections while a shop boy swept up the saw dust from the floor. As the customer left, the boy followed her to the door to flip the sign on the window to CLOSED.

I grabbed a meal at the Melting Pot and stayed till it closed, then went over to the Eagle, but not much was happening there either. I stayed anyway.

At about one, Otto had had enough of his day, so he called out last call. The few remaining paid their tabs and left. I walked out with Otto. He hugged me and went on his way across 5th Avenue to his house near 6th. Halfway down the street, I stepped out to the middle to get a clearer view of Lady Liberty. She was still there with her crown and torch lights glowing. She has aged. Her patina has grown. I know the number of days to my final closing time are very few.

Wednesday, October 1st

Silly baseball hope was all the Melting Pot could offer me today. No one greeted me because Sal was speaking.

"Well, my friends, a few years ago Casey asked whether any of the Mets knew how to play baseball.

"That team has just won the National League East division title." A guy at the counter overheard him and shouted over. "The mayor just proclaimed next week would be *Mets Week*."

I let them all enjoy their fun. I am content that, for once, the Mets have won more than they lost. Surprisingly, this accomplishment hasn't cheered me up as much as I had hoped it would. Achieving a silly goal reveals it for what it is. Frivolous and meaningless.

It's over anyway. *The News* reported on the other Cinderella team of baseball, who was winning even more than the Mets. The Atlanta Braves had won their last 27 of 37 games to win the NL West division. They would be the Mets next opponent.

The big favorite to win the World Series, was still the Baltimore Orioles. They had dominated the American League easily winning their division by 19 games. The betting odds had the Mets not going far. Silly hopes for an improbable dream.

Fathers and Sons and Other Village Idiots

Nevertheless, I found ten bucks in an overcoat pocket. I'm gonna use it to bet with Frankie that the Mets can win the World Series. Why not? Even if I win, it won't clear my debt, but it seems like the right thing to do.

Thursday, October 2nd

A blind man was crushed by a subway at Brooklyn Bridge station yesterday. He stumbled onto the tracks and could not climb out in time. The engineer slammed on its brakes, but the momentum pushed the train forward and it crushed the man against the platform.

Ed and I were sitting at the bar watching the TV when this story was covered. When you get a bunch of guys and no women present and there is drinking, the topics of discussion can often become crude. If a priest wanted to be one of the boys at the bar, he needed to tolerate this. Ed knew the rules. Many crude comments were made tonight.

"The blind man should have seen it coming," was the first crude.

"Hey Father, when a blind guy dies, can he see the light and walk to it?" Ed made a dismissive gesture that he would not engage in such a discussion, but it didn't stop others.

'I wonder if the City will issue him a lifetime subway pass?"

One rather big man added, "If he survived, but lost his arms and legs, could we toss him in the ocean and call him Bob?"

And they continued as they each tried to exceed the previous grossness.

I didn't think much of it was funny. Otto usually contributed with his own vulgarities, but tonight he didn't. Something touched him about the death. I'm only guessing but I think it might have been the bloody horrors he saw during his war. He finally spoke up.

"That must have been a horribly painful death. He might not even have died immediately. Poor bastard. If that corpse showed up at my funeral pallor, I'd tell the family to cremate the remains. Let's at least toast the poor bastard and hope he is resting in peace now."

161

Billy Warren

Everyone raised their glasses up then drank a swallow. The big man at the bar added, "To Bob." His buddy next to him, swatted him in the back of the head which caused his beer to spill all over the front of his shirt. He stood up to grab the other, when Otto, being an even bigger man, barked him down with "you deserved it." To which the man did sit down slowly with a long stare back at Otto. He might have been sizing up his chances.

"Let's try this again," said Otto while standing directly across the bar from the wet shirted man.

"To the poor bastard. Rest in peace."

Everyone drank up.

The wet-shirt man then said, "Let me buy a round for …," and he paused as he stared down Otto's eyes. He was not going to lose face over all this. "Since we don't know his name, let just call him …Robert."

Otto knew when to give a blowhard his out. He smiled and took a drink.

He and Anthony served up more drinks and Otto repeated, "To Robert."

Later, Otto was sitting with me and Ed at the bar, when it came time to settle up the wet shirt's bill. Otto told Anthony to not charge for the round. I heard him say to Anthony that it was a cost of doing business. Fights were more expensive to pay for.

While I sit with Otto and Ed, this whole incident reminded me of something I wanted to tell them both. For them both to see, I wrote, "Cremation," on my pad, then took my index finger and tapped myself twice on my chest.

"You don't want to be with Mom?"

"No," I wrote. "I have my reasons and the answer is no."

Otto read it and looked up at me then asked Ed what he thought of that as a priest. At first, Ed shrugged.

"He's a big boy now and God gave him free will in life. I think that you need to honor it."

"Humph. Okay Dad, where would you like us to put your ashes?"

He didn't expect that I already knew where. I quickly sketched out a stick figure sketch of the Statue of Liberty.

"The Statue of Liberty?" he said, and I nodded.

"In the Statue of Liberty?" I shook my head and made wavy lines before her feet then placed an X in the middle of them.

"In the water in front of the Statue of Liberty?" I nodded. Otto thought about it and started to stand up. I stopped him by grabbing his hand with my left hand and staring into his face. Then with my other hand I crossed my heart. Then I poked his chest with my finger.

"You are insisting that I promise you this right here and now?" I nodded and he paused.

"Okay, I promise," and I released his hand. He turned to Ed.

"Is any of this a sin, Father?"

"Oh, yes, probably so. We Catholics have such a long list of sins that I have trouble keeping track. I doubt it would be a mortal sin for you to be complying with a "last" wish such as this. Probably a venial sin where you might occur some purgatory time. Take your chances then go to confession to get it off your chest." Later, he clarified that cremation had been allowed by the Catholic Church for the last five years.

This was good. I have been meaning to take care of that little detail and now it is done. One step closer to closing affairs if things don't go well for me with my quest.

Saturday, October 4th

Mets' manager, Gil Hodges, was quoted as saying, "These boys have been underdogs since 1962." Despite a better record, the bookmakers were making the Mets the underdogs to beat the Braves to win the pennant.

Sunday, October 5th

I n the first game of the playoffs, the Mets beat the Braves 9-5. Baltimore barely won their first game, and it took the 12th inning. Maybe God does bless some underdogs.

Today is the 33rd Annual Pulaski Day Parade. It will march up 5th Avenue to celebrate the 190th anniversary of death of Brigadier General Kazimierz Pulaski, an American Revolutionary War hero.

For most New Yorkers, Pulaski Day is not as big a deal as Columbus Day or St. Patrick's Day, but it's important around the Eagle. After the parade, the marching Poles came back to the Eagle and started their celebrations again. Otto opened up the social hall and had hired a polka band. I left at midnight while the party was still going strong. I needed to get to bed as first thing in the morning, I had to do a task for Frankie.

Monday, October 6th

T he Mets beat the Braves again 11-6. The chatter at the Melting Pot was all about the game.

Frankie doesn't have me deliver messages anymore, but occasionally, I do need to deliver some bags to a barber shop in Bensonhurst on 86th street. I'd been there before. Frankie has had a lot of money changing hands lately, so I was frequently doing these money drops. I never asked questions. I had to do a drop this afternoon.

What surprised me was when I went into the back room of the barber shop, I saw Hector, Wilfredo's son, sitting in the backroom. Frankie must have gotten his hooks in this kid. Hector probably thinks he's working off his debt. In the back room, we both recognized each other but didn't say anything. The boy clearly looked alarmed. He's barely 18. I dropped the package and quickly left, but Hector caught up with me at the bus stop.

"Please don't tell my parents where I was today. Please, Mr. Baranski."

"Be careful," was all I could think to write.

"Yeah, I know. I will. Thanks."

"No, really. These are dangerous people. No matter how much you owe, get the money from your parents and settle your debt. These people are animals and will eventually get you hurt."

"Then why aren't you doing that?" he said as he looked into my eyes. He had me there. He continued, "Getting family involved is not a good choice, is it?" I nodded and he left me as quickly as he could. Hector is a good boy just trying to fix a mistake. Just another poor kid being used.

Later, I told Ed about what I saw. While he was visibly shaken by the news, he didn't seem surprised when I told him it was Hector I saw and where it was. He already knew the boy was in some trouble.

Tuesday, October 7th

Mets swept their division playoffs and won the NL pennant, but so did the Orioles in the AL. It will be just like the Superbowl. A Baltimore Goliath against a New York David. Placing a bigger bet is so tempting.

Wednesday, October 8th

Wilfredo's grocery store had a sign celebrating the upcoming Columbus Day and the parade in the city. The sign indicated the store would be closed in honor of Italian Americans. Wilfredo told me it was the second sign. First sign was put in by Frankie's people, then another guy, from Tony's people, came in and ripped up it up. The second visitor told Wilfredo that his bosses didn't believe in forcing storeowners to close. He also warned that if a store did close, they'd have trouble. The first guy came back with another sign and told Wilfredo that he better be closed.

"What are you going to do?" I wrote.

"I don't know."

When I told Otto about this, he told me that the Eagle also had the sign, but when Stan noticed it, he ripped it up. He told

Otto that he should remain open since he'd need a drink after that day was over.

Sunday, October 12th

Columbus Day was pretty quiet around the Eagle. In the newspapers, college presidents from around the country made an appeal to Nixon to start to pull out of Vietnam. The other news of the day was the Mets lost in first game of the World Series.

Monday, October 13th

The Mets tied the series yesterday. The next game will be back here.

In Manhattan, it was reported that one hundred thousand people marched down 5th Ave celebrating Columbus Day.

In the neighborhood, only the stores with the sign that were closed had broken windows. No problems for anyone open. It seemed a good indication as to which family was winning the war for our village. I live in what is supposed to be the land of the free. Instead, I live once again in the middle of a battlefield.

Tuesday, October 14th

I van once wrote,

A dry maple leaf has come off and is falling to the earth; its movement is exactly like a butterfly's flight. Isn't it strange? Gloom and decay—like brightness and life.

It was in his novel, *Fathers and Children.*

Fathers and Sons and Other Village Idiots

To my darling wife,

To bolster my spirit, I must find some shelter from this horrible world in which I still walk. Today, in the street, something beautiful caught my eye that reminded me of you. I decided that I must write a poem for you. I do hope you enjoy it. Writing for you has become my only way to remain sane.

Your loving husband

provocative now

your dress that you wear is
provocative
why change to so daring a
message now

your adornments that fully concealed you begin to reveal
voluptuousness
many who once causally walked by
leer now

should I ask why change to be a
temptress
but I know your need to change
right now

your lonely nights will arrive soon and you will be
naked
my beautiful maple you prepare for
winter now

Wednesday, October 15th

Tommie Agee hit a home run yesterday, but more importantly, he made two catches that saved at least five runs. Mets won 5-0 and are now ahead 2-1 in the series.

Father Ed showed up very upset at the Eagle this afternoon. He was wearing his cassock, rather than his clerical suit. Outside of church, this was unusual for him these days.

Otto and Henry were talking at the end of the bar and unaware of his arrival. There were a few others in the bar too. Anthony pushed Ed's usual daytime glass of diet coke across the bar. Ed then joined me in my booth. As he sat down, I stared at him, but he tried to start the conversation with his customary pleasantries.

"How are you today, Kaz," he muttered, but I could see that he wasn't looking for the answer. I continued to stare. When he finally noticed my stare, he started to unload.

Ed had known of how Frankie had his hooks in me, but he was also aware of how Frankie was starting to enlist kids in the neighborhood to work for him. He told me that he went over to Frankie's house to confront him for a second time about this. I asked if the first was back in August when I saw him leave in a hurry after William's discourse on the Battle of Brooklyn. He nodded. Back then in the Eagle, he spotted Frankie and a young man. He guessed that he was recruiting the kid for something illegal.

"Today, once again, he told me to stay out of his business. I tried to reason with him, but he just grabbed me by my arm, turned and pushed me out his front door.

"When he grabbed me, I felt like popping him one in the face. I had wished that I was not in my robes. I would have taken this collar off and I would have beaten some sense into him. I swear I would have." Others in the bar began to listen.

As bad luck would have it, at that very moment, Frankie walked in, probably for his liquid lunch. Everyone stared at him and then back to Ed. When Frankie saw Ed and heard the silence, he turned around and left. The silence lingered until Anthony broke into it.

Fathers and Sons and Other Village Idiots

"Well, enough's enough," he said as he ripped off his apron and came around the end of the bar. Henry was the first to step in front of him to slow him down, but Anthony quickly pushed him aside. Others including Ed ran up to help Henry restrain my grandson. Even Agnieszka joined us. Shouting began with the scuffling, as we all held on to the boy. Then the front door opened again and in walked Stan, still in uniform. Instinctively, he ran into the scuffle, which quickly subdued Anthony. No one wanted to explain to Stan what the pushing was all about. A family matter. We all turned to where we were before. Stan was happy enough with that outcome and said nothing. He only stared at the faces around the room.

We all know that something needs to be done, but it was just not as simple as just beating Frankie up on the street. Frankie probably had some real serious people willing to protect him, so beating him would only make things worse. Everyone calmed down. Everyone, except Ed. He seemed even more upset than when he arrived. Stan drank up but continued to observe us from over the rim of his mug.

Thursday, October 16ᵗʰ

B less the resistors of almighty power.

Life goes on and so does baseball. The Baltimore Orioles, a team that won 109 games this season, lost to our New York Mets again. The Mets were now up in series 3-1. Game 5 will be today.

Yesterday, Americans staged a moratorium to end the war in Vietnam. Over 5,000 protestors covered the stairs in front of St. Patrick's Cathedral for a candlelight vigil. In D.C., 30,000 peace marchers had carried candles past White House. The paper reported that there were 100,000 at Boston Commons doing the same. Americans around the world staged demonstrations, but still the *Daily News* ran a cartoon with a father imploring his son to support the president. The bastards.

Friday, October 17th

World champions! The Mets have become my *Saints of Lost Causes*. Somehow this win does settle my mind for today. My envelope from Frankie had some cash in it from my meager bet on the Mets. Not enough to change my life, but something.

Saturday, October 18th

It's no good writing if God hasn't given you talent. People will just laugh.

I am tired of people trying to tell me what I am capable of. First, my father, and now you, Ivan. Everyone wants to keep me in my station. I am tired of rules and expectations on me. Maybe I can't write, but maybe I can, if I continue to try. Those *Saints of Lost Causes* may not have solved my problems, but they have given me hope.

To all those bastards oppressing others to stay in their place, go to hell.

Sunday, October 19th

Tragedy has reached our streets once again. Hector was killed last night. Word was he was at the scene of a drug deal gone bad. He was just a poor boy of an immigrant father, like my sons. Hector was sent into the breach by the wicked, and he paid dearly for it. Something needs to be done about this cancer on our streets.

Monday, October 20th

Ed was furious today. In my kitchen this morning, Agnieszka, Ed and I shared our frustrations over the tragedy of losing Hector. Ed stood up and walked over to my window.

"Something had to be done, and we did nothing. Now it's too late for Hector."

Agnieszka asked, "Could we go to the police?" Ed quickly reminded her that whether the police already knew it or not, some of them were working for Frankie's bosses and we don't know which ones were. It was the way it was right now.

"Then we have to deal with him ourselves," said Agnieszka. This surprised both Ed and me.

I wrote, "There would be retaliation if we did somehow punish Frankie."

"He's a start. Kazimierz, you and I cannot sit here quietly any longer." With that, Ed decided to leave. Agnieszka sat with me, but no longer spoke.

I do agree. A cancer needed to be cut out. Just how and when, remain the questions.

Tuesday, October 21st

Kaz, I need to say that I am sorry." I must have looked perplexed because Ed continued and wouldn't let me interrupt.

"Yesterday, I feel I might have made it seem that it was our fault that Hector died. I am sorry if I did that.

"We all need to pray. A path will be shown. You must have faith, as I do that sometime will be done.

"You and I are being tested by God to do the right thing. Frankie will not prevail." And with that last statement, Ed was gone as quickly as he had come.

I agreed that Frankie must no longer prevail. How do I stop him, so that no one else in the neighborhood gets hurt.

Nothing much else happened today, but again, I'm thinking about Stan. I'm going to drop in on him tomorrow.

171

Wednesday, October 22nd

Hector's funeral was today up at St. John's Church. Most of us from the street attended the service. Some went with the family to the cemetery. Instead of going, I went looking for Stan and found him smoking on his stoop.

I told Stan everything I knew about Hector's involvement with Frankie and also my working for him. He asked about the scuffle in the Eagle the other day. He wasn't surprised by what I told him. He read my notes quietly but offered very little response. Then he ripped my notes from my pad and set them on fire with his lighter. The ashes laid curled up on his concrete stoop until a breeze blew them off.

"Kaz, you took a big chance coming to me because there are many in my precinct who shouldn't be trusted. Even I can't tell you who is safe. You need to get Father Ed under control, or he's going to get hurt. Innocent people will be hurt in order to protect some cops' secrets. These people would not only hurt you or me. They will not hesitate to hurt our families." We both sat in silence thinking about that.

"I'll keep my ears open for you, but, for now, all I can tell you is to stop talking about this and get Father Ed to do the same. Talking is not going to help."

I sat in silence. I was now more afraid than when I sat down. I don't think Stan will do anything to get me hurt, but I see now he has his fears too. He's also right. Talking will not help.

*

Hector's brother, Felix, and a few of his neighborhood friends, showed up in the Eagle trying to find out anything more about Hector's death. He was angry and looking for answers, but there were no answers for him there. Ed sat with him and tried to console him. Ed pleaded with him to pray, and God would provide a path.

When Felix left, everyone looked around at each other, but one said a word. We just sat there in our guilt. Ed told me that he needed to visit Wilfredo and his family again tomorrow before things got out of control.

Thursday, October 23rd

Wilfredo needed to reopen his store today. I was on a back aisle this morning and not really sure that he noticed me coming in. With mirrors at the end of the aisles, he probably knew someone was back there, but didn't know it was me. I heard the bell tinkle over the front door. Someone else had come in. It was Eugene.

"Wilfredo, my amigo, I wanted to stop by to express my sorrow for you. I was working during the nights of his wake and didn't want to trouble you yesterday at the church."

Wilfredo accepted his sympathies, and they conversed for a time. I shopped quietly while I continued to eavesdrop. I held my breath, wondering whether Eugene was aware of Frankie using Hector to work for him. If he did, he didn't bring it up.

Eugene was starting to say his goodbye and Wilfredo asked, "Will I see you on Saturday, at Father Ed's party, Amigo? It's now back at the Eagle."

"I didn't expect you'd be attending this year, Wilfredo."

"Oh, yes. Perhaps it's more important I come this year. My family needs love and support right now. Hector's death shows me more than ever that we need to put our trust in God. Maybe Jesus will not save us in this world, but I must believe He will save our souls. I must come."

He asked Eugene again, "So, will you be there?"

After a pause he answered, "Wilfredo, I was not planning to come this year."

"Why not? Are you working?"

"No, but I might be busy that evening. I've got some plans."

"More important than your community? Come just for Father Ed's photo."

"We'll see, Wilfredo. I'll see if I can make it."

"Come late but come Amigo."

"We'll see, Amigo." With that they parted.

I continued to shop and came forward a few minutes later. As I turned to leave the store with my groceries, he said, "See you Saturday, my friend. Don't forget God does love us all."

I wondered. Does he love us all, Wilfredo?

Friday, October 24th

Father Ed's big day will be tomorrow. He hadn't had the party at the Eagle in many years. This year, it appears to be especially important to him. He was making huge efforts to get all to attend.

Years ago, he worked it out with Otto to have both the bar and hall for this particular evening. Ed would buy food, and Otto would sell discounted beer. Ed would personally reach out to anyone in the neighborhood who might be having squabbles with anyone else. Interestingly, he never seemed to get his monsignor to attend. One year, the bishop dropped in for a drink. Seeing the positive response from the neighborhood, he became a protector of Father Ed. The bishop probably reined in the wrath of Ed's Polish monsignor.

At the Eagle this afternoon, Ed reviewed assignments with all present. He had everything down like clockwork, which appealed to Otto and his obsession with time. Suddenly, Ed left to deliver the other assignments to those missing. Before he left, Anthony asked, "Are you inviting Frankie?"

Ed quickly responded. "It is vital to include all. Without everyone, we're not an all-embracing community. God forgives those who forgive. All are welcome at this celebration and will be invited. In fact, Frankie had already accepted and will be bringing his girlfriend, Betty." Ed shifted his gaze over to Otto. "Nelson will also be coming." Otto stared back saying nothing.

Saturday, October 25th

What a night! I arrived at the Eagle about 4 p.m. to help Ed with setting up the hall, but surprisingly, he was already gone. Others were still there and by 6 p.m., the place was nearly ready. There was only one important task left to handle.

The funeral parlor closed at its usual 9 p.m. time, but Otto's discounted drinks were never served until after the 10 p.m. group picture. At the top of the hour, when Otto's clocks chimed and cuckoos inside stepped onto their perches, the photograph would be taken.

The remaining preparation was about time. At 6 p.m., Otto dialed *POPCORN* on the phone he kept under the bar. POPCORN was the telephone company's time service number. He would call aloud the current time for Anthony to set his watch. Anthony then proceeded to reset every clock in the bar. The only irregularity was that, in order to extend the evening's drinking, Otto had always had the times adjusted backwards one hour. The reason being tonight was the ending of daylight savings. At 2 a.m. tomorrow morning, the rest of the city would fall back to Eagle time.

I went home for a quick dinner about six-thirty and walked back in about twenty minutes to ten. The place was still rather empty. Because discounted beer was always the main draw, most would not arrive until a minutes before the party commenced. Slowly, the regulars started arriving.

As the cuckoos came out of their clocks for the quarter to the hour single chirp, Wilfredo and Felix arrived with a plate of food, followed soon after by Margaret, Tony and Izzie, all with food. Stella and Agnieszka arrived together brining more food. Nelson slipped in with them. Stan walked in about ten to. Anthony caught a dirty look from Otto when he walked in about the same time. Betty, Frankie's girlfriend, walked in about five minutes to the hour carrying a fruitcake, but without Frankie. She was quite angry about that, but others seemed to be relieved by Frankie's absence. All the food was placed in the hall, but everyone lingered in the barroom. Everyone but one notable exception; our host was missing.

Just a mere minute before the top of the hour, Ed rushed in with camera in hand. He explained his tardiness with the fact he had forgotten the camera and had to go all the way back to his cottage to get it. Immediately, he summoned everyone before the bar for the picture. I hadn't noticed until then, but Ed's bishop had also somehow slipped in.

When all the clocks started chiming, three photographs were quickly snapped. Surely, one photo would capture one of the cuckoos' appearances. After that Nelson, grabbed the camera for Ed to get himself into one. Then the drinks began to flow, the music started up, and the hall doors were opened.

The food filled the tables alongside the main wall. Polish ham, Hispanic rice and beans, Italian pastas and breads, and German or Jewish pasties, filled the tables. Even the bishop had brought a corned beef, which was maybe why I hadn't noticed when he arrived. He must have slipped in the side door into the hall. He stayed only for the photo and a few drinks and was gone in an hour. Frankie himself never showed up to the relief of all. Betty became more worried than angry about it. She, too, left rather early. Eugene arrived late and didn't make the photo.

This party never seems to disappoint. With his bishop gone, Ed was able to make a drunken fool of himself, drinking a lot, even for his standards. As the laughing and dancing intensified, some feuding neighbors even began to speak to one another. Others did not. Otto never went anywhere near Nelson the whole evening.

Ed and I left the Eagle about 2 a.m. He stayed at my apartment to avoid confrontation at the rectory. I'm finished writing tonight. I have no more to say.

Sunday, October 26*th*

It's now Sunday night, but the events of yesterday didn't end with Ed's party. I am only now getting time to write because the police have been questioning Ed and me all day. Let me start with what happened after I stopped writing last night.

By 2:30 a.m., Ed was in my kitchen pulling out some party leftovers for a snack. Only the refrigerator light lit the room. I was at the other end of the house finishing yesterday's entry.

Just as I had closed my journal, Ed ran into the room and shut off my lamp. I looked at him in the remaining dim light. He grabbed my arm and pulled me back towards the kitchen. I always forget how strong that man still is.

Standing to the side of the window, he pointed out and upward to the factory roof. I saw the dark shadows of two men moving across it.

Upon reaching Frankie's house, they slowed down their movement and stepped cautiously onto his roof. Within seconds, they were swinging their legs over the edge and onto the fire escape ladder. Big knapsacks were slung over a shoulder of each man. As we watched, one prowler followed the other down the ladder.

I went to the house phone to call Frankie's number. Ed surprised me by grabbing my wrist. We stared at each other. I knew what he was thinking.

After a moment, he released his grip. I still delayed another moment, then dialed Frankie's number.

It rang and rang, but no one picked up. It rang more, but still no answer. While I continued to listen, Ed whispered that he was going to the police call box on the corner. Before I could object, he was gone. I was alone.

I watched the intruders, who had reached the second-floor landing of the fire escape. Then, there was a muffled pop of breaking glass. Moments later, they were both inside and out of my sight. I was surprised how slight a sound they made. A simple pop. If I had been sleeping, I would have slept right through it. I doubt my neighbors heard anything.

With the window over there now open, I heard the ringing of Frankie's telephone. Then it stopped and my phone line went dead. I called back again but this time it didn't connect. I then noticed the intruders were quietly opening all first floor windows. At the time, I wondered why.

More silence in the darkness. I wondered what was taking Ed so long to get back. Maybe his bum leg was slowing him up. Maybe all the alcohol in his brain was too. Another five minutes past. Still no Ed.

Then a small boom filled the silent night air. Something had exploded inside Frankie's dark house. The curtains of the first-floor windows first blew out then pulled in. Red and yellow flames quickly covered the curtains. On the second-floor fire escape, the two men reappeared. Within seconds, they were up the ladder and back on the roof.

More popping and crackling sounds were coming from inside the house. Then, I heard a siren. How could the fire department be coming already? The siren got the men moving even more quickly but no longer quietly. They were running. Seconds more and they were out of my sight.

Up the alleyway, I could see the strobing blue, white, and red lights of a police car. I heard what sounded like a door being kicked open in and a voice yelling, "Don't be stupid. If he's in there, let him walk out himself."

It took the fire department another ten minutes to get there and by then flames were burning through its roof of Frankie's wooden house. The roof collapsed. If Frankie had been inside at inferno, he was history. The firemen fought from the factory roof and my backyard to keep the fire contained.

When Ed finally returned, he told me his story. The patrol car had rolled up to him at the call box without sirens. At first, the policemen thought he was drunk. While talking to him, they all heard the explosion and jumped back into their car.

Henry and Agnieszka came down to check on me and watch the fire from my backyard window. We weren't sure if we needed to leave. The whole neighborhood hung out their windows and watched for about an hour. Not much was left to Frankie's house. At least the cinderblock walls and tar roofs of the nearby factories stopped the fire from spreading.

Ed and I got to bed at about 5 a.m., only to be awakened by banging at my front door at 6. This is when we learned that the fire was not the biggest news of last night.

By early dawn, fireman continued to wander in my and Frankie's backyards. All morning long, uniformed police and detectives questioned Ed and me. Since we actually saw the intruders on the roof, we were questioned multiple times by various people. This seemed like too large a response for a fire investigation, and I was right. Someone let slip that Frankie was dead.

Since Ed had been standing with the police at the call box when the first explosion happened, he was being called an uninvolved but reliable witness. Each investigator wanted to talk to him. Another cop revealed to us that Frankie was dead, but he had not been in the house. He had died on a train track near Coney Island some ten miles away.

By noon, an unpleasant homicide detective named Sydney Hyman took over the case and dragged us over to the 72nd

Precinct, on 16th Street, but he wasn't from the 72nd. He was very annoyed that we already knew where Frankie had died. He questioned Ed and I separately for a few more hours. By dinner time, Ed and I were released. We walked back to 23rd, tired and hungry.

Now that I got all the excitement of yesterday and today into my journal, I need to go to bed.

Monday, October 27th

The philosophers table at the Melting Pot was filled today, but before I could sit down, Georgios was already asking me about the excitement in my backyard. While everyone gathered around, I wrote down what I knew, which wasn't very much. I did learn more from what they collectively knew.

The word on the street was that, while we were all at Father Ed's party, Frankie either jumped or was pushed in front of a train coming out of a tunnel near Coney Island. Someone at the table said that the engineer was our very own Basil from the neighborhood, but nobody had seen him yet. We learned the body was pulverized beyond easy recognition, but a wallet in the pants identified the body was Frankie's.

Sal lives in a second-floor walkup on 5th Avenue over Frankie's store. He liked to eavesdrop from his window on those who stopped to talk below it. All weekend, cops were posted in front of the store doorway. Apparently, the store had been ransacked sometime Saturday night, probably during the party.

Sal heard some cops below calling the murderer one stupid son of a bitch because he first tried to make the death look like a suicide about 10 p.m., then ransacked the store and burnt the house down hours later.

During police food breaks in his diner, Georgie overheard that Frankie's book was still unaccounted for. That cop said that the missing ledger was going to worry quite a few in South Brooklyn.

This explained why the cops on the case were no longer from South Brooklyn precincts. I'm thinking these early slips of the tongue were not accidents. Many were trying to sabotage the investigation by letting too much information out.

I sat at the table, still wondering about the whereabouts of Frankie's book and whether my name was in it. Everyone kept asking me silly questions about things I didn't know, so eventually, I got tired of writing and left the diner.

All weekend long, everyone who was at the party was questioned repeatedly by Hyman and his team. Since most of us were at the party all night, none of us had much to offer to him. Mostly we provided information about what we saw before the fire. Apparently, another neighbor was also up and verified what Ed and I reported to have seen.

The truth was that Frankie was so unpopular that most were glad he was dead. At the Eagle last night, many drank a lot of toasts to his killer. Some hoped it was a painful death under that train. I didn't care about most of that, but at least, until his mob can replace him, our neighborhood would be a little safer for our youth.

Knowing Frankie's criminal connections, most thought it was mob related. The two questions in their minds were who did it and was this business finished? I wondered about Mr. Green in Bensonhurst. Stan the cop thought that the murder appeared to be too complicated and slow for a mob hit.

The reality remained that we still didn't know who to trust. No one really spoke freely about what we knew. Hopefully, let our past sins die with Frankie. I heeded Stan's advice and kept my mouth shut. I might know something important that could get me killed. I did think that killing Frankie during the party was quite a nice coincidence. The party photo shows us all smiling at the time the train came out of the tunnel. Those not in the photo might have some explaining to do.

Tuesday, October 28th

Lady Liberty, I hope you appreciate my intentions for writing a poem about a demon who has usurped your glory.

Despite the recent excitement, I don't want to forget your birthday. On the radio they mentioned that you are 83 years old today. On last year's birthday, I had decided to write you a poem. It took me a year to finish it. It's based on two poems that I am fond of. *The Battle Hymn of the Republic (Brought down to date)* by Mark Twain, and the poem I first heard on the deck of the *Graf Waldersee*.

New Colossus (Brought down to date)

Not at all like the compassionate goddess, Clementia, of Roman fame,

With her welcoming arms to those across the seas;

Here at our walled street fortress shall stand

The bullish institution, whose breath

Imprisons the weak, and his name

Father of the Almighty Dollar. From his gaveled hand

Hammers worldwide warning; his demonic pyramid eye oppresses

The world's poor into submission.

Teach, new world, your storied dominances!" cries he

With joyous glee. "Give me your hungry, your rich,

Your elite chosen few yearning to capitalize on misfortune.

The ruthless and greediest of your kind.

Send these, the ambitiously evil to me,

For together we will take more than our share!

Sunday, November 9th

Birthday season is upon us. The Mother of Exiles had hers a few weeks ago. Dorothy Day's birthday was yesterday, or so Ed told me many times last night, as we celebrated our angels in the Eagle. Since he and I were buying, many were willing to pretend they cared about our angels. By the end of the evening, he was quite inebriated once again, but when I offered to let him sleep it at my house, he said quite loudly and for all to hear, "I no longer fear my little prick. Let him be dammed." He too has reached some sort of epiphany. Lord help us all. I wonder if Dorothy would approve. Maybe. She sounds like she is quite a rebel against authority. Birthdays mark the passage of time, something I can't afford to be wasting and yet I have.

I finally remembered what today's date is. My muse was born on this date in 1818. A century and a half after his birth and his words still have impact on the world. Ivan, what wisdom can you offer your humble student?

Every prayer reduces itself to this: Great God, grant that twice two be not four.

Humph! I never quite got that one. Should I be praying that an impossibility will happen or are you saying that all prayers are just irrational hopes? You're beginning to convince me that you don't know any more than I do.

Monday, November 10th

My silence must not be misunderstood. It's been weeks since Frankie's murder, and it seems to be fading from everyone's daily awareness. At the Melting Pot, we resumed talking about the war.

Sal mentioned that a 20-year-old boy hijacked a plane to Rome to escape and protest the war. Italy was refusing to extradite him. Sal added that two other jets were hijacked to Cuba last week.

David offered a story of Nixon appealing to his *silent majority* by labeling war protestors *the defeated minority*.

Washington police were now helmeted and preparing to beat down the next peace moratorium.

I think that I finally need to pick which side I am on. I can no longer be an idle onlooker of this war.

Tuesday, November 11th

Ed called me on the phone this morning and told me he was going to the next peace march in Washington. He asked if I wanted to come. I clicked my yes into the phone receiver.

Next, he asked if I thought it okay to ask William to join us. I answered with a yes again. When I asked him, William agreed to come then quickly ran out to tell Nelson about it. Nelson would be coming too. We all agreed to keep our plans to ourselves. No one would know where we were going.

Thursday, November 13th

I've been cautious too long. Today's my birthday, but it has no relevance if I don't get something done soon. I've got more important things on my mind than counting years between my birthday and my deathday. It's what we do between those two dates on our tombstone. What is the relevance of that dash between the two? I'm looking forward to Saturday's protest to give my dash some relevance.

Friday, November 14th

Traveling on the Aquarian peace train will offer me little time to write tomorrow. Before Henry gets up tomorrow morning, William, Nelson, Ed, and I will be on a Metroliner to Washington to join the protest. I am scared as hell. But I'm going anyway.

183

Saturday, November 15th

I'm still alive, but my jacket and this journal have some blood stains on them. As I write this evening, I'm on the Metroliner heading home. What's important is that my precious existence, which I have been overly protecting, survived. My life had become more precious than before.

I was terrified throughout most of the day, but boy, it was thrilling to be alive. I put myself in the breach this time, but for my cause, not a rich man's. I'm not dead yet.

Yesterday, as we reached the train terminal, William proposed that if we got separated, we would meet back at a specific phonebooth in Union Station. Each of us wrote down the number on that telephone dial. This proved prudent because this protest for peace didn't measure up to its name.

For many hours, the protest progressed along without any issues. It was just *US* yelling across barricades at *THEM*. At 4 p.m., our protest organizers decided to head towards the Justice Department. This was when the shit hit the fan.

One brick was thrown, then another. Groups of people swept past me going in opposing directions. This quickly separated me from the others. I was alone when I was jolted by a crash to the rear of my head. It felt like a lightning bolt. All I could see was whiteness. My ears heard nothing.

As I fell forward, time slowed. It was like an out-of-body experience. My knees reached the ground first, then my outstretched hands. My face flew towards the asphalt. In this slow motion state, my eyes watched darkness crashing in from all sides of me until I was in complete blackness.

I have no idea how long I laid there when I became aware of pressure in my armpit. Someone was yanking me upright, then pushing me in a direction. I wanted to turn to see who was there but could only keeping stumbling away. When I did turn, there was no one following me.

I found out later that William and Nelson circled back to where we had been together last, but Ed and I were not there. They followed the plan and returned to the telephone booth.

Ed was able to avoid any injury and being better acquainted with D.C. than I, quickly found William and Nelson. The boys

Fathers and Sons and Other Village Idiots

went back into the streets to find me, while Ed tried to keep the telephone line open.

I apparently continued to walk in the wrong direction for some time. A young girl looked at me and told me I was bleeding from the back of my head. She brought me over to a building a block away. There, on the steps, was a man with a first aid bag. I had been hit in the head with a rock and when I fell to the ground, I got stepped on as well. This man wrapped gauze around my head, then pointed me in the right direction to the station. I needed to circumvent many streets where the protest was still active. It took me quite a while to make it back.

Once there, I found the booth and Nelson and Ed. Within 20 minutes, William called the pay phone number to check in. With all of us accounted for, he worked his way back to the station while we stood in line to buy tickets. By evening, we were back on the train heading home.

Since I am alive and now on the train, I can write my accounts in my bloody journal.

Am I glad I went today? Yes, I am. I was able to let it be known how I feel about this war. I also exercised my free will, which seems to have become more important to me. I did survive that decision.

While dying was not what I came for, disappointing the Little Prick and not dying due to cancer would have some perverse satisfaction. I still don't feel that I am redeemed, so dying would have ended my quest in failure.

Protests are good, but peaceful protests are easy to ignore. I know violence will continue to erupt. I'm too old to be afraid of dying anymore. I am also too old to be silent anymore. For what it is worth, here's what I think about this day.

us them chanting
war not stop death not stopping
all souls losing out

Sunday, November 16th

The papers only reported about violence marring the peace march, but the real story was that 250,000 people showed up for this three-day moratorium. Yes, some protestors came wearing helmets with the intent to provoke violence. It was reported that most protestors turned their back on them.

This weekend, I stood before President Nixon's windows and let him know I don't support his war. No one else in the Eagle seemed happy we went. Even though Ed and I had invited the boys, Henry and Otto were angry at William and Nelson for taking us to such a place. I was not distressed. Neither was Ed. He, too, seemed more alive and pulled out of his recent doldrums of the past few weeks.

Tuesday, November 18th

To not incite violence, $20,000 had been demanded from moratorium organizers by who the papers called, "militant protestors." They had not been paid.

Wednesday, November 19th

U.S. troops massacred a village last March.

Last week was a story about a monk who lit himself on fire to protest the war.

Violence against others. Violence against self.

When is it right or wrong to violently resist the bully on the streets, or the tyrant with tanks? It's not as black and white as I used to believe.

Sunday, November 23rd

The papers were calling it, "the town that was." They reported that on March 16, 1968, a company of

American soldiers brutally killed women, children and old men in the village of My Lai.

The story reported was that the massacre was suppressed by the Pentagon for more than a year. Who knows how long the press knew about this before they finally revealed this story to America? Is everyone misleading me to manipulate me? Even God? I have my free will and so did those soldiers. Curse them. Curse God. Curse me if I don't voice my contempt.

There was a village that was.
Not unlike my village.
But no strangers came to Brooklyn tonight
to kill me.

Did our soldiers feel they had a choice?
Kill them villagers before
they kill us.

Did my president give them no choice?

Has God taken choice too?

God gave man the right of free will
to defy presidents and
if necessary
God himself!

People who perceive that they have no free will are destined to do wrong. Whatever my mind now tells me is the right thing to do, will be done. I don't care if it ends my quest, and I die and go to hell. If doing the right thing gets me dammed, maybe heaven is not where I belong. I feel a plan is coming into my view. I need a desperate act.

Thanksgiving Day

I feel little thanks today. I tried to stay out of the way at Stella's to let the others enjoy their day and wish thanks upon each other.

Instead, they watched football and shared no thanks.

Saturday, December 6th

In *Kasyan from the Beautiful Lands*, Ivan wrote this.

Strange things happen on this earth: You can live a long while with someone and be on the friendliest of terms, and yet you'll never once talk openly with him, from the depths of your soul; while with someone else you may scarcely have met, at one glance, whether you to him or he to you, just as in a confessional, you'll blurt out the story of your life.

After reading it late last night, I have decided to go to confession today to try once again to wrestle back my soul. To try something different, this time I went to St. Rocco's church to see a priest who was not my close friend. Since I don't need to protect the privacy of my own confession, I can write about it here. This one started out just as the last. Near the end, the priest asked if there was anything else I had done that I wished to confess.

I paused for a long while then finally wrote no.

Then he asked, "You still seem unsure to me and so let me rephrase, so that I can truly absolve you of your sins.

"Is there anything that you think may have been a sin or are thinking of doing something that you think would be a sin in the eyes of our Lord?"

I considered, then once again stood up and left. I guess this is why this path will not work for me. I have plans to sin further. Big plans. Big sin.

Sunday, December 7th

Four died yesterday in California at the hands of motorcycle gang members hired to be concert security. What should have been a peaceful rock concert turned into another hell.

There are events of a single day when perceptions of what it means to be safe, change forever. In truth, we are never safe, but a single event often forces us to confront this reality. In my life, there have been three such days that changed me forever. The day I hit my father, when Hitler invaded my Poland, and when God took my Marysia. One cannot stay naïve when confronted by such grief. I have had to grow up each time and acknowledge a new reality. I wonder if this rock festival will be a new reality for others. A time to acknowledge that fear is acceptable, but not acting is no longer an option.

I often think about what Helen Keller once said about safety. "Security is mostly a superstition," she wrote. "It does not exist in nature, nor do the children of men as a whole experience it. Avoiding danger is no safer in the long run than outright exposure. Life is either a daring adventure, or nothing."

I cannot allow my life to be nothing, and I cannot allow Little Prick's cancer from preventing me from having a life. Life is not safe, and it's too precious to be careful with. If I need to lose it to achieve happiness, then I will.

Tuesday, December 9th

My latest confrontation with God wasn't as comforting as the one in spring, but I no longer feel a need to be safe or to be redeemed. I need to assert my free will and not be held captivity by a church telling me to pay the ransom to them if I want to get to their heaven. I will not follow some religious recipe to get to heaven. I no longer see a safe path forward for me. Death will be here soon for me.

For tonight, I want to lie with Sancho on my bed. He is not feeling well. Right now, it is my job to comfort him. My needs will come soon enough.

Thursday, December 18ᵗʰ

Dear Marysia,

Sancho died last week. This has been why I haven't written you in a while. He died in his sleep in our bed. He bravely met his end and died peacefully.

Since you left, he has been my one reliable companion. When everyone else was out and about and busy with their lives, you and I had Sancho here to keep us company. Each night, he had been getting into my bed. I had Henry build me a series of little boxes next to the bed to aid him with the climb. It was as much for me as it was for Sancho.

I walk in from the street still thinking there is a meal I need to grind up for him. I look at his blanket near the vanity, expecting to see his face looking up. I climb in bed and expect him there. Now I am alone and when I think of it, I cry. I have lived too long and longer than another old friend.

With him gone, this releases me. Time to take action for myself. I just need to finalize the plan.

Your failed knight

Friday, December 19ᵗʰ

I hung out at the Eagle tonight. I didn't want to be alone, but I ended up being alone in a bar full of people. Ed found me there in my booth. He's beginning to be suspicious of me. Maybe he's figured out my plan. He has been trying to be with me as much as he can.

Near midnight, with only Ed and me remaining, Stan walked in. Otto pushed a filled mug across the bar to him, then asked us all a question.

"Did any of you guys read that story in the *News* a few days ago about bookies in New Jersey? It was about gambling with bookies. Gambling is so well accepted by people these days that the typical citizen just can't think their friendly bookie is a criminal. The article recounted stories of the real truth. Behind bookies were men with guns who use them.

Fathers and Sons and Other Village Idiots

"Gambling is so every day here, like jaywalking. People have gotten so used to it and think of it as a sport not a crime." I thought of the crime of losing Hector to this "sport." Stan spoke next.

"It's like prohibition. Criminals like laws that make things illegal. They're money-making opportunities for them." I thought next of Nelson, and the laws banning homosexuality. The mob was making money because of a law.

Otto asked Stan, "Can you tell us anything more about Frankie's murder?"

"Not much," was the quick response but after a look around the bar, he continued. "That investigation isn't going anywhere because no one wants it to go anywhere.

"You guys, and me, too, are off the hook, mostly because of your party, Father Ed. We all have solid alibis, which is a good thing because they would have loved to pin it on a local. That only leaves the mob or the police, and no one wants to know which one did it. Even Frankie's boss, Joey T., isn't cooperating.

"Once I was removed as a suspect, Hyman, the detective from the Coney Island, started sharing more information with me. He hoped I might know something important since I lived here. He was looking for dirt on someone here, like who might owe Frankie too much money. I said nothing." With that, both Otto and I shifted uneasily. Stan didn't look up and kept on talking.

"His chief detective told him that his initial finding of suicide won't fly with the DA because the press already knew too much about the case. Head Dick told him to confine his investigation to locals. If he couldn't find a chump, close the case as an unsolved mob hit. That's what Hyman eventually did.

"Even though he shared some with me, I still don't trust him. You all shouldn't either.

"Frankie's book has never popped up. If the press ever got their hands on it, it would blow up the borough. Maybe it got destroyed in the fire. That fire didn't make sense either. Why go to all the trouble to make it look like a suicide, then

191

burglarize his store and burn down his house hours later. No sense.

"It was well known that Frankie kept two sets of books. He bragged about it and called that second book, his life insurance policy.

"No one gonna miss Frankie, so who cares? Maybe that girl friend of his might miss him, but guess what? She's missing?"

"Betty?" both Ed and Otto exclaimed.

"Yeah. She was around the first morning after the murder but disappeared soon after that. If she didn't have such a good alibi by being here, she might have been the number one suspect. I'm not thinking anything good happened to her." We all just sat silently.

We talked awhile more until it was time to close. Stan offered to walk me to my door. Crime remains a cancer in our village because it's such an easy thing to do here. If we cut it out today, it grows back tomorrow. At least a part of the cancer has been cut out for now. It was the right thing to happen. We just need to keep cutting.

Little Prick didn't cut enough cancer out of me. His mistake, and so now I die, not him. If one is going to do something, one needs to be committed to do it completely. No half-ass good try will make it. It's time for me to commit to one final act. I am not going to let the cancer kill me and I am tired of seeking redemption.

Weak people never put an end to things themselves. They always wait for the end.

Ivan, I will be strong. I will wait no longer.

Saturday, December 20th

Are dreams supposed to be heaven? I wonder where we go when we die. I'm beginning to think we might live in other people's dreams.

I still think daily of Sancho. When I think of him during the day, I remember him old, but in my dreams, he is young. I had a dream of him with Marysia last night and both were young and healthy again.

It's almost winter now and I am rarely outside for long. Passersby don't know yet that Sancho is gone. In the spring, they will ask where he is. The truth is I will not be here in the spring to tell them. If all goes right, I won't be here by next week.

Sunday, December 21st

I hold no animosity towards the world but just don't want to be in it any longer. I plan to skip my Melting Pot visit tomorrow. I also decided that I won't be needing that cremation after all. I have other plans now.

winter stench arrives
hope lost for eternity
desperation reigns

Wednesday, December 24ᵗʰ

Christmas Eve dinner around my table this evening was with Henry, William, Agnieszka, and Ed. Each of us had an oplatek wafer on the plate before us. We had just finished giving thanks for the food we were about to receive and now it was time to go to each person in the room and share a personal conversation. It was a time to wish the other good health, profess one's love, and to ask forgiveness for past mistakes. Then, each person breaks off a bit from the other's wafer. As it melts on one's tongue, you embrace each other. Then you move around to another person at the table until everyone has embraced all the others. For those we missed tonight, we would repeat this ceremony tomorrow at Stella's, but Marysia and I always celebrated this tradition on the Eve.

Otto and Anthony were up at the Eagle getting ready for a Christmas Eve party in the hall before Midnight Mass. Neither Ed nor I would be attending the party. I have some important last-minute writing to do.

To avoid being pestered to join the party, Ed offered to let me stay at his house tonight. Tomorrow, we travel together to Stella's. While he continues to be very worried for me, he does not realize my intent for tomorrow. This will be my last entry into this journal. I plan to leave it in his guest room after I am done writing tonight.

Even though Ed is now retired, he had some assignments at the church in preparation for Midnight Mass. I am once again alone, which gives me the time I need to finish writing everything down in this journal and to write one additional note. Everything suddenly seems calm again in my life. All year long, I have worried about risking my life before achieving my quest. Tonight, with my decision to rush death, I have achieved a peace of mind and calmness and put an end to my hopeless quest. In case Ed doesn't want to show anyone this journal after I am gone, there will also be a note in my overcoat pocket. It simply states,

To all who ever cared for me,

I love you all very much, but I cannot let cancer kill me. It took away my Marysia, but it cannot have me too. My quest to achieve admittance into her heaven has failed and I have no purpose left. I have found no other path to follow that I am willing to follow. Please forgive me, but I must go now.

Your father, your friend, and your village idiot.

I will go to mass tonight to say my goodbye to my Black Madonna. In the morning, Ed and I will go to Stella's before noon for the Christmas lunch. I intend to hug everyone there one last time, then, during the afternoon, I will slip away for a walk. I will walk onto the bridge to finish my life. A storm is predicted for the afternoon. No one will notice me until it is too late. I will leave my coat with its note on the bridge.

I have no one but myself is to blame for my life or the ending of it. Given my circumstances, it seems to be the right thing to do. What other possible reasons might there be for me to remain here? Since I serve no further purpose, it's time to go to hell to meet my fate. I am sorry that I have failed everyone.

Dear Marysia,

I will always love you wherever my soul might be.

Your Kazimierz

Billy Warren

Christmas Day

D ammit. Whoever might be reading this journal someday, can plainly see, I did not die today.

Nothing ever goes right for me. Tonight, I sit alive at Ed's house and continue to write in this journal. Maybe this is my hell and only God is reading my writings. Maybe it's only Satan reading them, and he is enjoying my suffering. Are you, my tormentor?

This morning, Ed and I got up to go to Stella's. Because of the approaching snowstorm, we took the subway to avoid parking and travel problems. As planned, I had left this journal here for him to find today. I put on my overcoat with my note and wallet in its pockets, and we left.

Ed and I sat on a subway platform bench and waited for the train. I was overly dressed for the warm morning temperatures. Before I sat, I removed my overcoat and folded it over my lap. Ed sat next to me and soon another elderly man with a sad scent of homelessness walked up and sat next to him. He also had a folded overcoat on his lap. I assumed he planned to ride the trains throughout the storm.

"Merry Christmas, my son," Ed greeted the stranger, but he didn't reply. He did nod that he had heard him. He clearly was not there to talk. He seemed at peace within his own thoughts. His presence kept Ed from chatting with me. There were a few others on the platform but who kept their distance from us.

We sat close to where the train would enter the station from its tunnel. I heard rumbling coming from the darkness and got up to look down the tracks. Our stranger stayed on the bench with Ed. The train was almost in the station when I heard Ed call out, but it wasn't to me. I turned and saw the stranger drop his coat while running towards the tracks. At the edge of the platform, he leaped out. As he flew by me, he nearly knocked me along with him.

There, between the tracks, he stood motionless, arms by his side. I looked to the tunnel. The train almost there. Horrible squealing started. The engineer had seen him and had locked his brakes for an emergency stop, but, without a doubt, the

Fathers and Sons and Other Village Idiots

train would reach the man. The other onlookers froze and just observed.

Ed limped across the platform, yelling to the stranger. "Jump over to the next track," as he pointed across. The man ignored him and only stared at me.

I knew that Ed couldn't help in time. The train kept sliding. I still don't know why, but I dropped my coat and jumped down with the man. I wanted to push him towards the other track, but instead I fell to the ground when I landed.

Just like when I got hit in the head at the protest, time slowed down. I knew neither of us was going to make it across. I looked back up at Ed's face and was surprised by it. His look was not what I had expected. His head tilt seemed causal and the inquisitive expression on his face seemed out of place for the horror of the moment. Ed was watching something interesting and enjoying it. Was my last thought going to be what the hell was he thinking? The train was about to hit us.

Suddenly, the stranger pushed me down into the gutter between the rails and laid on top of me. I felt the train pull his body away from me, but I felt protected. There was no scream from the stranger. I heard only the roar of the train passing over me, then passed out. Somehow, I survived.

I woke up in a hospital bed, but I was unhurt. Hours had passed because I could see the snowstorm was raging outside the window. Medical people came and went, but they saw no blood or injury on my body. They left me alone to care for urgent cases in the ER from the storm. As they left my room, one of them said, "let's send the priest in to sit with him until we can do a more complete exam."

While still alone, I sat up and swung my legs over the edge of the bed. I heard the door of my room open, but the curtain around my bed concealed who it was. Footsteps approached me. Ed drew back the curtain to look upon my face, then collapsed to the floor. I couldn't shout out for help but went down to where he was. I wondered if there something wrong with my face.

Hours ago, at the station, he seemed serene when I was about to die. Here, he seemed shocked that I was alive. What the hell? There, on the floor, he explained.

197

At the waiting area, the nurses had told Ed that his friend was dead. Police had found the suicide note in my coat, along with my wallet. Witnesses had told them the man sitting next to the priest had jumped onto the tracks trying to save the man who died. I had become the stranger who lived, and Kazimierz Baranski had died.

On the floor, Ed and I embraced each other. The embrace reminded me of when I was a little boy in my father's strong arms. I felt reborn.

As I write tonight, it appears to me that God was not going to let me pick and choose the time of my death. Ironically, while I was glad to be alive, I also felt cheated. I wondered again whether I truly did have free will.

Ed realized he had to tell someone outside the room that a mistake had been made. The police would be contacting my family.

We pulled each other off the floor and he turned away towards the door, but I refused to let go of his arm. I dragged him over to the bed. We found a piece of paper and pen in the bedtable.

"Please, wait," I wrote on the paper. I was trying to think what this all meant. He waited. I believe he, too, was a bit short on his wits. I started writing again.

"You believe this some sort of miracle. Don't you?"

Ed looked wide-eyed at my note then at my face but remained silent as he handed my pad back to me. He saw something that he wasn't telling me. I wrote more.

"Ed, this must have purpose. Right? Maybe we shouldn't correct it. Maybe it wasn't mistake."

Again, Ed's expression was not what I was expecting it to be. I had expected an immediate rejection of my note. The dead man was somebody. The truth needed to be told, but Ed was not arguing. He was still not telling me something. Finally, he spoke.

"I saw something." With my hands, I gestured, "what."

"When you were both on the tracks, I saw something. I think I saw an angel."

Fathers and Sons and Other Village Idiots

Ed believes he saw his angel. He also believes he has finally seen his miracle. We shared more confusing bits of what we saw.

I convinced him to not yet tell anyone at the hospital. We should first go home to figure all this out. Surprisingly, he agreed. He stipulated that later, we could come back and say that we had both been in shock. We needed time to consider what happened. I got dressed in my clothing and the stranger's overcoat.

It seemed surprisingly easy, but because the hospital was on backup emergency power and most of the hallways were dimly lit, we walked out of the hospital unnoticed. Through the snowstorm, we were able to get to the station. There was power in the subways. It was a quick ride back to the 25th Street station. As the train pulled away, the two of us looked across the tracks to the southbound side where it all started this morning.

We climbed the stairs and stepped back into the storm. I looked down the street towards the water but could not see Lady Liberty in the harbor. Even the steeples of OLC above were hidden by low, dark clouds. I heard nothing in my head from Ivan. I had an eerie sense of abandonment in the middle of this swirling mess. But I did have Ed.

Together, we braced the winds and reached his cottage. The power was out in the neighborhood. The telephone was not working.

All this could not be an accident. I don't think I achieved redemption today because I tried to save a stranger, but I do feel I was saved. Did God save me for a purpose? Salvation but not yet redemption. Maybe I should still have hope.

I retrieved this journal and have started writing all these events in it. Ed went over to the church to pray, which left me alone. Tonight, by candlelight, I write. My writings have become my prayers.

*

The storm had gotten far worse and it's very cold outside. On a battery-powered radio, I heard two more inches of snow were expected before midnight. The phone and power

199

remain off. Winter and death had returned again. I was awake when Ed returned from church. We didn't talk much.

We had been in the same place, at the same time, but had two different experiences. He saw something that he could not explain and was thinking it was a miracle. I was planning to kill myself and got stopped by someone killing himself. There must be some mistake. Ed finally spoke.

"We need to go to the police station and straighten everything out. I can just tell them I just didn't understand what they were telling me at the hospital." I was still not sure what we should do. The streets were already covered with half a foot of snow. It would take a long time to walk over to the nearest police station. We agreed that it could wait until morning, then Ed spoke again.

"The man's family needs to know. His family needs to receive his body. They need to make their burial arrangements. He was somebody."

I had no good argument to this. The man was somebody.

I wrote, "Was the man my angel or yours?" Ed had no reply.

I walked over to the closet to check the man's overcoat. Maybe I could figure out who he was. I had intended to die today but someone else was dead. Who was he?

I found no wallet, but there was a folded piece of paper in a breast pocket. It was a flyer for some farm commune called *Spanish Camp* in Staten Island. The paper was yellowed and brittle. It meant nothing to me. When I handed it to Ed, he went pale.

"This is very old, and I have seen it before. I've been to this place, Kaz. This is where I met Dorothy Day."

Neither of us knew what to say.

I remember Ed telling me about her in the spring. He thought of her as his living guardian angel. Before tonight, I didn't really believe in angels and dismissed the notion of saints as heavenly fictions of an earthly church. Nonetheless, today wasn't very explainable with earthly logic. Finally, Ed articulated a plan.

"Tomorrow morning, we drive over to Staten Island to find out who this man was. After that, we go to the authorities to clear things up."

He said no more and left the room. I had no objection to going to Staten Island. I would like to know more about the man who sacrificed his life today to save mine.

I am finished with writing tonight. I'll go to bed but doubt I'll sleep. I have already done a terrible thing to my family. They will never forgive me for not going home tonight or for intending to kill myself. I can never go back to them now after what I've done. I need to stay dead.

Ed and I both agreed that if anyone knocked on his door, we would not answer. No one came in this storm. We were on our own.

Friday, December 26th

Ivan wrote in his *Brothers Karamazov*.

Is the burden of free will too much for a human to bear?

Nothing ever goes the way I plan. I can't tell whether it is divine intervention or divine interference, but I certainly don't feel I have free will. I have another long story as to how I ended up where I am tonight.

The morning started as planned. Very early, we got up, intending to quickly drive over to Staten Island. Snowplows, however, had pushed three feet of snow onto his driveway.

As we shoveled, my heart raced. A thought crossed my mind that dying of a quick heart attack would be better than a slow death with cancer. In my mind, nothing has changed about that. I will not let cancer be the cause of my death, but I don't want to go back to being Kazimierz. I have not yet ruled out a plunge into an icy New York harbor.

We shoveled for more than an hour, until finally, we were on the highway and heading to the shoreline village of Annadale on Staten Island, the location of Spanish Camp.

The highway and Verrazano Bridge were constantly being plowed and those roads posed no problems. Hylan Boulevard was the problem. A trip, which should have taken only 30

Billy Warren

minutes, took us more hours. The snow drifts grew larger as we drove south.

Ed and I were two idiots searching for an angel. I didn't know what to expect at Spanish Camp. I know Ed wanted Dorothy there.

At first, we remained within our own thoughts, but after about an hour of slow driving, Ed spoke.

"Kaz, I have a question for you. When we first met, I was only a priest to you, and you to me were another member of OLC's congregation. Strangely enough, we grew to be best friends as well.

"You were able to juggle two relationships with me. One of me being the Catholic priest and you, part of a flock. For lack of better terms, I was Father, and you were a son of the church. But we have another relationship that I can best describe as being brothers." I nodded throughout all this. He finally got to a question.

"Kaz, you could not confess a sin to me as your priest. Would you like to talk to me as your brother?"

I didn't know how I wanted to respond to that. I never had a brother, but I did think of him more so as a human brother and rarely a heavenly priest.

At my first failed confession, I didn't want to confess to God that I felt responsible for my father's death and regretted all my hatred towards him. If I hadn't wanted to be a writer, those events in Poland would not have happened. I feel that my desires caused his death, but I didn't want to debate this with either priest or brother.

My most recent failed confession was mostly about my guilt for not acting to save Hector, and my intent to commit suicide. I don't want to give up my future sin if I need it. Even if it means a failed redemption for me. Could I discuss all this with a brother?

While stopped at a red traffic light, I wrote a simple question on my notepad.

"Brother, what secret are you not sharing?" While his face revealed surprise, only silence was his answer.

"Why don't you share your secrets with me, brother?

Fathers and Sons and Other Village Idiots

I stopped writing. If my brother can't tell me his secrets, I can't share mine.

Since I decided when Sancho died, that Kazimierz no longer needed to live on, Ed could sense the change in me. I, too, sensed some different in him. His abrupt retirement was my first clue. knew he was no longer himself and this has been lingering with him The light turned green, and we continued on our way through the storm.

*

It didn't seem possible, but the storm got worse, and we shouldn't be out driving in it. More than once, Ed lost control of the car. Here and there, the car skidded and swerved. He reduced his speed for a while, but eventually forgot and resumed his haste. Something was driving him.

While deep in his own thoughts, a traffic light turned red. By the time Ed noticed it, it was too late. He slammed on the brakes to avoid going through the intersection. With wheels locked, the car began to slide toward a utility pole across the street. We watched and awaited the coming crash into it.

Just before the bumper could hit the pole, our left front tire hit the curb, spinning us around it and further down the icy street. Once we stopped spinning, we looked at each other.

"I still drive better than you," was all he could say. Not a high standard. At least, we smiled.

We got out to look at the damage. None really, except a left front flat tire. We went back into the car to consider whether the two of us were strong enough to fix a flat in the middle of this storm. Our heavy breathing fogged the windows. What choice did we really have? We got out and went to the trunk to get the spare and jack.

The spare seemed fine, and the jack was where it should be, but there was no tire iron to remove the lug nuts. I looked at Ed, but he said nothing. With no clear idea which way we should walk, we returned to sit inside the car.

"Well, Kaz, even though you are currently a dead man, your luck with me hasn't changed in your afterlife." A smile came to my face and when he noticed it, we both began to laugh until we were startled. A police officer was banging on

203

my fogged up passenger window. A patrol car had come up from behind. His flashing red lights lighting up the swirling snow.

Once he determined that we were not hurt or drunk, he offered to help us change the tire. He knew we weren't going to get a tow truck out there soon. He called in to his precinct to report the situation, and they approved the assistance.

The tire swap didn't take very long for him. Soon, we were on our way. I looked at the dashboard clock. It was already 2 p.m. and the skies were as dark as night. The storm had gotten worse.

Ed told me that after we passed by the Village of Great Kills, we needed to watch out for a street sign for Lipsett Avenue. He said that we'd turn left on the following street, Poillon. It was the way Ed thought was right, but he hadn't been there in many years. A few miles later, I spotted Lipsett and pointed. Ed was able to turn left safely down Poillon.

Poillon was a steep downhill road. At the bottom of the road, I could see a Dead End sign on a wooden barrier. Beyond it was the stormy ocean.

Despite going as slow as he possibly could, the car frequently skidded forward whenever Ed locked his brakes. I wondered whether we'd be able to stop at the bottom or slip right into surf. Fortunately, it flattened off near the bottom and the car came to a stop at our intended destination, Spanish Camp.

Ed wiped the moisture off his side window, and we looked out. It didn't look like the commune was still operating. There were many empty lots. Ed said most of the structures weren't there anymore. A few bungalows in disrepair remained. One larger bungalow in the center was still intact, with a few other smaller ones around it. Some had flickering lights behind closed curtains. Smoke was coming from some chimneys. We walked up to the main house, and, as we stepped onto the porch, Ed shouted above the storm that this was the one where Dorothy had lived. After a forceful knock or two, a dim light approached a window and a man's face appeared. Inside, we heard the unbolting of the door. In the doorway before us stood the man.

Fathers and Sons and Other Village Idiots

Ed bared his collar and asked if Dorothy Day might be somewhere in the commune today. The man waved us in before replying.

The house was only a single large room where all living, cooking, and sleeping took place. Three others in the room watched us but didn't move from their huddle around the woodburning stove. This structure was never meant to be used in any winter, much less withstand a storm like this. It was going to be a long night here.

The man explained that Dorothy stayed in touch, but she hadn't been at Spanish Camp in a long time. There was a rumor that she may come back to live in retirement there. "After all," he said, "she is over seventy and needs rest as much as anyone else."

Ed asked if he might know a man who matched our stranger's description. He did not and added, "all souls were accounted for at this morning's group prayers." Ed showed him the flyer. He said that one hadn't been used in decades.

When Ed and I turned to leave, the man voiced that leaving was a foolish idea during such a storm. He said that his radio was forecasting the worst was yet to come. He offered us coffee and asked if we needed a place to spend the night. We declined, saying we had important business to attend to back in Brooklyn.

He offered again, but we restated we could not stay. He went over to the window and pulled back the curtain. "Is that your car? You will never be able to get up the hill to Hylan in that." We intended to try anyway.

"I can't let fools go and kill themselves when I know I can help. Let me go get some friends. Wait here." In five minutes, he had six people with him. All dressed in meager coats. They were ready to help push us up the hill.

It took a group effort, and we finally reached the main road. Once there, we turned onto a flat section and got out to say goodbye. Ed promised to return soon with some food and clothing. I could not make such a promise, so I took off my gloves and hat and gave it to a boy who was wearing none. I gave another man my subway stranger's overcoat. I got Ed to

205

tell him that I had plenty at home. Finally, we got back in the car and drove away.

After a minute of driving, Ed said, "Do you know what Dorothy would have said about that?" I shrugged.

"If you own two coats, you have stolen one from the poor. You, my friend, own no coats at this very minute. I wonder if that made you poorer or richer for that gesture." I shrugged again.

I looked at the large snowflakes sticking to the windshield in between the wiper swipes. I was thinking about what the man had warned and was afraid he was right. We weren't going to reach Brooklyn by car in this storm. I didn't want to kill Ed trying. We needed to reconsider.

At another red traffic light, I wrote, "Can you find the Great Kills railroad station?"

"You want to take the train home?" I nodded then wrote.

"Train to ferry, then subway back to Brooklyn. I've done it before in a snowstorm. It's reliable."

"Okay then," as he drove on.

With a stop or two along with a few U-turns, we found the station. There, we saw a note on the ticket booth window. "Line closed until further notice. Trees across tracks."

Ed said, "Maybe we should reconsider the offer from those good people."

I had another idea. I've always looked for a good excuse to contact her again just to hear her voice or see her face. This was as good as any.

I wrote, "I know someone who lives here. You do, too." He knew who I meant.

"I think that we may be better off with those good people back there, Kaz. Anyway, by now, Louise thinks you're dead, and she might over in Brooklyn."

I made a series of short quick nods of my head. Yes, I knew that if her phone was working, she would have known by then. It was approaching 5 p.m. Maybe we'll be lucky, and no one would be home. She might not welcome me.

With a little difficulty and a few more wrong turns and backtracking to the station, we found her mother's house, the place where she and I said goodbye. No lights could be seen

Fathers and Sons and Other Village Idiots

inside. He opened his car door and got out alone. We thought it would be best if I was not at the door when she opened it. I watched from the car, shivering as much from fear as cold.

After his banging on the front door, I saw a flashlight shine through a side window. The door opened and Louise stood before him. She let him in and closed the door. I could still see them through the side window.

When Ed pointed outside in the direction of the car, I heard a horrible and long scream above the wind of the storm. Next thing I knew, she's down the stairs across the snow and opening my car door. Instead of a hug, she yanked me out on to the snowbank, then started hitting me. These hits didn't stop until Ed could limp over to pull her off me. She started hitting him as well, to the point of him falling over into the snow.

Eventually, she stopped hitting, looked at him, then me. "And you two like to call other people idiots." With that, she ran back towards the house. Once there, she slammed the door behind her. Ed and I sat in the snow, and just looked at the house and then over to each other.

"That could've gone better," he said. I agreed.

The wind continued to whip. We didn't know what to do next. Fortunately, a moment later, the house door opened again. Louise looked at us, gestured her arms inward, then turned away. We scrambled up and inside.

There was no power, but Louise had a fire going in the hearth. She lit more candles and brought us over to the kitchen table where she sat us down.

The three of us settled in with me between them, so they could each read my notepad by the candlelight. Ed explained the mistaken identity at the hospital and the switched overcoats with my suicide note in one of them.

"Why didn't you straighten this all out yesterday?"

Ed answered before I could write. "We were confused."

"Confused?"

He sheepishly added, "Yes, confused. I thought I saw something."

"What could you have possibly seen to do all this nonsense?"

"I thought I was watching an angel at work."

207

Billy Warren

"An angel?"

"I know it sounds crazy and saying it out loud makes it sound crazier, but I thought I also recognized the face of our stranger. I thought his face transformed into a face of someone I knew a long time ago."

I looked over to him. He hadn't told me he had recognized the face. It might explain why it seemed so easy to convince him to not straighten out this mess at the hospital. Louise was not buying any of this and turned to me.

"And you. Who did you see? Jesus?"

I thought and then took my pad.

"I didn't see Ed's angel," I wrote.

"Well, good. That's at least that's one small step towards sanity for you old fools."

Next, I wrote one word, "God."

They read it and stared at me. I hadn't mentioned seeing God. Until that moment sitting with them, I didn't recognize it to be God or even godlike.

"You think the stranger was God?"

"No, not him. As the train was coming out of the tunnel, I looked at you and you seemed to be in a daze, looking at the stranger. I turned to look at him, and I swear, I think he winked at me."

Louise said in disbelief, "Winked?"

I continued to write as fast as I could.

"Yes, he winked at me when only I could see his face. It was a wonderful peaceful face. Then he looked over to the tunnel. I looked that way but didn't see a train anymore. There was a ball of light flying out of darkness. The stranger then placed me down into the gutter and put his body over mine. I didn't move. He seemed to vaporize above me and went along with the light. Within this warm light, I felt serene and protected, then I seemed to go to sleep. I woke up on the way to the hospital with no serious cuts or pains. I don't feel I passed out. I simply went to sleep."

We sat in silence. Louise was raised Catholic, too, but was not actively practicing since the divorce. She had about as much faith as I had in God making bad things good again.

208

Fathers and Sons and Other Village Idiots

Eventually, Louise offered to cook us some food. Her stove was very old but ran on propane without the need for electricity. A simple match was all that was needed to start it.

As Ed and I ate some bread, Louise was carrying a bowl of soup to the table when she asked, "Why are you both here in the middle of a storm?"

Ed told her that we hadn't started out to see her. When he reached the part about the Spanish Camp flyer, Louise dropped the soup bowl and fell to the floor with it. Her face showed disbelief. Given everything else Ed had already told her, I hadn't expected this.

"That camp is only a few miles from here"

"Yes, we know. We were just there."

"My mother and father lived there. It's where they met. From there, they moved here when it was only a farm. My father grew food for the commune. Mother and I would go down frequently. Dorothy Day was rarely there, but I did meet her a few times. My mother called Dorothy a living saint. Dorothy once overheard and quickly corrected that she was no saint. She didn't want to be dismissed so easily."

"Yes, she was too fond of saying that," said Ed, "and the diocese didn't like hearing it.

"Me, I believe that if a person is a saint in someone's heart, then they are a saint or maybe an angel. I heard similar stories about Dorothy when I worked with her here in Staten Island and also in the Manhattan. The bishops didn't like her, or her quip that she was better than the saints, but that was never what she was saying. I did hear one bishop say that she was putting herself above heaven. The church back then, didn't like that she called her newspaper *The Catholic Worker*. They wanted to distance the religion from her and what they believed at the time were unpopular socialist beliefs.

Louise got up and stepped over the broken dish on the floor to leave the room. She returned with a framed photo.

"Is this the person you saw?" handing Ed the frame. The photo was of Dorothy with Louise's mother and father. He looked at it. Yes, he confirmed. He saw Dorothy's face on the stranger. They turned to me. I didn't want to tell them who I saw. I lied and said I just saw a stranger's face.

209

"Father Ed, my mother and father loved Dorothy. I can't remember you never mentioning that you knew her."

"Dorothy was the single most important person in my life. My feelings for her were very confusing, but I loved her. I felt in conflict to my vows. It really wasn't until this last year that I have been able to reframe my feelings and talk about her with anyone."

"And you," Louise said, "why would you think you saw my father's face? You never met him."

"I had seen this photo before in your apartment. Maybe it was that," I wrote. Ed spoke next.

"Dorothy's teachings certainly limited my career in the church. I think that her teachings have made my values clearer. Her actions were always based on doing what she thought Jesus would do without compromise. I loved her for it. I was so smitten by her that if she ever asked me to leave the church, I might have. She would never have made such a request because she was never out to undermine the church. I was just one of many who adored Dorothy like a gift from God."

I think of both Louise and Agnieszka that way. They were gifts. True angels in my heart. Perhaps my life has not been so bad since I have walked with angels through it all.

Louise spoke next. "Father Ed, you have always made my life better. I wish that I could have come to you about the divorce, but I knew that it was needed and still do. I could not come to you about something that might pit you against your own beliefs. If I had only known that you, also, were guided by Dorothy, I would have known you'd given me honest counsel and not rigid church dogma. My life has been very lonely these past few years without both of you in it." We all got a bit glassy-eyed.

Louise turned her gaze to me. "So, how are you connected to Dorothy?"

I wrote, "I don't know. I don't think I am. Maybe I needed to see you one more time and this is how it was meant to happen."

"Are you still intending to kill yourself?" she asked. Ed's gaze had been down, but with this question he turned his head slightly towards me and waited.

210

Fathers and Sons and Other Village Idiots

"Probably yes, because I can never go back to being Kazimierz. It may still be necessary. I feel I have done all that I can get done, and my future has no further purpose.

"Also," I wrote, "I will not linger and let cancer kill me."

Ed spoke, "But if you had killed yourself yesterday as you had planned, you would not be here right now. Louise and I would not be here.

"This has been a joyous couple of days for me, and I owe it to you being alive. Maybe there is more for you to do tomorrow or maybe next week or next year. Maybe only one thing or maybe a hundred. Furthermore, if you commit suicide, you will not be allowed into heaven to be with Marysia."

Louise interrupted him. "To be honest, Father Ed, you can't be sure of that."

"And neither can you. None of us really know. So, all we have left is doing what we believe is true to our hearts." He turned to me again.

"Kaz, when you planned to commit suicide, in your heart, did you believe that to be the right thing to do for your family? You've always strived to do the right thing.

"Or did exhaustion lead you to that sad notion?"

What was in my heart was no longer clear. I had been so sure of my path these last few weeks, but Ed and Louise were being honest with me. Not like Little Prick, who tells me things that may not always be true. I was confused and couldn't write further.

After the mess on the floor was cleaned up, we ate. We hugged every now and then and shed a tear or two as well. It was a turbulent yet somehow rewarding evening. For a moment, I thought that maybe this could be my heaven, but quickly realized that this can't be heaven without Marysia. Wherever she is, is my heaven.

Ed asked to be alone for a bit, so Louise showed him to a bedroom then went to her own. I was to sleep on the couch. At the kitchen table, I started writing up all these events in this journal. Another hour went by before Louise came back into the kitchen. When she saw that Ed was not with me, she called out. "Father Ed! If you please, would you join us again in the kitchen?" Ed could not have been in bed yet, as he was with us

211

a moment later. The three of us sat at the kitchen table, as Louise leaned across it and took a hand from each of us.

"Now, I would never let either of you tell me what to do, even though you are the two of the closest people in my life. That is, with the exception of my William, of course. He need never be included in any of this madness.

"So, here's how I see it. For all this to work, we need to agree.

"Kaz, your wake is supposed to start in two days. Before the telephones died, Otto called and told me the hospital had already released the body. He didn't want to argue with anyone about your cremation request and planned to do that quickly. It's probably already happened. Our stranger's earthly body is gone."

"So, what is this plan of yours?" Ed questioned.

"Kaz, this is what I want to try to do for you. I, somewhat, want to respect your wishes, but I have my limits.

"If I see you trying to kill yourself, I'm going to stop you. I will not be a part of any suicide and will do anything I can to stop it. If you hurt yourself, you are betraying me. Do you understand this?"

I nodded. Ed took her pause to insert that he would do the same.

She continued. "As I see it, you might kill yourself if you return to being Kazimierz. If Kazimierz stays dead, maybe you can do some good as this stranger. A new life might allow you to do things you could never do as Kazimierz. We don't know.

"If our stranger's body was cremated today, there is little hope we will ever know who he was. I am proposing you take his place. You can live here with me. I'd tell the neighbors that you are an uncle of mine. When William comes to visit, you need to leave for a while. William must stay out of this. Maybe someday I will explain to him what this was all about. Right now, I'm not sure I can explain all this.

"If you choose to stay dead, I will help you do this. What do you want to do? We need to know and need to know now."

I had been wondering where I could live without money and Louise seemed to be offering a solution. I don't think I am

Fathers and Sons and Other Village Idiots

going to be around too much longer, and I could live with living with this angel.

I wrote down, "I could never repair the damage I have caused by my pretending to be dead these last two days. I want Kazimierz Baranski to stay dead."

Louise posed the next question to Ed. "Father Ed, do you have any objection to keeping Kaz dead?"

"Well, this plan has been very quickly thought out considering you joined this mad hatter party only a few hours ago. Given what I have seen and heard yesterday and today, it does make some sense. Others may not think so, but it does seem the right thing for us to do. Let me rephrase that. I know in my heart that it is the right thing to do. I will support the plan on one and only one condition." I waited to hear it.

"Kaz, my old friend, you must swear to me on our friendship that you will not try to take your life. Even if we get discovered and get punished for this plan, you can never go back on this promise. You are losing your free will on that one point. You don't get to pick when you go. Sorry, but that's the deal for me. If you can swear to this to me, then I have no objection to keeping Kazimierz dead."

I sat for only a few seconds then grabbed my pencil and notepad. I had already made up my mind.

"I can make that promise to you both. I will not take my own life, but my condition is you understand that I now view my life to be precious. Precious, and one that should not be wasted by being careful. No matter what happens, I live life on my terms and take as many chances as I choose to take. Even if my choices endanger me. Deal?"

I could see that they were both thinking about what I was proposing.

As we were still holding hands, I lowered my head. Once more, my eyes watered up.

"Deal." It was Ed's voice.

"Deal," came quickly from Louise.

Ed reached over and hugged me from his chair, as Louise came around the table and joined us. Their warmth felt like the protection I received when my angel covered my body with his, as a train drove over it. I flashed back to the moment I

213

walked into the Our Lady of Czestochowa and felt her warmth on my soul. I am sleeping in a house of angels tonight, in a world where earthly angels do walk.

I can't say how long we remained at the side of the table together, but it could never have been long enough. We stood up together and recomposed. Of course, it was Louise, our planner, who spoke of our next steps.

"Okay then, there we have it. Father Ed and I need to be in Brooklyn by tomorrow to let everyone know we are okay, or someone will start to look for us. Otto was going to have a wake with your ashes in two days. It will be held in the social hall and not the funeral parlor.

"Ed and I must be there. Kaz, you can stay here or hide out at Father Ed's. I'll stay on 23rd Street with William and Henry." We nodded agreement. Louise got up and brought to the table a bottle of whiskey with three glasses.

"Let's drink to that poor bastard, Kaz," she said.

"May he rest in peace, that poor old bastard," added Ed. And we drank.

Ed resumed, "Let's drink to our stranger. May he rest in peace, as well. If he wasn't an angel before, he might well be one now, because he performed a miracle and saved my friend's soul." We drank again.

I thought again about the face of this stranger. I had lied earlier to Louise and Ed. On the track, the face of the stranger had changed into a familiar one, my father's. Has my father forgiven me for my hatred and was trying to rescue me?

Louise went to bed hours ago. Ed left, as well. Alone at the kitchen table, I write. It is past 3 a.m. It seems like a good plan, but I am not as sure as the others that it can work.

I don't want to go back to being Kazimierz. His days are over. Just like my mother, I need to take a new identity in order for time to move forward.

Tomorrow, we go back to Brooklyn. I hadn't planned on being living today, so I seem to be on borrowed time that is still running out. For me to be happy with this new life, I must still do one more good thing. Tonight, I pray to my angels.

Saturday, December 27ᵗʰ

Well, damn. This day actually went according to plan.

The blizzard was still raging this morning and roads were worse. Since I left Poland, I've never seen a storm like this. Louise's radio came back on with the electricity, but the telephones were still out. We heard that public transportation was running a limited schedule, including the Staten Island railroad and its ferries. We decided we could walk to the train station to work our way back to Brooklyn. Louise gathered a few things for herself to stay a few days. I wore an old coat of her dad's and off we went.

When we reached the ferry terminal, Louise called the house to let them know that she and Ed were fine. Their story was that after Ed left the hospital, he went home in shock. Before he could gather his wits, Louise was calling and asking if he could come and get her, as her car had a dead battery. The ruse was that Ed drove out, but then got snowed in. Today, with so much snow on the roads, they decided to take the railroad and ferry. Not a great story, but it was as simple as we could come up with. We doubted anyone would consider any inconsistencies once Ed and Louise were accounted for.

At the ferry terminal, I picked up the newspaper. Photos of autos piled up on icy streets with many people being taken to hospitals. Thank God we didn't try to reach home last night. Once on the ferry, I watched Louise and Ed standing by a window with her arm around his. I never thought about how much they might have missed each other.

The ferry passed before Lady Liberty, where my surrogate mom first showed me Brooklyn. There seemed to be a brief break in the storm and through the opening, I could see the OLC steeple. It is easy to count over to 23ʳᵈ Street where I suspected my family sat in mourning. Our family has its conflicts, but I know that we loved each other. My death will pull them all together. I know it. If I showed up now, I might shatter what little good my death might have accomplished. I can't imagine how I can ever help them anymore. I'd only be a burden. I am dead and I need to stay that way. Maybe someday they should be told the truth. I hope that someday this journal will better explain than I could today. It has been a crazy year.

On New Year's Day, I will give this journal to Louise to someday give to the family. I only hope she is willing to take it. If found out now, someone may hold this plan against her. Louise might never be able to give them the full story. Doing the right thing may not be popular with everyone.

Today's journey went smoothly, and we reached Ed's cottage undetected. The storm continued and was expected to go on for a few more days. The radio was calling it the Big Nor'easter of '69. Ed and Louise went up to the house to let everyone know that they were okay. I am too tired to think or to write more tonight. Peace to all that read this journal.

Sunday, December 28th

More snow on top of snow. Three more inches were expected today.

Over the years, my lack of concern of time had Otto often say that I was going to be late for my own funeral. Well, he was wrong. I was not going to miss it and knew how I was going to do it. This storm was coming in handy.

I had a key to the Eagle's alley backdoor. Once inside, there is a stairway up to the loft where I could hide and observe my own wake from above. Kinda like I was looking down from the hereafter.

Before becoming the Eagle, this tavern was once a speakeasy. The alley was its hidden entrance into it. The windowless loft was where the speakeasy was. In the loft was a peephole that looked down on the social hall. When the police raided the hall, the drinking crowd in the loft got a signal from a watcher to remain quiet. Those in the tea party below would continue their noise. It worked for a while until the police figured it all out and closed the place down until the end of prohibition.

Anyway, the top of the stairs would be where I would spend the evening, watching my own wake. This was my plan, but it had one problem. The backdoor key was in my apartment. I needed for Louise to find it.

Fathers and Sons and Other Village Idiots

I could not simply tell them to unlock the backdoor because Otto had it rigged to always be locked to the outside. In this storm, we couldn't keep it partially open. The draft might attract attention.

Louise searched the drawers where I thought the key should be, but it wasn't there. William noticed her searching and kept asking her what she was looking for, so she needed to stop. I would need to get in there myself.

Ed told Louise to unlatch the backyard cellar door. I would be able to get into the house from Frankie's alleyway. I only needed to wait for a call from Ed at the Eagle to let me know everybody had reached the Eagle.

With the storm still dropping snow, it was easy for me to walk up 24th Street and through the alley. There was an old fence in my way to my backyard, but I was able to use some partially burnt boards from the fire to step on the fence until it pushed over. The rest went as planned. Once in my apartment and seeing the kitchen, I remembered the key was in a coffee cup on the top shelf. Since I expected this to be the last time I would ever be in the apartment, I went to Marysia's vanity.

I sat there and shined the flashlight onto our wedding photo. I knew I couldn't take it with me, as Henry might notice it gone. Instead, I grabbed Marysia's hairbrush, but I hadn't been paying attention.

I looked up through the street window, to see old Mrs. Trimpoli crossing the street and coming straight towards me. She was probably going to attend my wake. The problem was she saw the light from my flashlight in the apartment.

I shutoff the light and sat in darkness, but she came closer and stood and stared. She was probably thinking there was a prowler in the house. It has become too common for thieves to read the death notices in the newspapers and rob a house during the wake. SOBs. I hope they rot in hell.

Mrs. Trimpoli kept staring in. I didn't want her to think it was a prowler and run to call the police. I did the only thing I could think to do. I turned on the vanity lamp. Mrs. Trimpoli saw my face. It was not a prowler. It was a ghost.

With an expression of shock, she stepped back and made the sign of the cross across her forehead and chest. We stared

217

at each other for another moment, then I smiled and made the sign of the cross as well. After that, I raised my hand up towards her as if I was making a pledge and mouthing the words, "Peace be with you." I then turned off the lamp and backed into the darkness of the room. I watched as this old woman got down on her knees to kneel in the snow with her hands clasped in prayer. What else could I have done? I needed to improvise.

I ran down the stairs into the cellar again, through the yard, down the alley, and back onto 24th Street. I walked up to Eagle's alleyway and turned down into it. I could only hope that when I unlocked the door, there would be no one passing by. My luck was good again. No one there. I guess I only needed to live long enough to see my luck change.

The loft was pitch black. As long as I kept it that way, no one would notice the open peephole near the hall ceiling. I had only one thing to watch out for. Through the hall doorway that led to the bathrooms, I needed to keep an eye on the hallway to the right that led to the loft stairway. If someone went by, I'd have time to hide behind some boxes. All I needed to do was pay attention.

I looked through my peephole, and a sense of warmth filled me. The crowd was not yet allowed into the hall, but I could see that my boys did a great job setting up. They followed my instructions completely.

At my end of the hall was the Table. It had been moved in for my wake. On it was a whiskey bottle crate. The label on its side was Johnny Walker Red, my favorite.

Ashes from the cremation were supposedly in the crate, but Father Ed insisted on switching the stranger's ashes with some from his fireplace. Louise helped him make that switch. At some later date, the stranger's ashes would need to be disposed of, more respectfully.

On top of the crate was a platter with a bottle of Johnny and many shot glasses. Next to the crate was a sign. While I could not read the words on it, from my peephole, I knew it read that the drinks were finally on me.

Around the hall, tables and chairs we set up in party style. We hadn't spoken about all this in quite some time, but I got a

Fathers and Sons and Other Village Idiots

bit teary eyed to see my boys remembered that I wanted a party and not a wake to send me off.

I heard clocks chime 7 p.m. and Otto opened the doors to the hall and stepped in with others following. I was a little saddened to see that there were so few there to mourn me.

Everyone trickled in from the barroom. William was one of the last to enter, but he needed to push forward to see why people had stopped moving. Wives were holding their husbands' arms and not letting them go forward. A toast to my departure was not right in the wives' minds and they were not going to let their husbands commit blasphemy at a sinner's wake. William moved forward and read the sign. Without hesitation, he poured a shot and drank. Louise, Agnieszka, and Ed stepped up next and with no hesitation drank. With Father Ed's gulp, other men shrugged off their wives and stepped forward. Otto, Stella, and Nelson joined the line and Henry was the last. With the shot glass in his hand, Henry stayed upfront and turned to address the group.

"For tonight and for each of the next two nights, the drinks will all be on my father. Please go to the ballroom bar now to grab another drink."

Given my mourners were very small group, within a minute, Otto and Anthony were able to serve everyone. They all turned back to Henry and waited. I felt like I was looking down on them from heaven. Perhaps I sorta was.

"It is good that today's storm has limited the number of people in this room tonight. You are the ones truly important to him. Thank you all for joining us despite this terrible storm outside.

"Maybe it is fitting for it to be a stormy week because Dad had a stormy life. He immigrated to this street alone as a boy. Here he raised two village idiot sons as he rightfully called Otto and me.

"He and Mom had a beautiful life together on this street, but my father had to live through her cancer, then his own. He often said that he didn't want that little prick cancer doctor to ever hear that cancer eventually killed him. I guess he found a way around that. I am sorry he didn't find another way, but what's done is done and we can't change it. Since Mom got

219

sick, he rarely had any break in his storm. From his cancers to my divorce to his idiot sons to his gambling debts, his storms never stopped.

"He raised Otto and me well and we could not be prouder that he was our Dad. I only wish I had said that more often to him.

"He respected each and every one of us in this room and always did what he could to support us in our lives. More importantly than respecting and supporting us all, he loved all of us for who we are.

"Now that's not to say that sometimes we all questioned his choices in life and now in dying, but he was always guided by one thing, doing the right thing whatever that might be in his mind. He always told me the hard part was figuring out the right thing. Doing it was annoying but easy."

With this, Henry seemed to lose his way, so Otto spoke next from behind the bar.

"When Dad could toast out loud, he had a favorite. Let's toast him with it tonight." Otto raised his glass up, and everyone did the same.

"Here's to it, and here's from it, and here's to it again! If you ever get to it, and don't do it, you may never get to it to do it again!"

Louise let out a little laugh. Ed quickly took her in his arms and held her laughing face to his shoulder. Eventually, Louise recomposed enough to show her face to others. There were misleading tears on her cheeks.

A polka started playing from the record player in the corner. William grabbed his mom and started around the floor. Anthony grabbed Agnieszka. Stella grabbed Otto. The crowd either clapped or joined in the dance. My party had finally started.

Suddenly, Henry was walking across the dance floor and tapping on William's shoulder. William backed away and Henry stood there with his arms open and offering a dance. Reluctantly, Louise reached out and they then took a turn around the floor. She's seen and heard quite a lot and maybe she might be reconsidering things too. Maybe not.

I noticed that Mrs. Trimpoli had finally buttonholed Father Ed and was very emotionally relating something. She mimicked my "blessing" gesture that I made to her from the vanity. Ed took a quick glace up to where he knew the peephole might be and made a brief frown in my direction. He, too, had to improvise. He hugged Mrs. Trimpoli, and I could see him say, "This is wonderful!" Then he blessed her with a sign of the cross. This was turning into quite a night. Then I noticed a new face had come in.

He wasn't just a party crasher dropping in to get out of the cold or to have free beer. His clothing told me he could afford to buy his own beer. He hadn't even removed his overcoat. He sat at the hall bar with his drink, just watching the crowd. I don't recognize him, but maybe we did once know each other, and he was paying his respects tonight. It's nice that at least one casual acquaintance took the time to come here tonight. Christ, I have walked this village for 60 years, I should have made a few friends in that time. This one though didn't look friendly. He spoke to whomever sat near him, but it seemed he was doing most of the listening. I was happy when he finally left. Odd man.

Tonight, I am back at Ed's, writing all this up. Ed pretended to be angry about my prank with Mrs. Trimpoli, until we finally laughed about it.

We sat and enjoyed ourselves for hours discussing the night and our past together, but not discussing our futures yet. I'm not sure I really believe that I will have one.

Tomorrow will be night two of my wake.

Monday, December 29th

The storm ended this morning, and the sun was seen once again. Shoveled sidewalks and plowed streets resurfaced from their snowy blankets. The temperature rose into the high 20s.

Louise called Ed's home to tell us that Henry suspected that someone had broken into the house last night. During the day, he had noticed the back fence was down. When he went through the cellar to inspect the fence, he noticed puddles of water on the floor and the cellar door unlatched. He asked her and Agnieszka about it. Apparently, he never heard anything about Mrs. Trimpoli encounter.

Louise reported that he had gone through the house, and nothing seemed to be missing anywhere. All the locks to each apartment seemed fine, as well. He eventually thought it might have been someone looking for a place to sleep last night. He was puzzled as to why the cellar door was unbolted in the first place, but keeping it bolted should stop this from happening again. I won't be able to enter the house again that way if I needed to.

Because the storm was gone, this evening was trickier to walk around the streets without being observed. I had to walk blocks out of my way to avoid close encounters. Once again, I did successfully reach my spot on the staircase, but I was late. The wake had already started. Otto was right. I was late for my own wake.

To my great surprise, the room was packed. My obituary had been in this morning's *News*. Maybe I had made a few friends over the many years. Since Otto had needed to reopen the Eagle barroom tonight, Alfonso, his backup bartender, manned the bar for him there. Otto had assigned Anthony to the hall doorway to prevent uninvited guests from entering the hall for free drinks on me. Everyone in the hall were people I knew well.

Unfortunately, this wonderful community of friends will exist in Brooklyn, while I hide from them in Staten Island. I don't like that, but it seems there was no other way. I had made my choice. Nevertheless, now when I appreciate my community once again, I am also losing it.

My wake went on just like I always wanted my wake to be, with people laughing at stupid stories of how we got through life together. Outliving my own death had this upside to it. I got to watch everyone relive our lives together. I noticed someone again and it is beginning to concern me.

That well-dressed thug, for lack of a better description, from last night had returned. He couldn't get into the wake room tonight, but I watched as he retreated back into the Eagle's barroom. Through the open doorway I could see him

Fathers and Sons and Other Village Idiots

sitting at the bar and talking to anyone nearby. With his intense stare into a speaker's face, it seemed more like an interrogation. He's not a mourner. He was not an old friend. He's after something.

With my attention diverted, I had taken my eye off the doorway to the loft hallway. Suddenly, I heard below the door open. As the stairway light went on, I scrambled up off the stairs and into the darkness of the loft, but I was slow and noisy.

I heard the sound of someone running up the stairs two at a time and calling out. It was Nelson and he had heard me. The loft light came on before I could reach my planned hiding place. I turned to look at Nelson's face as he saw mine. We stared at each other with nothing to say. With the music playing below, probably no one there would have heard Nelson's call. The only thing I could think to do was put my finger to my lips. I think of this now, but the boy was having a ghost tell him to be quiet. What else could he do but be quiet. I got out my writing pad and started to write.

"As you see, I didn't die. Need for you to let me explain."

He read my words and nodded. I must commend the boy that he didn't shake as he returned the pad to me each time. He definitely was the stoutest-hearted person that I have ever known. Nothing seemed to rattle him, even conversing with the dead.

I explained as much as I could with as few words as I could write. In the end, he just shook his head in disbelief then reached over and we hugged until I pulled away.

"Please don't tell your father. Don't tell anybody. Don't want to involve and maybe endanger anyone else.

"In fact, don't talk to Father Ed or Aunt Louise even though they already know. Just stay out of this crazy plan. Probably illegal and its already bad enough I had to involve them.

"To get them to agree, I had to promise to not kill myself. Promise you the same, but the less people ever talking about this, the better."

I answered a few more questions for the boy, but his tone was that he was going to keep the secret. We hugged again before he left. I was alone once again in the dark and dead to the world. I do hope that real dying is not this complicated.

I decided it was time for me to leave and get back to Ed's. As I write tonight's events into my journal, I realize how exhausted I am.

Tuesday, December 30th

Death is going to be the death of me yet. I continue to wonder about what my future would possibly be. I just cannot imagine it. Today itself has been a quiet one for me, but we did have a change in plans.

When Ed and Louise found out that Nelson had discovered me in the loft yesterday, they insisted that it was time to get me out of Brooklyn once and for always. I reluctantly agreed. I was already quite satisfied that my wake had become a highlight of my life. Not many people can say that.

Today was a workday for many, so we needed to leave the neighborhood before crowds of workers filled the subway platform. The three of us caught an early subway to make the 6 a.m. ferry back to Staten Island. The plan was for Ed to take his car back on his own, and Louise would drive her car back this evening without me. There would be one wake night without the guest of honor. I am here alone with only my thoughts. This almost always leads to trouble and Ed and Louise knew this. It would be the first time since Christmas day that I would be unsupervised, so to speak.

I promised them I would be fine and that this was the best plan. The right thing to do. Ed left immediately upon reaching Great Kills, and, tonight, Louise went to my wake without me. She returned about 10 p.m. tonight with nothing notable to tell me.

According to my last wishes, my funeral plan should be that all interested parties would gather in the evening in Manhattan to take the 8 p.m. Staten Island ferry. They will all ride out onto the harbor and there dispose of my ashes before the Statue of Liberty. Ed was to go by subway with everyone from 23rd Street. Louise and I would go to Staten Island ferry

Fathers and Sons and Other Village Idiots

terminal for the 7 p.m. ferry to Manhattan. I insisted that I must be on board somewhere. This was the plan. My mourners would make the round trip to return to New York, while Louise and I would drive home to start my new life. All in all, not a bad plan. Living my last days on earth with Louise seemed wonderful. To possibly follow that up with eternity with Marysia, would be joyous. Better than I deserved.

My Dearest Marysia,

Tomorrow, Kazimierz, the idiot, will be buried at sea, just like my mom. Poets say your name means *Star of the Sea.* Perhaps the sea is where I belong to be with you in spirit.

I do feel my quest is as yet unfulfilled. After tomorrow, I will begin to fade from people's memories, but this quest must somehow go on.

Have I done the right thing, but failed? Is this a possible outcome? Could I have done the wrong thing, yet succeeded? In my heart, I feel that is not possible.

Have I succeeded or failed to reach heaven? I will only allow God, and not his church, to judge me.

Have I done the right thing or wrong for our family? I will allow only you to judge me.

One year ago, I resolved to do something good. All year, I refused to follow other people's rules. I only did what I thought was right. I did my best.

Your loving Kazimierz

225

Wednesday, December 31, 1969

This New Year's Eve, I sit in purgatory, a jail cell with my notebook and some very unhappy people around me. Let me explain what I think happened today, but frankly, I think I am truly insane. Nevertheless, something unexpected happened again.

In Staten Island this evening, I put on Louise's father's overcoat and hat to conceal myself once again. We caught the 7 p.m. ferry from Staten Island that would become the 8 p.m. from Manhattan, my funeral procession to eternity. When we reached New York, Louise joined the mourners in the terminal while I stayed on the ferry. She would reboard with them.

I sat off to one side to watch them gather near the rear of the main deck. A much larger group than I had expected. Who would have guessed so many were so happy to deep six me. Finally, the ferry was untied, and we were on our way.

Manhattan looked so beautiful to me tonight. High clouds hid the skyscrapers' tops. Only lights from the lower floors could be seen, and these reflected randomly on the choppy winter waters. Everyone was already gathering near the rear deck because it would be less windy to hold a little ceremony. It would take about ten minutes to be before Lady Liberty. There, my ashes would fly.

Only Louise, Nelson, and Ed knew that I was still alive, or so I thought. We were all wrong in that assumption. Even then, I continued to feel that something was not right about all this, but I couldn't stop it now.

Anthony and Nelson were standing closely together at the doorway looking through the window into the dark harbor waters. Otto stood off to the side, as stubborn as ever about accepting who his sons really were. Stella and Agnieszka sat together, almost like mother and daughter.

Louise sat with William and Henry, but with William between the former marriage. They have love of William in common, but my heart told me that I should never expect more for them.

Finally, my moment arrived. Someone slid open the heavy deck door, and my mourners walked out into the winter's air.

Fathers and Sons and Other Village Idiots

Inside, I sat on my wooden bench. I couldn't dare join them. I took the moment alone to look right to see to Lady Liberty, then left to my Brooklyn village. Somewhere in that darkness stood the steeple of my Black Madonna.

With his back to the waters, Father Ed turned to face my mourners. He appeared to be saying a few words. I worried what the bastard was saying about me. Some nodded in agreement.

Next, Henry stepped up holding a sack. A sack. Like a bunch of potatoes. Louise reminded me earlier that the ashes in the sack were from Ed's fireplace. Still, symbolically, I resented being carried in a sack. A vase would have been nice.

Henry poured some of my ashes over the rail and the wind carried me away. No parting words of my passing. He just dumped me in like one dumps ashes from an ashtray.

Otto stepped up and silently did the same. Just dumped me overboard me into the darkness. Couldn't I have a few last words from anyone? Apparently not and the ceremonial dumping of Kaz continued. Even my beloved Agnieszka dumped without a word. Just like that, I was all gone.

Otto retrieved the sack from her and thoroughly shook it. Let's be sure to get rid of all of the old coot.

Some lingered there, but most needed to get inside from the cold. There were tears on some cheeks. I wanted to come over to comfort them, but I couldn't. Being dead has its drawbacks. Then Louise looked over in my direction. I had warned her not to do that.

Next, Ed looked my way and as he stared, his eyes widened, like he was looking at a ghost. He knew I wasn't dead. Something was wrong. I did not know what the hell was going on. They appeared to be looking right through me, and I now know, they were.

I had a crazy notion that perhaps I really was dead. Did I actually die last week on that subway track? This thought was shocking, but not upsetting. Maybe I saved that stranger, and he was my redeeming deed. It was he who Ed took back to Spanish Camp. We didn't talk much that drive. Had I been misunderstanding the events of the last few days?

227

But if I was dead, where's the goddamn light that I am supposed to be walking into?

Louise looked over to me and I moved a bit. She clearly saw me. I stood up and Nelson noticed. Next, Ed yelled at me, "Kaz, look out," and pointed to something behind me. I turned to see two men running at me. One of them was the thug from my wake. Were they somehow associated with Frankie or Mr. Green? Maybe the mob came to my funeral but not to praise me. They were here to bury me.

I started to run toward the doors as fast as a 77-year-old man could run, but they grabbed me within moments. To my surprise, instead of shooting or stabbing me or tossing me overboard, they handcuffed me. All I heard was one say that I was under arrest.

They held me by my arms as my mourners came forward. Mrs. Trimpoli walked up to me, and I offered her a weak smile back. With her finger, she poked my chest. Once satisfied that I was real, she slapped me across the face and turned away.

"You and you and you and you," said one of the policemen while pointing in turn at Ed. Louise, Henry and Otto, "You're also under arrest. Come with us." They brought us down to two police cars on the car level of the ferry. During the drive back to Brooklyn. I learned about what had been transpiring for the last few days.

On Christmas Day, hospital staff reported to police that some things didn't add up, and then I disappeared. The police started to investigate. The hospital cooperated with the investigation and sent over an empty sealed casket to the crematorium. I was still missing, and they were waiting for me to show up before they moved in. The remains of the subway stranger's body had been tagged as a John Doe.

From the nearby neighborhood, I hear fireworks exploding. New Year's Day 1970 has arrived, and I start it in jail. Ivan's voice has returned to taunt me.

... was coming to that troubled twilight time, a time of regrets that resemble hopes, of hopes that resemble regrets, when youth is past ...

Before they bring me before a judge, I must express my regrets.

I have tried to write poetry,
but written poorly.

I have tried to love,
but done so miserably.

I have tried to heal the soul of my family,
but wounded it mortally.

I have tried to get through the gates of heaven,
but failed.

I can take my only comfort in knowing that
even though I have

written poorly,
loved miserably, and
failed so completely.

I tried because of my love for another,
always thinking it was the right thing to do.

New Year's Day, 1970

Anyone who doesn't have hope for the future is a fool. What other choice is there? For one whole year, I have been swearing that I would not still be alive on this day, yet I am here and writing once more.

God didn't allow my death or for me go to prison. All year, He has seemed to be both saving me for my quest while resisting me in achieving it. He just won't let things play out like I plan them.

When the ferry docked in Staten Island, the police took us away in their patrol cars. The others needed to return to Manhattan and work their way back to Brooklyn. Stella took Agnieszka home with her. Nelson and Anthony went back to their apartment.

Last night, Otto, Ed, Louise, Henry and I sat in a holding cell filled up with New Year's Eve drunks. At 3 a.m., we were brought before the night judge. He seemed entertained by our story being different. Because we were well identified and not a flight risk, he released us to return to him the following Monday. He had serious issues piling up before him, and our group seemed harmless. By 4 a.m., we were all released.

It was when we all returned to 23rd, we discovered that William was missing. Henry called Anthony and Nelson, then Stella, but William was not with any of them. Anthony and Nelson walked down to the house, while Stella and Agnieszka drove over to our house.

Stella and Agnieszka finally arrived back about 6 a.m. As we sat around the living room, Nelson mentioned that as boys, he and William would often go down to Shore Road when they were pissed off with their fathers. He and Anthony decided that they should go down there to see if William might be there. Stella offered to drive them back and she would sit at her house in case he went there. Everyone who was going off to search for him agreed to call here every hour. Father Ed said that he would go check out OLC. He returned in 20 minutes, alone.

It was Agnieszka who said, "What about Coney Island?" I knew that she had gotten the idea from my journal. At least she was thinking clearly because this thought had never occurred

Fathers and Sons and Other Village Idiots

to me. Coney Island might be a possibility on this very day. It was my place of broken promises. Since it was a large area to search, several of us got into Ed's car and went to Coney. Otto stayed back at my house in case William showed up there.

Within 30 minutes, we were walking onto the boardwalk. The Coney Island boardwalk goes for miles, so it shouldn't have been easy to find him, but we did. We found him, still in his suit and tie, near the Stillwell Avenue subway station on the stretch of beach where the Coney Island Polar Bears took their dips.

William told us that he went out drinking all night and ended up at some party where he fell asleep. After he slept off most of his drunkenness, he thought he'd come to the beach.

He said that all night long, he was angry with us. While sitting on the boardwalk bench, he remembered his other times of being at Coney Island. The New Year's Day visits. The summer beach times. The visits in the middle of the winter to get a hot dog. Happy times as a family. When Louise and Henry reached out and hugged him, he seemed to melt in their arms.

His dad told him about sitting in a jail cell with the drunks. As we huddled together in the cold, we had a few chuckles about the ridiculousness of the night. Louise spotted a phone booth down the boardwalk and went over to notify the others.

More and more garbage cans on the beach were starting to blaze with bonfires. A few minutes later, someone blew a conch shell and people began to disrobe around their cans. The Polar Bears were assembling as they had been since I came to America. It was a gathering of all the clans of New York. In the freezing cold, skin colors seemed to disappear. I felt like the world was represented in that community out there. No one seemed alone or by themselves.

William then announced that he was going to join them. He looked over to his dad. Henry looked at me and I at him. William said that it would only take a minute and that it was something he was considering before we arrived.

I could tell that this was not Henry's dream. It was no longer mine either. The plunge would surely kill me.

231

Billy Warren

Meanwhile, Ed was trying to explain everything in Polish to Agnieszka, who couldn't follow everything that was being said in English. Once she comprehended, she turned to William and sent him on his way with a kiss on the cheek. As she turned away from him and towards me, she winked at me and, with a little smile, said in Polish in a low voice only to me, "Someone should do it." I felt ashamed. Was all my determination to no longer be cautious, be so hard to live up to? At least, William was resolved that this was what he came to do. Louise had still not returned from the telephone booth.

William removed his shoes and socks then went down the stairs onto the cold sand. Still in his overcoat and suit, he started walking quickly towards the nearest burning can, but before he got too far, Henry shouted out that he would be joining him. Agnieszka, Ed and I remained on the boardwalk at the rail watching, as father and son ran shoeless towards a flaming trashcan. They were going in. It was a simple plan, but nothing was ever simple in this family.

Louise eventually returned to the group and wondered what was happening. Once we pointed out to the beach, she started screaming at everyone. Ed and I tried to restrain her, but it also took Agnieszka's help. Louise would not stop struggling, until both Henry and William turned back to her and waved. The scene of her smiling son and ex-husband standing on the beach in their underwear, quieted her down.

From the boardwalk, I noticed someone on the beach that no one else had yet spotted. A dark figure in blue was running up behind them. Upon reaching them, the policeman grabbed their clothes and threw them into their chests. Without decent bathing suits, he was not going to let them into the water.

Apparently, William and Henry didn't move fast enough to his liking, so he grabbed their arms to turn them away from the water and towards the boardwalk. They were not going to get past him. I needed to help.

I started down the stairs. Since I could not yell, I needed to attract attention and Ed helped me out. As I stripped off all my clothing, and I do mean all, Ed started yelling as loud as he could. Soon Agnieszka joined him. Henry and William looked up and so did the cop.

232

Fathers and Sons and Other Village Idiots

I was running in my birthday suit to the next flaming can further down the beach. Ed told me later that Louise was in complete shock and didn't move a muscle. He also said that Agnieszka was laughing so hard she cried.

As I ran bare-assed, the cop released my boys' arms and started out to intercept me. The race was on. My job was done, but now I really wanted to make it into the surf.

Despite my running as hard as I could, I was still freezing to death in the wind. My old joints were tightening up. I looked over the shoulder of the approaching cop and saw that Henry and William were heading back to the surf.

The cop chasing me started to blow his whistle. Another cop responded from the other direction. I could beat the second cop to the water but knew the first cop was nearly upon me, but I no longer want to fail. I really wanted to make my plunge and cry like a newborn baby. I wanted to be reborn.

In my head I yelled one simple prayer to God, "Please let me have this one." I raised a fist at the sky as this one thought screamed inside my head. "Let me have this one."

The cop was nearly on me as I approached a pile of driftwood. I didn't have the time to go around it, but surprisingly, I was able to jump over it. He wasn't expecting that of me and was intent on grabbing me, but he had taken his eyes off the driftwood. He tripped and went down with a thud. I ran even faster. I knew that was all the help I was going to get. I had to do the rest on my own.

Being knee-deep in the water, I stumbled on the first little wave I reached. I tumbled into probably only a foot of water. I stayed down and enjoyed my moment in the surf. Next, I was being dragged out by the second cop.

As I was being dragged along the beach by both cops, Louise reached us with my clothing in her arms. As she wrapped me in my clothing, she thanked the policemen for saving her father. Ed finally limped up with his cane, flashed his collar and also thanked the cops for rescuing his senile old friend.

"He is very demented, but as you can see, he's quite nimble. He slipped away from us on the boardwalk before we realized what he was up to." Having a priest's collar on helps one get

233

away with such bullshit. I, now half dressed, apparently gave the officer a vacant stare. The second policeman started laughing at his fellow officer, telling him what the captain would say if they arrested a senile old man. He told his partner, "This guy is in a dreamland. Look at his face. Let go of him." The first officer eventually agreed that it would be no good arresting me.

What a day this has been!

I sit in my house tonight and write in this journal for the final time. I never thought I would be here again. While no one is in the apartment with me right now, I don't feel alone in it anymore. I feel a part of something larger than just myself. I'm part of a community. Ed told me that his Dorothy used to say that community was the answer to that great loneliness. This village with all its idiots have always been my solution.

Did I achieve my quest for redemption by acting unselfishly for once? I really don't. Love made me start my quest and my village enabled me to love more. I don't have regrets anymore. I took my dip.

These truly are my final farewells.

To My Precious God,

You have given me enough time to find my own path. I believe that I do have the free will that your Father Ed always said I had. Thank you for saving me so many times. I would still greatly appreciate it if you would also redeem me.

To My Know-It-All Muse,

Maybe artists are full of shit, but at least we create.

To My Sacrificing Mother,

I have tried to do the right things in life.

To My Black Madonna and Mother of Exiles,

As beacons, you both have guided through my darkest hours.

To My Beloved Wife,

Thank you for loving me and enriching my world.

To My Unfortunate Father,

No one deserves to be hated, and I now pray that you forgive me. I look forward to seeing you soon in either heaven or hell.

To My Idiot Sons,

Take more chances and always love your children for who they are.

To My Inspiring Underdogs,

Thank you for your tenacity.

To My Fellow Village Angels,

You have been brought to me as angels to shepherd my soul. I know now I was never alone. I always had community.

I hope all souls can find their village and take their emotional dip to rejuvenate their spirits. I had always been a fearful idiot, but at least I was not a fool. I did have skeptical hope. It's okay to doubt and question, but always persevere against those trying to put you in your place.

Peace be with you all,
Kazimierz

Epilogue

A few days after the events on the beach, Grandpa came down with a pneumonia that would be his real demise. He died a few weeks later in late January.

At the hospital, he apparently had a successful confession. At his wake held in the Eagle social hall, he was laid to rest in a split lid casket with a platter on top, serving his Johnny Walker Red. He had a full funeral mass at OLC and was buried in Queens with Grandma. I still think his first wake in December was more memorable.

In a hospital during the week before his death, Grandpa floated in and out of consciousness. Everyone, including Grandpa, knew this would be his time. When he was awake, he revealed that he was happy that cancer was not going to be the death of him. He lingered in the hospital for a few more days. The family shared times sitting with him in his hospital room. When he was coherent, he would pass notes to us to hold short conversations.

On the day before he died, the two of us were together while he wrote on a hospital pad. He wrote for over a half hour, and I had thought that he might have forgotten that I was there, but the note was for me. I saved it and have included his note here.

Fathers and Sons and Other Village Idiots

My dear grandson,

Life is too precious to be careful with, and the alternative to dying before one is dead is to continue to pursue happiness while one is still alive. I have finally succeeded, but it took too long a time. It was my realization of selfless love that finally pulled me through.

Will I get into heaven? As my Ivan too often said to me,

One cannot know what one doesn't know.

I know that I was an underdog in life who was maybe fighting an unwinnable quest. God, and only God, can judge whether I achieved success as a soul.

I don't really know whether my father somehow redeemed himself in life. I pray he is in heaven and finally taking good care of my mother. In these last few weeks, I have hoped for this to be true. Maybe he has been sitting in Purgatory awaiting his son to pray for him.

Hate does no good and I was very wrong to carry it so long. Please remember that loving enriches the world, not hatred. In the end, it was my love for my family and friends that saved me. My angels showed me I always had community.

William, you must pursue your happinesses to your deathbed. Enjoy everything you do as if it might be the last time you get to do it.

Here's to it, and here's from it, and here's to it again!
If you ever get to it, and don't do it,
you may never get to it to do it again!

Your loving grandpa

237

I remember that when I read this, I just sat quietly. Next, he gestured that he wanted the loose papers from his bedside drawer. He no longer collected his writings in his notebook. He looked through the notes until he found what he was looking for and handed it to me. It was a Tanka, a poetic form he indicated that he had never tried before. He wrote it was about time to try something new. I have pasted it below along with one more quote from his beloved Ivan.

I hope that you have enjoyed my grandfather's story. If he were here today, I'd bet he would tell you to be a little reckless and take that plunge. Even if it kills you, you were going to die anyway. Why not live a little before you go?

William "Duke" Baranski

winter just a pause
when pursuing happiness
this end savored
sweet smell of death it can be
when happiness follows death

— Kazimierz Adama Baranski 1970

Every man hangs by a thread, any minute the abyss may open under his feet, and yet he must go and invent for himself all kinds of troubles and spoil his life.

— Ivan Turgenev, Fathers and Sons 1862

Fathers and Sons and Other Village Idiots

The End

ACKNOWLEDGMENTS

Even though this, my debut novel is self- published, I have so many people to acknowledge and thank.

My editor and new friend, Lew Istre, from the Lake Wildwood, California Writers Group. Working with Lew was so invaluable to me. His efforts are significantly responsible for whatever readership my work achieves.

Several family and friends read early drafts or segments of a very ill-conceived story. These include Ellen Wahle, Ed Chan, Joe Chuckla, Joe Wu, Dave Fleck, and Stephen Wahle. I'm sure it was a painful experience and do hope they read the final version. Their feedback helped me improve the tale.

Mary Datoc, in the Interlibrary Loans section of the Santa Clara County Library (SCCL) district, had to scour the nation for another library willing to loan their copies of the 1969 *New York Daily News*. Thank you to the University of Central Oklahoma for loaning 24 microfiche reels to me in 2017. Thank you to Jeff Binschus, circulation manager at the Morgan Hill branch of SCCL, who facilitated the many reel shipments between institutions.

Thank you to everyone above!

Lastly, I wish to thank again my wife, Theresa. She was the first and last person to read this manuscript before I could publish it. It wouldn't be in print without her.

ABOUT THE AUTHOR

Billy Warren was born and raised in a South Brooklyn neighborhood under the shadow of the local Polish Catholic church steeples and the watchful gaze of the Statue of Liberty. He is 2nd generation Polish American whose ancestors immigrated to America around 1910. He is a graduate of City College of New York BS '75, and San Jose State U. MA '81. He remains grateful and proud of his Polish and Brooklyn heritages, and public school education.

He has had diverse professional experiences that include being an air traffic controller, spinal cord injury center therapist, technical writer, and healthcare executive.

Today, he writes historical literary fiction full time from northern California. He is married, father of two sons, and a male breast cancer survivor.

While he cannot promise to answer all emails, all will be read. His contact is billy@billywarren.com

TO MY READERS

Self-published works can only thrive if you, the readers, seek out Indy Presses, such as Billy Warren Books.

Please keep independent authors on your reading lists, and please post your reviews on their social media author sites.

I maintain author pages on Amazon.com, goodreads.com. BookBub.com, and Bookshop.org. My website has links to all.

Please visit billywarren.com

COMING IN 2026
"BEYOND GOOD AND EVIL AND MURDER"

There was an unsolved murder in *Fathers and Sons Other Village Idiots*. Somebody did it. Do you know who?

Billy Warren's next novel, *Beyond Good and Evil and Murder*, solves that puzzle. It's a historical fiction murder mystery set in 1970 South Brooklyn but again with some literary undertones.

Someone kills a local bookie but does it in such an odd fashion that it's deemed too complicated to be a mob hit. The question becomes why.

The most likely suspects are all from the neighborhood, but most have an airtight alibi.

Months later, another neighborhood bookie working for another crime family gets murdered in the same place and in the same way, and again during a neighborhood party. Again, most in the neighborhood have a strong alibi. Why did the killer pick that night?

The mobs want to know. So does city hall. Few want justice but all want payback. Some local cops are on the take, but you don't know which ones. No one can be trusted, maybe not even within your *family*.

In order to protect the community, it's up to a local priest and bartender to solve these murders before another one happens.

Beyond Good and Evil and Murder starts with a premise that *What is done out of love always takes place beyond good and evil*. It is a historical fiction whodunit that questions traditional concepts of good and evil.

These novels do not need to be read in sequence. Enjoy!

Printed in the USA
CPSIA information can be obtained
at www.ICGtesting.com
LVHW091153191024
794186LV00033B/650/J